AS THE CROW FLIES

A P.J. BENSON MYSTERY

AS THE CROW FLIES

MARIS SOULE

FIVE STAR
A part of Gale, Cengage Learning

Detroit • New York • San Francisco • New Haven, Conn • Waterville, Maine • London

GALE
CENGAGE Learning™

LIBRARY OF CONGRESS CATALOGING-IN-PUBLICATION DATA

Soule, Maris.
    As the crow flies : a P.J. Benson mystery / by Maris Soule. —
1st ed.
        p. cm.
    ISBN-13: 978-1-59414-952-8 (hardcover)
    ISBN-10: 1-59414-952-6 (hardcover)
    1. Women accountants—Fiction. 2. Michigan—Fiction. I. Title.
PS3569.0737A9 2011
813'.54—dc22   2010048393

First Edition. First Printing: March 2011.
Published in 2011 in conjunction with Tekno Books and Ed Gorman.

Printed in the United States of America
1 2 3 4 5 6 7 15 14 13 12 11

Dedicated to Bill, my hero,
and in memory of
Ch. Roho's Baraka
October 1971–November 1980

ACKNOWLEDGMENTS

Many thanks to my critique partners—Bonnie Alkema, Dawn Bartley, Annette Briggs, Sue Crouse, Lynette Curtis, Ardyce Czuchna-Curl, Renci Denham, Julie McMullen, Joe Novara, and Bob Weir. All of you make me a better writer. A special thanks to Lynette Curtis for arranging an interview with Detectives Executive Lieutenant Victor Ledbetter, Sergeant Karianne Thomas, and Jeffrey K. Johnson of Kalamazoo Public Safety's Criminal Investigative Department. They not only helped me understand how a witness with dementia would be interviewed and assisted, but showed me around the department. Thank you, Cheryl Moulds, for keeping me on track with the title, and thank you, Dr. Marion Gorham, who is my Rhodesian Ridgeback's veterinarian, for taking the time to look up the effects of toxic poisoning. If I didn't get that right, it's not her fault.

ONE

```
P.J. Benson, C.P.A.
speaking on
HOW TO
PROTECT YOURSELF
FROM SCAMS
2:00 p.m.
Friday, June 12
```

"Here." A silver-haired woman about my height but three times my width shoved a battered, black briefcase into my arms. "You take this."

"I don't understand," I said, shifting the cumbersome piece of luggage to a more comfortable position. "What's in here?"

She gave a quick, furtive glance around the library meeting room, then stepped closer and lowered her voice to a whisper. "Something they want."

Something heavy, I decided, and set the briefcase on the carpeting. "Who wants it?"

"Them." Her pale blue eyes held a feverish glow that reminded me of the look my schizophrenic mother got when she was sure aliens had landed. "The ones he talked to. He told them if they want what he has in this briefcase, they'll have to pay for it."

My internal alert alarm went off, and I stepped back ar

glanced at the nametag on the woman's cotton blouse. *Ida Delaney.* "Ida, that sounds like blackmail."

"I know. And that's why you have to help him. Help me." Her chin began to quiver. "I know what happens to blackmailers. I've seen it on my afternoon shows. They get arrested or they get killed. I don't know what I'll do if they kill him."

Just the idea of getting involved in another murder sent a shiver down my spine. "I can't help you, Ida," I said. "You need to go to the police."

"No." She shook her head, the loose-skinned wattle under her chin swinging back and forth. "No, I can't do that. Donald said if I bothered them again, they'd make me go into a nursing home. I came here because the sign outside said you'd tell us how to protect ourselves."

"From scams." I thought I'd explained that during my talk. "Not from . . ."

I was going to say stupidity, but stopped myself and looked around, hoping to see either Emily Anderson, the librarian who had introduced me, or my grandmother, who had convinced me to talk to her senior citizens' group.

At least two dozen gray-haired seniors had stayed after my talk, most of them now gathered around the refreshment table. I didn't spot either the librarian or Grandma Carter in the group. My grandmother's absence didn't surprise me. My bet was she'd stepped outside for a cigarette. She hates all the *No Smoking* regulations Michigan's lawmakers have come up with.

Well, I felt no pity for her today. Although summer wouldn't officially start for another nine days, today's weather was perfect—temps in the mid-seventies and not a cloud in the sky.

"The police think I'm crazy," Ida whispered, bringing my attention back to her.

I knew from experience how that felt, but I had to agree with them in this case.

"Sometimes I get things a little mixed up," Ida said. "But I really thought it *was* my house. Otherwise, I wouldn't have crawled through that window. I mean, my gosh, I almost got stuck."

"You crawled through a window into someone else's house?" I tried not to smile, but picturing Ida Delaney squeezing her broad rear-end through an open window was more than I could suppress.

She frowned at me. "It wasn't funny, and I really don't see why they had to call the police. Donald told them it did look like the house I used to live in."

"And who's Donald?"

"My nephew." She looked down at the briefcase by our feet. "I think he's sorry he threatened them. He asked for way too much money." She sighed, a look of sadness filling her eyes. "It's all because he thinks he needs to hire someone to be with me when he's gone. He worries that I'll get lost if I go out on my own. But I found my way here. I saw the sign last week, and I remembered."

She pointed out the window toward Portage Street, where for the last two weeks the marquee in front of the Washington Street Branch Library had announced my talk. Portage is a heavily traveled street, so in addition to helping Grandma's senior citizens' group, I hoped the publicity would gain me a few new clients. P.J. Benson's Accounting and Tax Service has been in existence for six months, and all I can say is I'm glad my grandfather left me some money as well as his farm when he died.

Starting a home-based business wasn't easy. What I needed were clients, not a situation where someone was trying to blackmail someone else. "Ida, much as I'd like to help you, I'm afraid I can't. I'm a C.P.A., not a detective. You really need to contact the police."

She frowned, a multitude of wrinkles gathering across her

11

forehead and sagging downward. "But they'll just . . ." She stared down at the briefcase, then back up at me. "Could you please just look? See if you can figure out what's in there that someone would want?"

She asked so sincerely, I decided why not? If I found something, I would call the police. Even my crazy mother was right sometimes.

I was about to bend over and pick up the case when I heard the librarian's voice. "Ida? Now, you're not bothering Miss Benson, are you?"

"I need her help," Ida Delaney said, looking to my right.

Emily Anderson came up beside us. I'd met Emily the day my grandmother brought me to the library to set up the talk, and then, again, a few hours earlier today, when I arrived to give my talk. Wearing gray pants and a flowered blouse, low-heeled pumps, and wire-rimmed glasses, she looked exactly as I expected a librarian to look. I guessed her age to be mid-forties, but she patted the older woman's arm in the same way a mother might pat a child's. "Ida," she said, "I think P.J.'s talk should help all of us. Is your nephew here?"

Ida Delaney shook her head and looked down at the carpeting. "No, Donald doesn't know I'm here."

"In that case, how about if I give him a call, so he can come pick you up," the librarian said, and then turned to me. "P.J., a couple of the ladies over at the refreshment table were telling me about phone calls they've received. You should go talk to them."

I felt it was more an order than a suggestion, but I welcomed the excuse to escape. "I'll do that," I said, and took a step back, away from the two of them. The briefcase remained on the carpet. "I'm sorry I can't be more help, Ida. Maybe Miss Anderson can help you."

"But I . . ."

A peal of laughter from the refreshment table drowned out the rest of what Ida Delaney was saying. One of the women—an elegantly dressed blonde who looked too young to be attending a gathering of senior citizens—turned toward me. "Come join us, P.J.," she said. "We're telling stories about scams that haven't worked."

"Tell them our story," a slender octogenarian with blue-tinted hair said.

"No, you tell it," insisted the blonde. "It's your story, Nita."

"Well, okay." The older woman grinned. "This all started a month ago when two men came to my house and told me they were going to be in the neighborhood resurfacing driveways. They said, since they would already be there, they could do my driveway really cheap. They also said, if I didn't get it done soon, I was going to have major cracking. Now I figured I probably did need to have the driveway sealed, so I told them okay. But after they left, I started worrying about my decision, so I called my friend Grace." She nodded to the blonde.

"I'm a real estate agent," Grace supplied. "We hear all sorts of horror stories about shoddy workmanship, contractors who don't finish a project or use substandard materials. As it turned out, the day Nita called, I'd talked to a client who had been scammed by these same men."

"Rather than chastise me for my foolishness," Nita continued, "Grace said 'Great.' And then she told me her plan."

"And Nita played along beautifully." Grace hugged the older woman.

"We got them." Nita grinned at the others in the group. "Got them good."

"What did you do?" one woman asked.

"While these men were applying the sealer, I stopped by," Grace said, looking smug. "Along with a friend who works for the Michigan Department of Transportation and a couple of officers from Kalamazoo Public Safety. While we all stood there, blocking the men and their truck, my friend tested the sealer they were applying. As we'd presumed, it was merely a coating of oil."

"You ought to have heard the things those men said as the officers took them away." Nita tsk-tsked and shook her head, but her blue eyes sparkled with amusement. "That'll teach them to underestimate a senior citizen."

I nodded. Anyone who underestimates my grandmother is really in for a surprise. I was about to say as much when I felt a tap on my shoulder.

"You about ready to go?" Grandma Carter asked.

I could smell cigarette smoke on her and knew I'd been right about where she'd been. I glanced at the clock on the wall and realized how late it was. I needed to return to Zenith and let my dog out, shove a pan of lasagna in the oven, and hopefully straighten my house up a bit before my gentleman caller—as some of these older women would say—arrived. "Sure," I said. "Just give me a minute to gather my notes and thank the librarian."

I'd given everyone in attendance my business card and a copy of an article on scams directed at seniors. I slipped the extra cards and copies, along with the three-by-five cards I'd used as prompts for my talk, back in my briefcase, and then went over to talk to Emily Anderson. "Thanks for rescuing me from that situation with Mrs. Delaney," I said. "I wasn't sure what to do. Did you look in the briefcase? Was there anything . . . anything unusual?"

Emily Anderson smiled and patted my arm. "Yes, I looked. It was filled with lab reports and site maps. Oh, and some boxes of dirt. Nothing I wouldn't have expected. Her nephew is a soil tester."

"Anything that could be used as blackmail?"

"As blackmail?" Emily chuckled. "Not unless I missed something in one of those aerial photos . . . and I don't think I did."

She looked past me, toward the outside door. "Poor Ida. Her mind is getting worse and worse. I do feel sorry for her nephew. He's a very patient man, but I don't know how much longer he's going to be able to care for her. He usually brings her and picks her up when she comes to the library. I tried calling him just a while ago, but he didn't answer. Since Ida was gone when I came back, I'm assuming he picked her up."

"So where'd she get the blackmail idea?"

Emily fanned out her hands. "With Ida, who knows? It could have been something she saw on one of the soaps she watches. I'm not even sure that briefcase is one her nephew uses. It looked pretty old. Maybe her nephew gave it to her, and she put those papers and boxes of dirt in it."

Reassured, I thanked her again. Outside the library, I walked around to the parking lot at the side of the building. Grandma was already buckled in and listening to her favorite talk station when I reached my car. I'd given her a key months ago, when her car had to go into the repair shop and she borrowed mine for a couple of days. That was before I moved out of the city into what she calls "the sticks." She's never given the key back, and I've never asked for it. I figure if I ever lose mine, I know where I can find a spare. Meanwhile, if she and I are out somewhere, and I take longer to get to the car than she's willing to wait, I often find her sitting in it, listening to the radio.

"That was a good talk," she said as we drove back to her house. "But I'll tell you, I don't understand how anyone can be fooled into believing you won a prize in a contest you never entered. Or why someone in Nigeria would contact me or you for help."

"They wouldn't keep doing it if people didn't fall for it," I

15

said. "Look at how many of those get-rich scams Mother has fallen for. Did you ever get rid of all those envelopes she was supposed to address?"

"Recycling now has them."

"How's Mom doing?" I asked, hoping the news would be good.

"Cross your fingers." Grandma did cross hers. "She's still working, and still taking her medicine."

My mother has been a schizophrenic all of my life. In fact, getting pregnant with me probably triggered the disease in her. For the last two months, however, she's been on some new medicine that seems to be working wonders. Of course, even when she's crazy, she's not *completely* crazy. It's just difficult at times to weed through the bizarre to find the reality. I learned that the hard way.

I pulled up in front of my grandmother's house, but I didn't get out. "Thanks again for setting this up," I said.

"You're not going to come in?"

"I've got to get home and let Baraka out." My dog is good about not having accidents in the house, but he's only six months old, and I don't like to make him wait too long. "And Wade's coming by."

"Ah yes, Detective Sergeant Wade Kingsley of the Kalamazoo Sheriff's Department," Grandma said with a grin. "So how are you two doing?"

"Fine . . . I guess."

"You sound a little unsure. Trouble in paradise?"

Wade and I started dating two months ago, and up until last week, I would have said we were getting along great. Now . . . ? "He and his son are spending the weekend on Wade's boat. I wasn't invited."

"Maybe he wants to have some man-to-man time with the boy."

"Yeah, maybe," I said. "Or maybe he's afraid his ex would have a fit. She's sure I'm a bad influence."

"What a lot of poppycock." Grandma slid out of the car, then leaned back in. "By the way, I put that briefcase in your trunk."

Two

"She told me you were her accountant," Grandma said as the two of us stared at the battered briefcase in the trunk of my car. "She made it sound as if she'd known you for some time."

"I never met her before today," I said.

Grandma pointed at the case. "So what are you going to do with it?"

"I don't know. I guess return it to the nephew. But not today." I closed the lid to the trunk. "When I have a chance, I'll take a look inside and see if I can find the nephew's address or phone number. That or I'll call the librarian. I know she has his number."

I gave my grandmother a hug and watched as she paused on her way to her front door. She picked up a tennis ball from her postage stamp-size lawn and tossed it onto the neighbor's yard. I hope I'm as spry as she is when I'm in my seventies . . . and as healthy, both mentally and physically. In many ways she's been more of a mother to me than mine ever was or could be. If anything ever happened to Grandma, I'm not sure what I would do.

The first thing I noticed as I approached my house was the ~een Chevy parked in my driveway. Closer, I saw the gate to fence I'd recently had installed around my house was open, someone was at my front door. I slowly pulled into my ay. Even from the back, I recognized the wide hips, bib

18

overalls, and work boots. The woman standing on my porch was Nora Wright.

Last I'd heard, she was out on bail, awaiting trial for attempted murder.

Mine.

Months ago, when I first met Nora, I considered her harmless. Back then I also thought Rose, the woman Nora lived with, was her sister. That shows how naive I can be. It wasn't until Nora tried to eliminate me as a possible rival that I took her threats seriously. I couldn't prove she tried to poison me, but when a couple of shots barely missed my head, she forgot to hide the twenty-two rifle she used. Ballistics, along with gunshot residue on her jacket, were enough evidence for the DA to prosecute.

So far I hadn't heard when her trial was scheduled. What I had heard was Rose left town, and the judge attached a restraining order to Nora's conditions for release. Her presence at my house was in clear violation of that order, and I didn't like it . . . not one bit.

Nora turned away from my door and lumbered down the porch steps. As she marched along the gravel path toward my car, she reminded me of the army sergeant she used to be. Keeping watch of her, I decided to leave my engine running. I didn't see any weapon in her hands, but she was holding a piece of paper. Though paper cuts probably wouldn't be lethal, I only lowered my window partway down.

"Your dog barked at me," Nora grumbled as she neared my car.

"Good." I was glad to hear he was becoming territorial.

"If he ever bites me, I'll sue."

"You're not supposed to be close enough to me for him to bite you. In fact, you're not supposed to be anywhere around me." But obviously she was, and it made me nervous. "So why are you here?"

"I heard you're planning on cleaning up this place. Before you do that, I have something to show you." She pressed the paper she held against my car window. "This is a note from your grandfather promising me the woods after he died."

My window was dirty, and the writing was small and hard to read, some of the letters running into each other. It took me a while before I figured out the note said when my grandfather died the ten acres of woods that butted up to the back of his house—my house now—would be given to Nora. The signature was almost indiscernible, but it might have been my grandfather's.

Staring at the paper, I wanted to scream "No!" Maybe those woods were filled with the junk my grandfather had dumped there over the years, but they were part of my heritage . . . and they separated my property from hers.

I didn't want Nora owning them.

Never ever.

I knew I was crazy to argue with this woman, that I should just call the police, but she made me angry. While looking her straight in the eyes, I placed a hand on the gear shift, ready to switch into reverse and get the hell away if necessary. Heart in my throat, I said, "Nora, you're not getting those woods. Once a jury hears what you did, you're going to spend the next ten or twenty years in jail."

Her nostrils flared and her eyes narrowed, but all she did was take a step back. "That's not what my lawyer says. And I'm not worried." She waved the paper in the air. "This is legal."

"Oh yeah?" My adrenalin was pumping. "Well, my grandfather didn't mention anything in his will about giving you the woods. Until someone official tells me otherwise, those ten acres are mine."

"You touch anything in those woods, anything at all, and

you're going to be sorry."

The look in her eyes was hateful, but I refused to be bullied. "Just talking to you makes me sorry. Now get off my property, or I'll call the police."

I reached for my cell phone, and she glared at me all the way around the front of my car. She jerked open the door to her Chevy, and then slammed it shut the moment she was behind the wheel. She gunned her motor, and a spattering of gravel hit the side of my car as she spun her tires. I don't think she even looked for traffic when she pulled onto the road. I watched her head west, then make a right turn onto the road that led to her house. Only when her car was out of sight did I put down my phone.

Heart pumping wildly, I closed my eyes and sagged back against the seat. I hated feeling afraid, but I couldn't stop my body from shaking. What was I going to do if a jury didn't convict her? How could I live in my house if legally she did own those woods? From the edge of the tree line she could see into my house. Might show up at any time.

Calm down, I told myself and tried to relax. *You'll deal with that situation if and when the time comes.*

I was still on edge when I opened my front door. Baraka was happy to see me. His tail thumped against the sides of his crate, and he bowed and stretched, his lips curving up into a smile. Quickly, I let him loose and went outside with him, allowing him beyond the confines of the fence. While Baraka was tending to his business, I gathered the mail and newspaper. One bill, the weekly edition of the *Zenith Press,* and a credit card offer made up the day's postal delivery.

I watched Baraka sniff each of my car's tires, using his doggy abilities to gather information about where I'd been and what other dogs had marked my tires. He cocked his leg at one—a talent he still hasn't perfected—nearly lost his balance, and then sauntered off as if it had been his decision not to wet the tire.

I bought Baraka with the idea of showing him, and he was developing into a beautiful Rhodesian Ridgeback. Last time I checked, he was twenty-six inches at the shoulders and weighed seventy-five pounds. I'm betting, by the time he reaches maturity, he'll hit twenty-seven inches and ninety pounds.

Thing is, even though he has a perfect ridge and wonderful confirmation, I was no longer sure I wanted to put him—or me—through the rigors necessary for a dog to win at shows. Living by myself out in the country, I liked having a dog wary of strangers . . . one that would bark at people and liked to play growly. I've found it can be a lifesaver.

The phone in the house started ringing, and I called to Baraka. He beat me to the door, and I caught the call on the third ring. It was Wade.

"I'm not going to be able to make it tonight." He sounded exhausted. "We had a case break, and I have a pile of paperwork that has to be finished before I leave. I could stop by, but it would be late. Very late and—"

"And you and Jason are supposed to leave early in the morning," I finished for him.

"Right." He paused, and then added. "I am sorry. I hope you didn't go to a lot of trouble for tonight."

Trouble? I wanted to say. *Like spending two hours chopping onions and green peppers, browning them with hamburger, sweet sausage, and mushrooms, then simmering the mixture with tomatoes and fresh herbs to make the sauce for the lasagna I'd planned on serving tonight? Trouble like rushing home so I could clean my house before you arrived?* "No, no trouble," I said. "I just . . ."

I didn't finish. What was I going to say? That it had been a week since I'd last seen him. A week without even a phone call. That he'd promised he'd be here tonight, and I was looking forward to a little nookie? That I didn't understand why he hadn't invited me to go along this weekend?

If I said anything, I'd start sounding like his ex, who, according to both Wade and his sister, constantly complained that he spent too much time on his job. But darn it all, I'd been looking forward to tonight. Now I'd be eating alone, sleeping alone, and who knew when I'd see him again.

My silence must have clued him in that not all was well. "It's not as if I planned this, P.J.," he said, sounding defensive.

"I know."

"Actually, if Linda had let me, I would have picked Jason up tonight, and you and I wouldn't have had any time together."

"I see." As if hearing that would make me feel better. "Look, just have a good time with your son. Okay? Now, I've got to go. I've got work to do."

"P.J.—" Wade started, then said, "Just a minute."

I'd heard another voice in the background asking him a question. Wade's "Yes, yes, I'll be there in a moment," was obviously directed to the person speaking to him, and then he came back to me. "Look, I'll call you sometime tomorrow."

"Yeah, sure," I said, maybe a little too curtly. "Talk to you then."

After I hung up, I mentally kicked myself. I *was* starting to act like his ex, getting all grouchy because his job had interfered with our getting together, feeling upset because he wanted to spend a weekend on his boat with his six-year-old son and hadn't included me. It wasn't like he was my husband. We weren't even engaged or officially anything. In the last two months we'd slept together, gone out on dates, and even spent a weekend on his boat in South Haven. But that was it. He didn't owe me anything, and I didn't owe him anything.

So why was I feeling depressed?

I knew the answer to that, but I didn't want to admit how much I liked Wade. Maybe this was what I needed. Time away from him. A cooling-off period. A reality check.

I didn't remember I'd forgotten to tell Wade about Nora's visit until I picked up my copy of the *Zenith Press* and saw there was going to be a meeting Monday night about a proposed road change. The change would take land from some farmers, and they weren't happy. I could understand their mindset. Nora's determination to take a portion of the land I'd inherited from my grandfather bothered me more than her ignoring the judge's restraining order or any danger she might pose.

I had no idea why she wanted those woods, but I was almost certain she'd killed my grandfather to get them. Trouble was I couldn't prove that. The official cause of death on my grandfather's death certificate was heart failure, and I didn't have enough evidence to order his body exhumed and tested for an overdose of sleeping pills.

My hope was Nora would go to jail for her attempt on *my* life. Then I'd feel some justice was served. And if she bothered me again, I would call the police . . . or more accurately, the sheriff's department since I live over twenty miles outside of Kalamazoo's city limits, and Zenith is too small for a police department.

Baraka padded over and sat down in front of me, looking at me with those big brown eyes of his. I knew he was asking if it wasn't time for his dinner. "Not yet," I told him, but decided I might as well go ahead with my dinner plans. So what if Wade wasn't going to join me? I liked lasagna. "If you're lucky," I said, giving Baraka a pat on the head, "I'll share some of my dinner with you."

I turned the oven temperature up high so it wouldn't take too long for the lasagna to heat, set the pan on the middle rack, and then opened the bottle of merlot I'd bought special for tonight, and poured myself a glass. Since I no longer had a reason to clean my house—and I've never been one who felt cleanliness was next to godliness—a glass of wine and the local paper seemed like a good way to unwind after an afternoon of talking to seniors.

However, before I even sat down, I remembered the briefcase in the trunk of my car. That old lady might not have all of her marbles, but she was persistent. Sooner or later, I was going to have to look inside that briefcase, if only to figure out how to return it to her.

With nothing better to do, sooner seemed better than later.

THREE

I set the briefcase on the end of my dining room table, next to my glass of wine, and for a moment simply stared at its battered and worn exterior. Soft-sided, with outside pockets designed to carry a computer and cell phone, and an expandable midsection, the case was designed for multiple functions.

I immediately checked for a laptop and found none. Same result with the cell phone pocket. The briefcase's zipper had a lock, but it wasn't engaged, and I easily slid it open. Which made me think the librarian was right: This was probably an old briefcase Ida Delaney's nephew gave her. It seemed to me, if the briefcase contained something the nephew was going to use as blackmail, he would have locked it.

Five cream-colored, pint-size cardboard boxes sat on top of a pile of papers. One by one I removed the boxes. Each had to weigh at least a pound, and each was marked with a combination of two numbers and a letter. They were sealed with clear shipping tape, but I could tell they had been opened at some time and resealed.

"Her nephew is a soil tester," Emily had said.

So were the boxes filled with dirt the nephew was testing? Or dirt Ida had dug up herself?

As I contemplated looking in one, I took a sip of wine . . . and nearly spit it out.

I'm no connoisseur of wine, but I know when something tastes like vinegar. And to think, I actually spent more than my usual ten dollars for this bottle of merlot. All to impress Wade. Who now wasn't coming. What a bummer of a day this was turning into.

I set the glass back on the table, and decided to postpone opening a box. I wanted to look through the papers beneath the boxes. Somewhere in that pile might be an incriminating document or picture Ida's nephew could use to blackmail someone.

The top paper immediately piqued my curiosity. It reminded me of a treasure map. Two curved lines divided the sheet into three sections that might have represented bodies of water or land. I couldn't tell. A series of Xs were scattered over all three sections, a trio of numbers and letters penciled in next to each X. Five of those combinations matched the labels on the boxes now sitting on my table.

Beneath the map-like page was a fourteen-page printout listing various chemicals and their toxicity: nitrogen, selenium, benzene, fluorine, mercury, and lead. I scanned the pages, and noticed certain paragraphs had been highlighted. I figured I'd come back to those later.

I found photographs under the printout. Twelve in all. Evidently taken from an airplane or helicopter. Five of the aerial photos included farmhouses that looked somewhat familiar, but since I'm not accustomed to looking at houses from above, I couldn't be sure. Also several of the photos had ink marks on them—dots and Xs that seemed randomly placed. *Put there by Ida?* I wondered. *Or by her nephew?*

I thumbed through all twelve of the pictures several times. Looked at them upside-down and sideways. I even found a magnifying glass and studied the photos. If Ida Delaney's nephew discovered something in one of those pictures that he thought he could use to blackmail a person, I sure didn't see it.

At the very bottom of the briefcase lay a small, spiral-bound notebook with a scratched and dirty green cover. I picked it up and slipped the photos back into the briefcase. The notebook contained names, addresses, and phone numbers, along with dates and notes. The notes made no sense to me, but several of the addresses were local, and I recognized two of the names. One was a crop farmer who had recently received an award and had his picture in the *Zenith Press*. The other was a dairy farmer who didn't live far from me.

A couple of dates in the notebook were fairly recent.

So, Donald, did you give this to your aunt, or did she take it?

If she'd taken it without his knowledge, he was probably looking for it. I hadn't found anything that looked like it could be used to blackmail anyone, but I also hadn't found anything with the nephew's name, address, or phone number on it. Which seemed strange. Most men carry extra business cards in their briefcases, or have some form of identification in them, just in case the briefcase was lost. With that in mind, I began digging through the inside pockets.

When my fingertips touched a slender, rectangular, hard plastic object, I carefully lifted it out. My first reaction was surprise. With a pocket designed for holding a cell phone on the outside of the briefcase, it seemed strange to find one placed where it wouldn't be easy to access. My second reaction was envy. I own an old, flip-top style cell phone with a small screen that shows a phone number, caller's ID, or a line of a text message, but that's all. The phone I now held was one of the newer, very expensive kinds that could do everything—make phone calls, text messages, access the Internet, take pictures, listen to music. Everything.

I lost my cell phone once. The person who found it tracked me down by redialing my most recently called numbers. Looking at this phone, I hoped I could do the same. Besides, I wanted to give the phone a try, see just exactly what I was missing.

What I was missing, it turned out, was a password.

For a moment I stared at the white box on the phone's screen, the request for a password mocking my efforts to be a good citizen. Shaking my head, I looked down at my dog. "Know any good passwords, Baraka?"

He looked up from the rawhide bone he'd been chewing on, closed one eye, as if winking, and went back to the bone.

"Yeah, well, me neither."

I turned off the phone and set it on the table next to the five dirt-filled boxes. I decided, if I couldn't open the phone, I'd open one of the boxes.

A plastic bag filled the inside, a twist-tie holding it shut. As the librarian had said, the box was filled with dirt. Plain, ordinary, everyday dirt.

I opened the plastic bag, gave its contents a sniff, and tested its texture. As far as I could tell, there was nothing out of the ordinary about the sample, nothing out of the ordinary about the "treasure" map and lab printouts. Nowadays lots of farmers tested their fields so they knew what types of fertilizer to apply and where.

I reached for the map page that had the Xs and coded letter/number combinations. My hand was just above the page when the timer on my oven went off.

Baraka must have thought the buzzer meant his food was ready. Rawhide bone forgotten, he leaped to his feet, ramming into my side, and knocking me against my dining room table. My hand hit the glass of wine. I could see it tipping and grabbed for it . . . but not fast enough. In an instant, a pool of red covered the "map" I'd been about to pick up, along with part of the lab report.

"Baraka!" I yelled, righting the wine glass and moving everything away from the spilled liquid. "Darn you!"

He stopped at the entrance to the kitchen and looked back. I hurried by him, silenced the timer-buzzer with the tap of my finger, and yanked a slew of paper towels off the roll. Back at the table, I sopped up the wine and patted the wet pages. The "treasure map" and half of the report was soaked. The exposed sides of the boxes looked like spatter paintings.

"Now what do I do?" I asked, as if Baraka could answer.

He simply sat and cocked his head, the black hairs outlining his eyes and the wrinkles between his eyebrows giving him a quizzical expression. I grabbed more paper towels and dabbed at the mess I'd made. The papers had taken on a pinkish tinge, but so far the ink hadn't run. Ida Delaney's nephew might not be happy with pink reports, but the data was readable.

I did need to place the papers on a flat surface to dry, and since my table and buffet were covered with files, books, and a coffee maker, the top of my washer and dryer seemed the best bet. I carried the wettest pages into the laundry area between my bedroom and bathroom and created an absorbent bed for them using more paper towels. As soon as I had those pages in place, I returned to the dining room.

I wiped down the rest of the papers and boxes and resealed the box I'd opened. Notebook, papers, and boxes went back in the briefcase, where they would be safe from my clumsiness. I was reaching for the cell phone when the smoke alarm in the kitchen went off, and Baraka started howling.

I'd turned off the timer's buzzer but not the oven.

FOUR

Smoke, burned pasta, and blackened cheese greeted me when I lowered the oven door. I opened a window and grabbed a dish towel. Waving the cloth back and forth under the smoke alarm, I finally moved enough fresh air by its sensor to silence the irritating sound. The lasagna, however, was beyond saving.

I settled for a peanut butter sandwich and filled Baraka's dish with his usual quantity of kibble. Our dinners eaten, I began to clean the kitchen. Baraka watched me scrape the ruined lasagna into the garbage, his eyes following every clump of charcoaled pasta, cheese, and meat sauce that disappeared into my wastebasket. That's the beauty of a dog. Even when I burned dinner, he was willing to give it a try. I did find a small amount of meat in the center that looked edible. He thought it tasted great.

I stuck a Jackson Browne CD in my player, cranked up the volume, and sang along as I scrubbed the lasagna pan. That's another nice thing about dogs. They don't criticize an off-note, and couldn't care less if the words don't exactly match the music. Baraka simply stretched out on the kitchen floor and gave a deep sigh.

I thought I might be wrong about Baraka's critical ear when I hit a wrong note, and he barked and jumped to his feet, the hair on the nape of his neck bristling. Then I heard the knock at my back door.

Heart pounding, I turned away from the sink. It was past

nine o'clock, and even though the sun hadn't set, none of my neighbors would simply drop by at this late hour. Not for a casual visit.

When I moved into my grandparents' old farmhouse, I thought living in the country would be safer than living in the city. I quickly learned that wasn't true. If anything, the isolation made me more vulnerable.

My first thought was Nora. She'd ignored the judge's restraining order once. No reason she wouldn't do it again. Get rid of me, and there'd be no one to protest her claim on those woods.

I grabbed the cast iron fry pan from the stove. It wouldn't provide a lot of protection, but it was better than a wet dishrag. And then I glanced out the window. Instead of a green Chevy, I saw the front of a tan Jeep, and my fear turned to anger.

"What do you think you're doing?" I demanded, jerking open the door. "You just scared the living daylights out of me."

Wade Kingsley looked at me through the screen door, then at the frying pan I held. "I thought I was coming to see you?"

"You said you weren't coming."

"My partner said he'd finish the paperwork." Wade glanced past me. Jackson Browne was introducing another song, his words somewhat muted. Wade frowned. "Did I come at an inopportune time?"

That he even thought I had another man in the house angered me more. "What! You think I called someone the moment you said you weren't coming? And yes, you came at an inopportune time. I burned your dinner."

"I can tell." Wade opened the screen door and walked in. "But I'm not hungry for food."

"Oh, so you get a hard-on and decide you can make time for me?" I glanced down at the crotch of Wade's khaki trousers. Baraka was also investigating that area.

"That's not what I meant," Wade said and casually pushed Baraka's nose away. "Are you going to hit me with that?"

I still held the fry pan in a defensive position. Turning, I placed it back on the stove. "I should. You could have called and let me know you were coming."

"I wanted to surprise you."

"Well, you did." I kept glaring, but I was glad to see him.

I don't know what it is about Wade Kingsley, but from the first time I met him, I've found him attractive. He fits that old cliché of tall, dark, and handsome, and even though he's a homicide detective and doesn't have to wear a uniform, the way he holds himself and walks telegraphs his authority.

Initially, I was entranced by his eyes. They're blue, but it's more like a sea blue than a sky blue. More like the color of Lake Michigan on a sunny day. And his lashes. A man shouldn't have eyelashes that long and sexy.

Attraction or not, he's a man—irritating one minute and absolutely wonderful the next. In a way, I owe my life to him. Or maybe he owes his to me. I'm still not sure about that. Some things he won't tell me. He says he can't, and maybe because of his job, that's true. When it comes to discussions about law enforcement, we often disagree. He sees things in black and white, legal or illegal; I'm not always sure it's that easy to determine.

Tonight, it wasn't a legal issue that had me upset but an emotional one, and most of the conflict was on my part. "So why are you here?"

"I wanted to see you. It's been a week."

That's not my fault, I almost said. Instead, I shrugged. "I've . . . I've had things on my mind."

Again, I said nothing, and I could tell my silence was getting to him. He glanced away and took in a deep breath before tilting his head to the side and smiling. "I have missed you. Missed talking to you."

"Yeah, right." Lately, we hadn't been doing a lot of talking. Not unless you counted the moans and groans we'd made in bed the last time he stayed over. "You could have called."

"It's not the same as being here." He stepped closer and gently ran the backs of his fingers along the side of my face. "Being with you."

Dammit all. The giddy sensation that spiraled through my body, lodging itself between my legs, made denying what I wanted impossible. Within five minutes, we were in my bed, the door closed, Baraka on the other side, whining.

It was midnight when Wade left.

I never did tell him about Nora or Ida Delaney and the briefcase.

FIVE

The next morning I awoke feeling strangely alone. If all had gone as planned, Wade and his son were now fishing on his boat somewhere off the shores of South Haven. Just the two of them: father and son. They might even head up to Saugatuck, Wade had said. Might anchor just inside the breakwater or on Kalamazoo Lake and spend the night on the boat.

That's the way it should be, I told myself. *He only gets to see his son every other weekend, so stop feeling sorry for yourself.*

I pulled on a pair of shorts and a T-shirt, and then headed for the bathroom. The moment I came out of that room, Baraka greeted me. Although he sleeps in his crate, I no longer close the door. So far he hasn't had any "accidents" or chewed anything left on the floor. I know a lot of people sleep with their dogs, but if I'm going to share my bed, it's going to be with a man, not a dog.

Baraka led me into the kitchen. Coffee comes first for me. A trip outside is his priority. I let him out the kitchen door to do his duty.

As I rinsed out the carafe, I thought about Wade. "Stay safe," he'd said when he left me last night. Not exactly a declaration of love. But did I even *want* him falling in love with me? Did I want to move our relationship into anything more than good friends and bed partners?

Ten percent of the world's population has schizophrenia. The child of a schizophrenic has an even higher risk of getting the disease. With men, the onset usually starts in their teens. With women, it can show up much later, even into their mid-thirties. I'm only twenty-eight. My symptoms could show up at any time, which is why, in the past, I've avoided long-term relationships. Why I still needed to avoid anything serious.

"I'm fine with or without you, Wade Kingsley," I said aloud, determined to vanquish my feelings of loneliness. So I felt left out. No big deal. I'd get over it. I had my dog. Baraka wouldn't care if I acted crazy or not.

He barked just then.

Rhodesian Ridgebacks aren't a breed that barks a lot, and I was curious, especially since this bark had sounded fearful. Although I'd let him out the kitchen door, I could tell he was now in front of the house. I set the coffee carafe aside and headed for my dining room.

The fencing around the house keeps Baraka from dashing into the road or chasing a deer into the woods, but it wouldn't stop a skunk from entering the yard. Just two days ago my neighbor, Howard Lowe, said he'd seen one of those black-and-white "kitties" around. I hoped I wouldn't be spending my morning deodorizing Baraka with a tomato juice bath.

The old, two-story farmhouse I inherited from Grandpa Benson still had its original windows, mainly because they weren't standard and it would be difficult and expensive to replace them. The window by my front door was at least five feet high and eighteen inches wide. I could easily see my dog through it. He stood on the porch, facing the driveway, his body rigid and his neck and head extended. The hair running from the top of his head to his tail, including along his ridge, stood on end. Coming toward him on the gravel walkway that ran from the driveway to my porch, was not a skunk but a burly, brown-haired man wearing tight-fitting, faded jeans, a white polo shirt, and a denim jacket. Sunglasses hid his eyes, but I could tell from the narrow line of his mouth and the furrow of his brow that he wasn't pleased with my dog's aggressive stance.

I, on the other hand, was delighted. I didn't need to worry about a skunk squirting Baraka, and twice in two days he'd become a protector of his territory.

My delight in Baraka's protective qualities was short lived. The man said something, and Baraka immediately began wagging his tail, the hair along his neck and haunches returning to normal, and all signs of aggression disappearing. He backed up, allowing the man to climb the steps onto the porch.

I opened the door before the man had a chance to knock, but not all the way, and I left the screen door closed.

"Beautiful dog," he said, looking down at Baraka. "He's one of those African lion dogs, isn't he?"

"Some people call them that." I cracked the screen door open just enough for Baraka to wiggle inside. Maybe my dog hadn't been as protective as I might have liked, but I would rather have him by my side than near this man. I wasn't sure why, but something about the stranger made me wary. Once my dog was inside, I said, "What can I do for you?"

He showed me my business card. "This is you, isn't it?"

"Yes." Although I don't have my address on my card, I do have my phone numbers—home and cell—and anyone with a little Internet knowledge could track me down. "Where'd you get that?"

"I understand you talked to Ida Delaney yesterday, that she gave you a briefcase."

"Ah, yes." I'd seen her take my card. In fact, I think she may have taken more than one. "You must be her nephew."

He didn't confirm or deny my assertion; in fact, he didn't say anything. Although he hadn't taken off the dark glasses, I could feel his eyes boring into mine. Then he looked beyond me, into my dining room, and smiled, just slightly.

37

I have an office. It's not much, simply a section of my living room where last month I had a contractor build a wall and put in a door so I could keep my business equipment and files out of sight. Thing is, I still like working at my dining room table, and, as usual, I had a pile of paperwork—and the briefcase— clearly in view.

"I see what I'm looking for," Ida's nephew said, and jerked open the screen door.

"Wait!" I tried using my body to block his entrance.

Which was a mistake. At five-feet-two, and less than a hundred and five pounds, I presented no obstacle. He pushed his way past me without as much as an "excuse me."

"Hey—!" I spun toward him. "You can't just barge in here."

But it seemed he could. And if I'd thought Baraka would defend me, I was wrong. Instead of attacking the intruder, my dog ran into the kitchen.

"If you'll just wait." I grabbed at his jacket sleeve, hoping to stop him so I could explain what had happened.

A quick jerk of his arm tore his sleeve from my grasp. "Is this everything?"

I glared at him. "You tell me."

"You looked inside?"

"Yes, I looked inside. I was trying to find a name. A phone number. A way to contact you." Though now I was sorry I'd bothered. "Look, I didn't ask your aunt to give that to me. She put it in my car. I would have gotten it back to you today."

He chuckled. "So you looked in the briefcase, and you didn't call the police?"

"Should I have?" I stepped back, closer to the door. Ida had said he was trying to blackmail someone. What had I missed?

He ignored me and zipped the briefcase closed.

"She's worried about you, you know." I felt he should understand why she'd given me the briefcase. "I don't know what you have, but trying to blackmail someone could be really dangerous."

He lifted the case from the table, scattering some of my papers in the process, and turned back toward me. "Be glad you don't know. In fact, you'd better forget you ever saw this briefcase . . . or me."

"Trust me, I'm not going to forget you."

Not a wise thing to say I realized when the back of his hand hit the side of my face. The blow propelled me against the edge of the door, my head slamming into the metal stile so hard it jarred my teeth. My legs collapsed beneath me, my thoughts jumbling, and I fell to the floor with a thud. For a moment I couldn't see anything, but I heard Baraka growl—a deep-throated rumble.

And then his growl turned into a yelp of pain, and I knew the brute had kicked him.

"Damn you!" I yelled. "Leave my dog alone."

"Shut up," Ida Delaney's nephew demanded, towering over me. "You listen to me now. I wasn't here, and you've never seen me or this briefcase. Do you understand?"

I stared up at him.

"Do you understand?" he said, firmer than before.

I gave a slight nod.

"Good." A cruel smile touched his lips. "Not a word to anyone. Not if you don't want me to come back here."

I waited until he left the house before I tried to get up. Slowly I struggled to my feet, dizzy and confused. Holding onto the side of the door, swaying slightly, I watched him drive away. "Bastard," I muttered and felt blood in my mouth. I pushed open the screen door, stumbled outside, and spat on the lawn.

I squinted to see the license plate on the car. It was a Michigan plate and either had two number ones or two Ls. The car itself was tan, but I don't know one model from the next. It did have four doors and was fast. My assailant must have floored the accelerator the moment he pulled onto the pavement.

Assailant. I've been around Wade too long. I've started thinking like a law officer.

Inside the house, I checked on Baraka. He'd slunk under the dining room table and was licking his side. "Poor baby," I murmured as I pushed on his ribs. "You tried, didn't you? But that mean man was just too big for both of us."

Nothing seemed to be broken, but I knew I'd be watching Baraka closely for the next twenty-four hours to make sure he didn't have any internal injuries. I hoped being kicked wouldn't make him shy . . . or overly aggressive.

The numbness on both sides of my face had begun to change to pain, and I couldn't stop shaking. For a moment I wasn't sure what to do next—put ice on the bruises, take aspirin, or call Wade. I might have indicated I wouldn't say anything to anyone about what had happened, but there was no way I was staying silent. This guy needed to be stopped.

I dialed Wade's cell phone number.

Two rings and a recorded voice stated the number I had called was not available. I disconnected and called nine-one-one.

Six

"He hit me," I told the dispatcher, the shock of what had happened still leaving me dazed. "Slammed me right into the side of my front door."

"Who hit you?" she asked, her voice calm and controlled.

"I don't know." I could feel tears welling in my eyes. Tears of anger. I didn't like being a victim.

"Is that person still in the house?"

"No," I assured her. "He left. He took what he came for, hit me, and left."

"And what did he take?"

"A briefcase."

"Anything valuable in this briefcase?"

"Obviously he thought so."

"Yes, of course. What I mean was it full of money? Drugs?"

"Boxes of dirt," I said, then realized how ridiculous that sounded. "They were marked with some sort of coding. And there were papers with similar codes . . . and pictures. The kind taken from an airplane."

"But no drugs?"

"No, no drugs. No money."

"When the officer arrives, tell him exactly what happened."

"I will. I just . . . I mean . . . He took me completely by surprise. I didn't want to take the briefcase in the first place. He—"

She cut me off. "Do you need an ambulance?"

41

"An ambulance?" I touched each side of my face, then looked at my hand. No blood. "No, I guess not."

"I can send one."

"Don't bother." I didn't need a bill for an ambulance run that wasn't necessary.

"If you're sure." She asked me to wait a moment, then came back. "An officer is on his way. Do you want me to stay on the line until he arrives?"

"No. I'm fine. Thank you." I hung up, and sank onto one of my dining room chairs. Baraka came out from under the table and put his head on my lap. "I'm sorry, baby," I murmured as I stroked his head. "You tried. He was just bigger than both of us."

I was mentally rehashing exactly what had happened when I remembered the papers I'd spilled wine on the night before. I got up and went into the laundry area.

My scheme to keep the papers from wrinkling didn't work as well as I'd hoped. In the process of drying, the edges had curled, and the paper had become quite brittle. Even though I couldn't see how anything on these pages could be used to blackmail someone, I decided, while I waited for the deputy to arrive, I'd make copies of everything.

It seemed like hours before a sheriff's patrol car pulled into my yard. The moment the uniformed officer stepped out, I wished Wade wasn't in South Haven fishing. The tall, skinny deputy walking toward me had come to my house several times two months ago. Neither he nor his partner had believed me when I told them someone had been in my house while I was gone. They told Wade I was as crazy as my mother, and for a while, Wade had believed them.

"Whatya do, run into a door?" Deputy Chambers asked the moment he stepped into the house.

42

"As a matter of fact, I did." I lowered the bag of frozen peas I'd been holding against the side of my face. "With a little help from the guy who hit me."

While waiting for the deputy to arrive, I'd looked in a mirror. My face could have been the inspiration for a Picasso. Although I'd been hit with the back of a hand, Ida's nephew had obviously been wearing a large ring. I could see the impression on my left cheek. Not anything that would give an idea what the ring looked like, but the area where it had hit had already doubled in size.

The side of my face that had slammed against the edge of the door looked even worse. I had a welt from my temple to my chin that was darkening to an odd shade of black. Even my nose appeared puffy and was tender to the touch. My eyes are brown, but the whites around my irises were streaked with red.

I'd tried to brush my short curls into a semblance of order, but quickly decided my hair could stay the way it was. So what if it looked like a brown mop. My scalp hurt.

"Sergeant Kingsley do this to you?"

That Chambers would even suggest such a thing upset me. "Sergeant Kingsley is out on Lake Michigan, fishing with his son."

"His son is only six."

"I know that." Obviously Chambers didn't think six-year-olds could fish. "Wade didn't hit me. Some guy hit me. A big guy. I think he might be Ida Delaney's nephew."

"And who's Ida Delaney?"

Good question. "A woman I met yesterday. An old woman. She gave me a briefcase. She said her nephew was trying to blackmail someone. She wanted me to help her."

"Why you?"

Another good question. "I don't know. I gave a talk on how older people could protect themselves from scams. For some reason she seemed to think I could protect her . . . or her nephew."

"What's the nephew's name?"

"Donald. Maybe Donald Delaney, if he and his aunt have the same last name. Maybe not."

"And who's blackmailing this Donald guy?"

"It's the other way around. He's blackmailing someone. And no, I don't know who."

"I see." Chambers glanced around my dining room, at the door I'd slammed into earlier, and then back at me. "Was Detective Kingsley here last night?"

"Yes." I frowned, wondering what Chambers had seen to make him ask that.

"What time did he leave?"

"Around midnight. Why?"

"Well, we've all noticed how Kingsley's been on edge lately," Chambers said, drawing out the words. "Argumentative. So I'm thinking maybe you said something he didn't like hearing. Something that made him hit you."

I stared at Chambers. I couldn't believe this man. Two months ago, he'd made me sound like the guilty person. Now he was trying to involve Wade. "I didn't say anything to Wade that made him hit me because he didn't hit me. Some guy I've never met or seen before hit me. Hit and threatened me."

"Because you were trying to blackmail him?"

"No." I was lightheaded, and a throbbing headache made me nauseous. "Can we sit down?"

Chambers gave me a quizzical look, and then reached for his radio. "I think I'd better call the paramedics."

"No. Don't," I said, maybe a little too fast. "I'm fine." I really didn't want the Zenith fire department sending a truck out. If they did, within the hour everyone in town would know what had happened. That's the way it is in a small community. "I just need to sit down."

"You don't look fine," Chambers said, showing the most concern he had since arriving. "But yes—" He motioned toward one of the chairs at my table. "Do sit down."

I eased myself onto the nearest wooden chair, and Chambers sat across from me. He pulled a notebook and pencil out of his pocket. "Okay, again, from the beginning, tell me exactly what happened."

I did, starting with my talk at the library Friday afternoon and ending with my call for help this morning. I gave what I thought was a pretty good description of the guy who hit me. Chambers made notes as I spoke, but when I told him about the car and license plate, he shook his head. "That's not much to go on."

"I was still stunned . . . from being hit."

"You say this guy's name is Donald Delaney?"

"I said it might be." While talking to Chambers, I'd been thinking about that. "The librarian said Ida Delaney's nephew is nice. Very polite. Believe me, this man wasn't nice . . . or polite. So maybe he's the person the nephew is trying to blackmail."

"Threatening him with something in the briefcase?"

I started to nod, but a sharp pain along the back of my head stopped me. "Yes."

"What?"

"I don't know. According to the librarian, the nephew analyzes soil samples for farmers. Everything I saw in that briefcase—the aerial photos, boxes of dirt, and lab report—could have been related to his job. In fact, until that guy showed up here this morning, I figured Ida Delaney was going senile and only thought her nephew was trying to blackmail someone."

Chambers nodded and glanced at his watch. I could tell he was eager to leave. Which was fine since there wasn't much more I could tell him. However, I still wasn't sure he believed my story. "I have something to show you," I said and stood, cringing at the pain any motion created. "I spilled some wine last night. It got on some of the papers. One of those papers looked like a map. It wasn't in the case when the guy took it. I'll get it and the others for you."

I didn't rush. The two aspirin I'd taken weren't touching the throbbing in my head. Back in my office, I grabbed the original wine-stained papers, but I left the copies in the machine. I wanted to show them to Wade the next time I saw him.

I returned to find Deputy Chambers kneeling and rubbing Baraka's ears. He stood as I approached and brushed his hands on his trousers. "Your dog's grown since I last saw him. Think he'll get much bigger?"

"Maybe an inch taller." I handed him the papers. "He'll fill out. Get a lot more muscular."

"Big as he is, I'm surprised he didn't try to protect you."

"He did. The guy kicked him."

"All around nice guy, huh?" Chambers thumbed through the pages.

"That's the one I think is a map," I pointed at the page with the Xs.

"Looks like a kid's drawing." He turned the page upside down, then on its side. Now that he mentioned it, it did sort of look like a child's drawing, except for the numbers and letters next to the Xs.

"Some of those number/letter combinations matched ones on the boxes," I explained.

Chambers took time to read a wine-stained printout before he asked, "You ever have the soil on this farm analyzed?"

"No. That is, there's a farmer who leases the farm land I own. He may have had an analysis done. I don't know. Why?"

"Just curious." He looked back at the map. "You said there

were aerial photos of farms in the briefcase. Any idea where they were taken?"

"A few looked familiar, but from the air one farmhouse or field looks about the same to me."

"And you have no idea where the old woman and her nephew live?"

"Just that it's somewhere in Kalamazoo. I think the librarian would know."

"Doesn't really sound like you *know* much of anything." He smiled and slipped his notebook back in his pocket. "How's your mother doing?"

I could see where this was going. "My mother is doing fine, Deputy Chambers. *I* am doing fine. This is not something I made up." I pointed at my face. "I do not go around slamming my head against a door. And no, Wade did not hit me. Some creep I've never seen before did this, and he threatened to do worse things to me if I told anyone, so you'd damn well better find him before he comes back here."

"No need to get snippy, Miss Benson," Chambers said and started for the door. "I will follow up on this. Meanwhile, I think you need to see a doctor, get some x-rays."

The way my face ached, I was beginning to believe he might be right. Something could be broken.

Before pushing the screen door open, he paused. "Is there someone who can drive you to the hospital, or do you want me to call an ambulance?"

"Don't bother." I just wanted him gone. "I'll have a neighbor drive me in."

After Chambers left, I considered calling Howard Lowe. He owed me a favor or two. I actually picked up the phone and dialed his number, and then I hung up. I wasn't so bad off I couldn't drive myself into Kalamazoo. Why make someone wait around for hours while I had an x-ray or two taken? Baraka seemed to be okay. He'd be fine in his crate until I returned. And this way, I could go see my grandmother after I left the hospital. I wanted her take on what had happened.

SEVEN

I arrived at my grandmother's house five hours after signing in at the hospital's emergency room. Considering that I'd arrived at the ER on a Saturday morning and several of those in the waiting room sported bruises similar to mine—many of them, I gathered, won in barroom fights—I guessed my wait wasn't too long. The first thing I was asked by the ER nurse was if I had been in a fight. I wasn't sure how to answer that question. "To fight" implied a combat of two or more people. My attacker never gave me a chance to engage in combat.

"Come in, come in," my mother said when she opened the front door, a cigarette dangling from her lips. Then she noticed my face and frowned. "What did you do, run into a door?"

"Got slammed into one," I said, glad the shades were drawn and the lighting was dim inside the house. Even with dark glasses, light was bothering my left eye.

"You telling me that policeman boyfriend of yours hit you?" Grandma asked, coming out of the kitchen, holding a dish towel. She shook her head as she neared. "Boy, he did a job on you."

"It wasn't Wade," I said, upset that everyone seemed intent on blaming him. "He wasn't anywhere around." I headed straight for the living room and Grandma's sagging, overstuffed couch. The TV was on, a squeaky-voiced newscaster questioning the sudden disappearance of Kalamazoo Township's drain commissioner. This was big news since only a few years ago

49

another drain commissioner had been accused of sexual harassment and misdemeanor extortion. That one had a massive stroke while scuba diving in Florida and ended up in a nursing home. No one seemed to know what had happened to this one.

The shot I'd been given for pain was kicking in, but the newscaster's voice was putting me on edge. I grabbed the remote and pushed mute. "It was either Ida Delaney's nephew who hit me," I said. "Or someone who knew she'd given me that briefcase."

"Her nephew hit you when you returned the case?" Grandma sat down beside me and leaned close to get a better view of my face. My mother remained standing, a cloud of cigarette smoke encircling her head.

I took off the dark glasses so the two of them had a better view of my eyes, and both gave a low whistle. "You need to see a doctor," my mother said.

"I just came from the hospital." I patted the pocket of my jeans. "They gave me a shot for pain and a prescription for Motrin. X-rays didn't show any broken bones, and they didn't think I had a concussion. They said I'd feel better in a few days."

Not exactly what I'd wanted to hear considering how bad I felt when the doctor said that, but now that the pain medicine was taking effect, I thought I might live.

"If you got whiplash, it will take more than a few days," Grandma said and gave my arm a pat. "You want to stay here?"

"I can't. I have Baraka to take care of." And even without him, I wouldn't have wanted to. Living with two smokers I'd learned was like being stuck in a chimney.

"So what happened?" my mother asked, sounding perfectly normal, to my continuing relief. As long as she stayed on her medication, she was like any mother—loving and concerned.

The problems occurred when she decided she no longer needed her meds.

As I explained what had happened that morning, my mother did sit down. Every so often she or my grandmother interrupted to ask a question, but mostly, they listened. When I told them about Deputy Chambers and how he'd treated me, Grandma shook her head. "You'd think, after what you went through two months ago, he would treat you with some respect."

I shrugged. We'd agreed, after the events that turned my life around and introduced me to Homicide Detective Wade Kingsley, not to discuss that incident, especially not in front of my mother. Considering her illness, we weren't sure how she might process the information if we kept talking about it.

An alarm clock upstairs went off. My mother jumped to her feet and snuffed out her cigarette—I think it was her third since I'd arrived. "Time for me to change. *I* have a date."

Her grin was a delight to see, and I waited until she'd gone upstairs before I mouthed to Grandma, "A date?"

"It's a guy she met at work," Grandma explained, keeping her voice low. "I've met him a couple of times. He's a little odd looking, but he seems nice enough."

"He also works at Goodwill?"

Grandma nodded. I wanted to know more about this new man in my mother's life, but Grandma was focused on what had happened to me. "How did this guy know how to find you?" she asked.

"He had my business card." I thought about that. If the man at my house had been Ida Delaney's nephew, as I'd originally assumed, it would have been logical for her to give him my business card. But if the guy wasn't her nephew . . . "I don't know how he got it. I don't know how he knew I had the briefcase . . . unless Ida told him."

"Do you know her phone number?"

"No." It was the same problem I'd had when talking to Deputy Chambers. I didn't know Ida's phone number, where she lived, or if her nephew's last name was Delaney.

"I'll get a phone book," Grandma said and headed for the kitchen. "Do you want anything? Water? Coffee?"

"Nothing," I called after her.

She came back with a phone book, and we scanned the listings for a Donald Delaney or Ida Delaney. Neither one was in the book. Grandma called the library, but that led us nowhere. Emily Anderson didn't work on Saturdays, and the librarian I talked to either had no idea how to reach Ida's nephew or wasn't about to tell me. When I discovered Emily had an unlisted number, I gave up. "I guess I'll never know how he got my card or knew about the briefcase."

"Well, what did your boyfriend say when you told him what happened?" Grandma asked.

"He doesn't know what happened."

"You haven't told him?"

"Evidently there's no cell phone service wherever he and his son are fishing."

I looked away, surprised by the tears forming in my eyes. Grandma noticed. "That bothers you, doesn't it . . . that he's not available when you need him."

At first I considered denying her statement, then I decided to confess all. "It's more than that, Grandma. He didn't call me once last week. Didn't ask me to go fishing with them this weekend. And then he broke our date last night. He had work to do, he said. It didn't matter that I'd been looking forward to seeing him, that I'd spent half the morning fixing his favorite meal."

"Men don't think of those things."

"Yeah, well, I'll tell you what they do think about. Hours later he showed up at my door, all horny and ready to . . . ?"

"Hop into bed," Grandma finished for me and grinned. "So you feel he's taking you for granted. Is that it?"

"Maybe. I mean, I feel like I'm always second. Second to his son. Second to his job. Second to—" I stopped myself and glanced upstairs, where my mother was now getting ready for her date. "Shoot, I don't know what I'm saying . . . or what I'm complaining about. Until I know I'm not going to turn out like her, I don't want to get involved with a man. I mean, I shouldn't . . . should I?"

"Why shouldn't you?" Grandma asked. "What are you going to do, wait until you're fifty before you allow yourself to fall in love?" She scooted closer and slipped an arm around my shoulders. She weighed even less than I did, but I felt the strength in her embrace, along with the support. "Honey, you've got to stop living in fear of becoming a schizophrenic."

"Sounds great, but how do I go about doing that?"

"Make an appointment to see a doctor. Have some tests run. If you're not showing any signs of the disease, try to stop worrying about it. Don't forget, stress is one of the factors that can bring it on."

What she was saying made sense.

"And as far as your detective . . ." She grinned. "Maybe what he needs is to see you with another man. I'm not saying jump in bed with someone else, but a little competition wouldn't hurt."

EIGHT

I spent the rest of that day and all of Sunday lying on my couch feeling sorry for myself. Ice packs helped reduce the swelling around my eye, but reading anything was impossible, and the idea of doing housework never entered my mind. Not that I think that often about doing housework.

Even Baraka was content to lie around, though when it came time for his meals, he was eager and waiting. That he had a good appetite and his stools showed no signs of blood reassured me that he'd sustained no internal injuries. For both of us, it was simply going to take time for the bruises to heal.

Baraka's reddish-brown coat covered any discoloration of his skin. I wasn't as lucky. By Sunday afternoon, I had a mottling of black and blue that gave a fair image of where the guy's ring and my flesh had come in contact, along with a line on the other side of my face that mirrored the edge of my front door.

It wasn't until late that evening that I started to feel halfway human. As the sun began to set, Baraka and I sat on the edge of my front porch and let the croaking of the frogs and the chirping of the crickets entertain us. Although Friday had been warm and comfortable, a front had swept across Michigan, and all day Saturday and Sunday the temperature and humidity had risen to sweltering levels. A cooling breeze had finally come up, bringing with it the aroma of fresh mown hay.

"Good thing the wind's not blowing the opposite direction," I said, inhaling deeply. As much as I like Bill and Sondra Sommers, a westerly wind brings a pungent odor from their dairy barn.

Baraka licked my cheek, and I draped an arm over his shoulders. I could see a car coming down the road, its headlights on. In the city, I never paid attention to cars going by, but in the country traffic was minimal, more than three cars passing in five minutes seeming like a traffic jam. I watched the car near, slowly recognizing the blue Ford. It belonged to Howard Lowe.

He honked as he passed, but didn't stop. A couple months ago I would have thought that was because he hated me for putting *No Hunting* signs all around my property. Since then, we've come to an understanding of sorts. He still thinks I'm a city slicker who doesn't know squat about living in the country, but he agreed not to hunt in my woods and even brought me some peas from his garden just the other day.

As the sky grew darker, the hoot of an owl signaled the changeover from daytime birds to the night hunters. Across the road, I saw a flicker of light, then another. I watched as the flickering became more numerous, the dots of light appearing close to my house as well as far away. "Lightning bugs," I said to Baraka, as if he needed an explanation. "Fireflies."

I remembered coming out to my grandparents' house when I was a child, and catching fireflies in a jar. It wasn't as easy as it sounded, and my father had laughed at my efforts and told me he'd done the same as a child. Those were good memories.

Sad memories.

The ring of my telephone interrupted my reminiscing. Scrambling to my feet, I went back inside. I recognized Wade's voice the moment he spoke.

"P.J., what the hell happened?"

No *How are you?* or *Are you all right?* His tone turned me defensive. "I got mugged, that's what happened."

"And you told Chambers I hit you?"

"No way."

"That's what I'm hearing."

"Well, it's not coming from me. Who said I said that anyway? Chambers?"

"No, a couple of the guys. They said Chambers took the report, and that you wouldn't come right out and say it was me, but he could tell you were lying, especially when you kept changing your story."

"I did not change my story. If anyone is lying, it's Chambers." Which I wouldn't put past the creep.

"Did you give him some sort of kid's drawing and pages you'd printed out from the computer?"

"That wasn't a kid's drawing, and I didn't print that report, someone else did. Before you start accusing me of things, look at what I did give him. Read his report."

Silence lay between us, long and uncomfortable. I was about to hang up when Wade finally spoke. "Are you all right?"

I was spitting mad, that's what I was, but I kept my voice neutral. "Sort of."

"What do you mean, 'Sort of'?"

"I mean sort of, that's what I mean," I snapped back. "I have a very sore neck, a face that's turning colors, and a puffy eye. But I feel better than I did yesterday, so I'm sort of all right."

"You should see a doctor."

"I did."

Again, there was silence. The next time he spoke, his voice was gentle. "You should have called me."

"I tried. Several times. All I kept getting were messages that your phone was out of service."

"Oh, yeah. I forgot. I had a little accident Saturday morning."

I could hear the embarrassment in his voice. "What kind of accident?"

"Right off the bat, Jason hooked a whopper, and in the process of hauling it onboard, I dropped my phone."

"On the boat?"

"In the lake."

I didn't want to laugh, but I couldn't stop myself. "Yeah, I guess you could call that a 'little accident.' So your phone's now at the bottom of Lake Michigan?"

"Actually, my sister gave me a floaty thing for the phone, just in case something like this happened. It worked, and I was able to snag the phone with my net. But it got wet, and I don't think it's working too well."

"Maybe not at all."

"Maybe." I heard him take a deep breath before he said, "I'm sorry, P.J. I should have been there for you. Do you want me to come over?"

"No." Not the way I was feeling. "It's late."

"You okay?"

"Yeah," I lied and felt a tear slide down my cheek. "Just tired." Tired and still a little angry. "I imagine you are, too." I forced myself to ask. "Did you and Jason have a good time?"

"We did. It's just that . . ." He didn't finish whatever he was going to say. Instead, he said, "For dinner tonight, Jason and I cooked up the Coho he caught. It was delicious."

"I bet." I love salmon. It would have been nice if Wade had invited me to share some with them.

"P.J. . . . ?"

"Look, let's just leave it tonight. Okay? I'll talk to you later."

"P.J., I'm sorry I accused you. It's just that the way things have been going lately—"

I cut him off. "I said I don't want to talk about it. Not tonight. Maybe tomorrow."

I hung up on him and cried, tears of anger mixing with tears of sadness. Wade's call had really bugged me. I wasn't sure where our relationship was headed, but he should have known I'd never tell Chambers he'd hit me. Did he think I was crazy?

That thought made me stop.

Wade and I have talked about the possibility I might turn out like my mother. Maybe the reason he didn't invite me to share the weekend with his son was because he was sorry he ever got involved with me. Maybe . . .

I stopped myself from going on. I really was tired. My face and body hurt. Everything seemed dismal and negative.

Although going to bed sounded good, I decided to watch the eleven o'clock news. Mostly I was interested in what the weather would be like tomorrow. Even though I'd driven by several newly mown hay fields, and I knew those farmers wanted it to stay dry until they got those grasses baled, we really could use some rain.

I expected the lead story to be more speculation regarding the whereabouts of the county drain commissioner. For the last week it seemed that was all our local news people could talk about. Where had he gone? What did finding his car parked at the airport mean? Were any funds missing? I certainly wasn't prepared for the picture that flashed on the television screen along with the headline: *Breaking News.*

The photo showed Ida Delaney and a younger, slender, blonde-haired man standing in front of a two-story house. "Today," the squeaky-voiced female newscaster announced, "the body of Donald Crane—shown here with his aunt, Ida Delaney, who lived with him—was found in the basement of his home."

The camera switched off the picture and onto the newscaster as she continued. "The police are releasing little about the cause of death, but have asked anyone with information regarding the whereabouts of Ida Delaney to contact them immediately. She is described as . . ."

The newscaster went on with a description of Ida's height, weight, age, and general features, but I wasn't listening. All I could think of was the man who'd come to my house the day before. As I'd suspected, he was not Ida's nephew.

That he knew I had the briefcase meant only one thing . . . Ida had told him.

So where was she? What had he done to her?

NINE

Monday morning, I called my grandmother. She has caller ID, so without even saying hello, she asked, "Did you see the news about Ida Delaney's nephew?"

"I did. I guess she was right to be worried about him."

"They're not saying how he died. She's probably dead, too."

That's what I'd been thinking; nevertheless, hearing my grandmother say it aloud sent a shiver down my spine. "I hope not."

"Think it was that guy who hit you?"

"Could be."

"You need to move back into town."

I almost laughed. "Grandma, Ida and her nephew lived in town."

"Oh, right." For a moment she said nothing, but I knew she was thinking. Finally, she said, "What are you going to do?"

"Nothing. He has the briefcase. I described him to Deputy Chambers, and this morning I called and left a message on Chambers's voice mail identifying Donald Crane as the nephew I'd been talking about. It's up to the Sheriff's Department or Kalamazoo's Public Safety officers to find him."

"What if he comes back?"

"I'm hoping he doesn't." But he had threatened to return if I told anyone about him . . . and I had.

"But what if he does?"

"If I see him coming, I'm locking the doors and hiding." I

had an ideal place down in the cellar. "Listen, if you hear anything more, let me know. Okay?"

She said she would, and I hung up. A little while later, Baraka started barking, and I heard a rumble outside my house. I immediately tensed at the sound. It wasn't as if I truly expected that bully to come back, but I was relieved when I looked out the window and saw the ten-yard Dumpster I'd ordered weeks before being delivered. I left Baraka in the house as I directed the driver back around the far edge of the house near my grandparents' old chicken coop. I had him set the Dumpster exactly where a body had lain two months ago, and after the delivery truck left, I stared at the giant trash bin and wondered if throwing out the garbage my grandfather had collected throughout his lifetime would help erase the memory of the gun fight that had occurred at that spot.

I've never owned a gun, but back in April, after finding a man dying in my dining room and having my house broken into several times, I agreed to borrow my neighbor's Smith and Wesson AirLite. I had that gun in my pocket the night I discovered who was behind the murder and break-ins. Wade insists I didn't fire the killing shot, but he also insists I saved his life. All I know is a hero of mine died that night, and it's not something I like to remember.

As soon as I let Baraka out of the house, he considered it his duty to sniff every inch of the base of the Dumpster. It smelled stinky to me. For my dog, it must have been a plethora of delightful aromas. I swear he was smiling when he finished his job.

Soon I would be adding new smells: moldy old magazines and newspapers, cans and bottles that held decades-old scents, dust, dirt, and spider webs, along with nesting boxes and soiled straw. But not today. Bending over still made my head throb.

I started back to the house, but stopped at the sound of Baraka's low, guttural growl. I barely heard him over the clamor the crows had been making. When I looked back, I saw Baraka standing near the Dumpster, facing the woods. His body was rigid, his eyes focused on something in the trees behind the chicken coop.

I couldn't see anything, but I returned to his side and placed the palm of my hand on his shoulders. Tension had turned his muscles to steel, and the rumble of his growl traveled the length of his body. With me, tension started my legs shaking.

"What is it, boy?" I asked, keeping my voice low.

He gave me a quick glance before turning his attention back to the woods. I still couldn't see anything, and all I could hear were those incessant crows, who seemed to feel it their sworn duty to tell every living creature exactly what was happening. How I wished I understood crow.

"Was it a deer?" I whispered, as if Baraka would answer.

Deer often cross through my woods. Or it could have been a fox. About a month ago, while in my woods looking for Morel mushrooms, I found a fox hole. And a couple of days ago, while driving home, I saw a coyote dash across the road. Then there was that skunk my neighbor saw. A skunk would be better than one possibility.

I did not want to see that man from Saturday morning come walking out of those woods.

I stared at the path that cut through the trees, my body poised to run back to my house. Something moved, and Baraka barked. He lunged toward the fence, but I stood where I was. A person came into view. Not the guy from Saturday, but Nora Wright.

Maybe I should have been as frightened of her as I was of that bruiser, but simply knowing she was on my property fired up my temper. I couldn't believe her audacity. "What are you doing here?" I shouted over Baraka's barking.

She looked at me as if I were the one trespassing, glanced at the Dumpster, then at Baraka. "Can't you shut that thing up?"

I wasn't about to tell him to be quiet, but he stopped on his own. Even the crows quieted some. I repeated my question. "What are you doing on my land?"

"I heard a lot of noise." She glanced around. "It sounded like a bulldozer."

"You probably heard the truck delivering this." I pointed at the Dumpster.

"Don't you go putting anything from my woods in there."

"Your woods?" I scoffed and moved closer to my dog. "They're my woods, Nora, and at the moment, you're trespassing."

"It's only a matter of time before they're my woods," she said with far more confidence than I liked.

"That's it!" I snapped. "I've had it. I'm calling the police." I turned away from her and started for my house. "Come, Baraka."

I didn't look back to see if Nora left. I didn't even check to see if my dog was following, but he was by my side when I went up the steps to my back door. I also didn't get a chance to call the sheriff's department. My phone started ringing before I even reached it.

It was Wade.

TEN

"I read Chambers's report," Wade said, an apologetic tone to his voice. "He should have called the paramedics. Should have taken some pictures. From what he wrote, you got pretty banged up. You're sure nothing was broken?"

"Nothing showed up on the x-ray." I ran the palm of my hand over the side of my face. My cheekbone was still tender.

"No concussion?"

"Maybe a slight one." I appreciated Wade's concern, but I wasn't ready to forgive him for his attitude the night before. "I'll survive. Oh, and I called and left a message on his voice mail this morning, but just in case Chambers forgets to add it to his report, I'm now sure the man who hit me wasn't Ida Delaney's nephew. I saw the nephew's picture on TV last night. He's dead."

"I know. That's why I called."

And here I'd thought he was concerned about my welfare.

"You need to call Kalamazoo Public Safety."

"Why? On TV it said to call if you had information about Ida's whereabouts. I have no idea where she might be."

"You may have been the last one to see her alive."

"She's dead?"

"No. That is, they haven't found her body, but from what I've heard, the nephew died from multiple blows to the head and body. If a woman her age was hit with that much force, I don't see her surviving."

"You think the guy who hit me killed the nephew?" The thought made me slump onto a nearby chair. I remembered too clearly the power behind that bruiser's slap. The idea of being punched by him, of being hit over and over again, made my stomach turn and my legs start shaking again. I know my voice quavered when I asked, "Do you think he'll come back here for me?"

That Wade didn't immediately respond with a positive "No" was as telling as when he said, "I think you should consider buying a gun."

Although he couldn't see me shake my head—and the action instantly caused pain—Wade must have heard the jiggle of my brains. I'm sure he understood my silence. Softly, he said, "I know you don't like them, P.J., but neither you nor I would be alive today if not for a gun."

"I killed someone I loved."

"You saved my life."

I wasn't sure if he was finally admitting my shot was the killing shot—for the last two months he'd been telling me it wasn't—or simply reminding me that if I hadn't borrowed Sondra's gun, when I did find the man behind all the mysterious break-ins and a man dying in my house, Wade might also be dead.

"At least be careful," he said, perhaps understanding my reluctance. "And drop by the station. You can look at some mug shots. We might get lucky, might have one of the guy who hit you."

"I will," I said. "But I don't think I'll do it today. I just don't feel up to driving into Kalamazoo."

"You sure you're okay?"

He sounded concerned. "I'm sore, but I'll live."

"You call nine-one-one if you start feeling worse. And call Kalamazoo Public Safety. Tell them what happened Friday, what that old lady said to you, and what happened Saturday morning."

"Okay." I would do that. "I hope she's not dead. She was a little daft, but evidently not as crazy as I thought. Will you be assigned to the case, Wade?"

"No. The murder occurred within the city limits. That makes it Kalamazoo Public Safety's baby."

"Some baby." Death, in my mind, did not equal birth.

"You take care of yourself, P.J.," Wade said softly. "Don't let anything happen to you."

"I'll do my best," I said, feeling less than confident. "You take care of yourself, too."

We hung up then, and I leaned back in my chair and closed my eyes. Too much had happened in the last three days: Ida's demand I look in the briefcase, the face-bruising hulk threatening and hitting me, and the nephew found dead and Ida missing. And then there were my mixed-up feelings about Wade, and Nora's constant harassment.

Nora.

Once again, I'd forgotten to tell Wade about her. I started to dial him back then changed my mind. Wade dealt with homicides, not women who disobeyed restraining orders and trespassed on land. To report Nora's actions, I would need to call another department, explain everything that had happened, past and present. I just wasn't up to that. Not at the moment.

By early afternoon the temperature had risen to the mid-nineties. Way too hot, in my opinion, for the middle of June. Clouds covered the sky, but the humidity made the air feel like a steam bath. My grandparents never installed central air, but I'd purchased a window unit for my office—to keep my computer equipment cool—and found several floor fans stored in the attic. I had one going in the dining room, so even with the windows and doors open, I never heard the blue pickup pull into my yard. It was Baraka's bark that alerted me to its presence. I automatically tensed, but a moment later a slender, middle-aged brunette, wearing jeans, a T-shirt, and a baseball cap, stepped down from the cab, and I relaxed.

The woman had a hand on the gate latch when I came out on the porch, Baraka by my side. Before I could stop him, he raced down the steps toward the gate, barking and wagging his tail at the same time. The woman stepped back from the gate.

"Are you P.J. Benson, the accountant?" she called over Baraka's barking.

"I am. Baraka, down!" I yelled when he jumped up on his side of the gate, rattling the hinges.

The woman smiled at him then looked back at me. "I need a bookkeeper."

"In that case, you probably should contact one of the employment agencies. I'm a CPA. My fees are higher than a bookkeeper would charge."

"The lady at the bank said you're good. Really good. She said you could help me set up the proper accounts for my business so everything was legal, that once you did, I could probably handle most of the paperwork."

God bless a small community. People did help each other. "So you're looking for someone to set up your books?"

"Yes." Her gaze returned to Baraka and the gate. "Can I open this, or will he run off?"

"He won't run off. Just close it behind you."

I watched her enter the fenced-in section of my front yard. She took a moment to let Baraka sniff her before she closed the gate and started toward my house. Baraka followed, tail wagging. I came down the steps and met her halfway. "What kind of business are we talking about?" I asked.

"A boarding kennel, dog grooming, and eventually obedience

training." She smiled and gave Baraka a pat on the head. "He's a Ridgeback, isn't he? I've seen them at dog shows, but never around here."

"There aren't many around," I said, remembering how much trouble I had finding a breeder. "Baraka came from just outside of Chicago."

"I'm Abby Warfield," she said and extended her hand in my direction. "I live about a mile south of here. That is, as the crow flies. A little farther if you take the road out of Zenith."

I shook her hand and tried to think why her name sounded familiar. What she said next explained why.

"If you recognize my name, it's because I'm the one fighting to get the curves taken out of that road. You wouldn't believe how many cars and trucks have ended up in my front yard because they were going too fast and couldn't handle the curve."

"I did see something about that in the *Zenith Press*." Except with everything that was going on, I hadn't read the article.

"I hope you're planning on coming to the meeting tonight."

"Meeting?" I guess I should have read the article.

"The one about straightening the road." She gave me a quizzical look. "At least, come if you think the road should be straightened. I need all the support I can get. That farmer and the old lady who live across the road from me are doing everything they can to stop the road commission from making the change. They don't want to lose a few lousy feet of land. They don't care how those curves affect me."

She looked back down at Baraka. "How would you feel if you boarded your dog, with me, and while he was there a car slammed into the kennel?"

"Has that ever happened?"

"Not yet, but not long ago one came close. And if a dog was ever injured or killed while under my care, I'd be out of business."

I could see her problem. I could also tell she needed to vent. Barely taking a breath, she went on.

"They say straightening that road will take farm land away from them, that they'll lose money. Well, I'm a widow, and I need money, too. I don't have any children, but I love dogs. All kinds of dogs. So when the company I worked for went bankrupt, and I couldn't find a job, I started boarding dogs. I don't make a lot of money from that, but when I add in the grooming and obedience classes, it will be enough to pay the bills. I love what I'm doing, but if that farmer and old lady get their way, it'll only be a matter of time before something bad happens. So what do I do?"

I knew what she wanted to hear. "You get the road straightened."

"Exactly." She nodded her approval and smiled. "So will you come tonight? Come and support me."

"I'll try." That was as much as I was willing to promise.

"And will you set up a bookkeeping system for me? What I have now is a mess."

"Sure." *Why not?* I needed more clients, and I could understand Abby's frustration at not finding a job. Michigan's poor economy made layoffs and unemployment a common occurrence for way too many people. I might even reduce my fees. I liked her openness.

"Good. Great." Her smile widened for a moment, then turned into a frown. "What happened to your face?"

"I ran into a door." It was becoming my set response.

"I hope you hit that door back."

"This one took me by surprise."

"Then I'd suggest staying away from it." She gave a sigh and crouched down, so she was eye level with Baraka. "You're not very old, are you, big boy? But you are a handsome one."

Anyone who thinks my dog is handsome is a-okay with me.

Baraka must have felt the same way. He licked her face.

"He's six months old," I said. "I was going to show him, but I'm not so sure about that, now."

Abby slowly stood, groaning a bit as she did, and then ran her hand over Baraka's ridge, checking its length and the symmetry of the crowns. "Ridge is perfect," she said, "and looks to me like he's going to have good confirmation, though you can't always tell at this age. So why aren't you going to show him?"

"I don't know." Insecurity wasn't something I could easily explain. "I've heard showing is very competitive, and with judging being subjective, big-name kennels often win even though their dog may not be as good as yours."

"Yeah." Abby nodded in agreement. "I showed my Lab when he was a year old. Even though he came from great bloodlines, he rarely got a second look if one of the big-name handlers was in the ring with me. Oh well . . ." A shrug of her shoulders indicated she'd accepted that. "Worse things to worry about now than *pretty*. My dog's only seven, but lately he's started looking and acting much older. He sleeps all the time, and has been losing weight. Some days he won't even eat."

"That's not good. What's your vet say?"

"He checked him over. Said Dexter's heart and lungs sounded good. Gave me some pills that were supposed to give him more energy and perk up his appetite, but I've had Dex on them for a week, and I haven't seen any change. I'm going to take him back, but to be honest, I've been feeling really punky myself lately. Migraine headaches. Upset stomach. Probably all due to stress." She grinned. "Neighbors like mine will do that to you. So, about the bookkeeping . . . ?"

"Come on inside, where it's cooler," I said, glad I had Baraka's shots up-to-date and hoping my own immune system was functioning properly. "I'll fix some iced tea, and we can talk about what you need."

ELEVEN

Before Abby left, she reminded me once again about the road-straightening meeting. I wasn't eager to appear in public with my face looking the way it did, but Abby's plea for support convinced me I should show up. That evening a generous application of foundation did cover some of the bruising, but I wear makeup so rarely, I felt like I'd put on a mask. The moment I stepped into the meeting room, I knew the effort had been wasted. "How are you doing?" was the general question people asked. Along with, "Have they found the guy who did that to you?"

I don't know how news can spread so quickly in Zenith, but it does. They say there are six degrees of separation. In this town I think it may be two or three.

The turnout for the meeting was good. Most of the chairs had already been taken by the time I arrived. A hand waving above the heads of others caught my attention, and I saw my neighbor, Howard Lowe. He was motioning me over to the empty chair next to him, and I headed that direction.

"Figured you'd be here," he said when I sat down. "Saw Abby Warfield's truck at your place this afternoon. She's been trying to get everyone around to come tonight."

"She was there on business, but she did mention the meeting," I said, not wanting to admit Abby was the one who'd convinced me to attend. "She is definitely adamant about wanting the road straightened. What do you think?"

"I think it's gonna raise our taxes. That's what I think." He looked around the room, finally pointing at a lean, wiry-looking man somewhere in his sixties, wearing bib overalls. "Leon there don't want it. The road would cut right through one of his pastures and part of a corn field."

Leon stepped to the side, and I saw Grace, the sophisticated blonde I'd met at the library, the one who'd shared the story about the phony blacktop. "Is that his sister?" I asked Howard, remembering Grace had said she had a brother who lived in Zenith.

"Yup. She's a Realtor. Lives in Kalamazoo, but grew up here in Zenith."

"I met her the other day when I gave a talk in Kalamazoo." I wanted to talk to Grace after the meeting, see what she knew about Ida Delaney.

"The woman next to her is Olivia Halsted," Howard said. "She's the other one here who would lose part of her property if this road thing goes through."

I studied the woman Howard had referred to. From the gray hair, wrinkles around her eyes and mouth, and the flowered blouse and polyester slacks, I guessed Olivia Halsted to be in her late seventies. In a way, she reminded me of my grand-mother, and I wondered if the man standing next to her was her grandson.

Howard must have read my mind. "That's her lawyer, she's talking to," he said. "One of them uppity city fellahs. Don't know his name, and I'm not sure where she found the money to pay him. Owen died owing a pile of back taxes. Olivia had to sell a part of the farm to pay those off."

"Maybe he's doing it pro bono."

Howard snorted. "Never met a lawyer who gave anything away for free. You gettin' one to represent you?"

"You mean against the guy who did this?" I touched the side

of my face where the bruiser's ring had hit.

"No, I mean to stop Nora from takin' those woods of yours."

Again, I was surprised by Howard's knowledge of what was going on. "You know about that paper she showed me?"

"She told me 'bout it when I found her sneaking around them woods of yours."

"You were in my woods this morning?"

"No, this was yesterday. Sunday."

"Both you and Nora were in my woods Sunday?" I should be charging a toll. "What were you doing there?"

"Looking for Jake. He slipped his collar and got away again."

Jake, I knew, was Howard's prize coon hound. I also had a feeling Howard used Jake's "gettin' away" as an excuse to go where he wasn't supposed to be.

"I weren't hunting," Howard said, raising his right hand as if that signified he was telling the truth. "I know you don't want nobody hunting on your land." He rolled his eyes. "You got enough signs posted sayin' so."

"Sounds like you need a new collar for Jake."

"Probably do." He grinned. "He did kill a rabbit while he was back there. I knew you wouldn't want it layin' around, stinking up the place, so I brought it back to my place."

And probably had it for Sunday night supper. I doubted I'd ever really stop Howard from hunting in my woods. "So what did Nora say? What was she doing?"

"She said it was none of my damn business what she was doing there, and that she had a paper signed by your grandfather giving her the woods. As for what she was doin', I don't rightly know. When I saw her, she was diggin' around in some of that junk your grandfather dumped out there. You're gonna need a bigger Dumpster than you got if you think you're gonna clean up those woods."

He was right about that. "The Dumpster's so I can clean the

chicken coop and wood shed, and maybe some of the stuff behind those two buildings."

"Yeah. Lots of junk back behind that chicken coop."

He should know since I once found him there, barely alive. I was going to mention that, but the township supervisor started rapping a gavel on the podium set up at the front of the room, and everyone stopped talking. Officially, the meeting had begun.

The meeting lasted more than an hour and a half. Michigan's Department of Transportation, the Department of Environmental Quality, and the Environmental Protection Agency all gave reports. The representative from MDOT had a chart showing how many accidents had occurred at the site over the years, while the men from the DEQ and EPA assured everyone that straightening those three curves wouldn't affect the water table or any endangered species. The number of accidents seemed small compared to highway statistics, but some people had lost their lives, and I could understand Abby Warfield not wanting cars or trucks barreling into her yard and possibly hitting her dog kennel. She mentioned this when it was her turn to talk.

She looked tired—pale—and I vowed to take some extra vitamin C just in case she'd exposed me to whatever she had. I might even mix a few more vitamins in with Baraka's food.

When Leon Lersten argued against the change, I could also see his point. If the road was straightened, a section of a hill that edged his property, along with dozens of fruit trees growing on it, would be removed, and the irrigation system he had set up to cover one of his fields would be divided into two parts. He'd have to drive heavy farm equipment across the pavement to reach that portion of his farm. To make matters worse, while construction was going on, his land would be torn up and unusable.

Olivia Halsted's lawyer spoke for her. His name, he said, was

Neal Wager, and he was pleased to be able to help a woman of Mrs. Halsted's character, which made me think he must be representing her pro bono, no matter what Howard said.

Neal Wager had a deep, husky voice I could have listened to forever. And he wasn't bad looking. Average height and build, he reminded me in many ways of North Carolina's former senator, John Edwards. Even Neal's blonde hair was styled in a similar manner, and I wondered if any barbers in the Battle Creek/Kalamazoo area charged four hundred dollars a cut.

I'm terrible at guessing ages, but I put Neal Wager somewhere in his mid-thirties. *Just the right age,* I thought, then mentally kicked myself for even considering that idea. I was having enough trouble dealing with my feelings about Wade. In spite of Grandma's suggestion that a little competition would be good for Wade, I certainly didn't need to be looking at another man as a potential date. Heck, I didn't even know if Neal Wager was married.

I glanced at his left hand. No ring.

Stop thinking that way, I told myself, and tried to listen to what he was saying.

He gave a compelling argument why Mrs. Halsted's front yard shouldn't be torn apart, leaving her house dangerously close to a road where cars would be whizzing by at over sixty miles an hour. He played on the audience's sympathies by having Olivia Halsted stand beside him, looking weak and helpless. I had a feeling if Neal Wager practiced in front of a jury he won a lot of cases. He was convincing me.

No one stood up to represent the acreage that had once belonged to the Halsteds. I guess they assumed if Leon and Mrs. Halsted could convince the township not to change the road, the acres that lay between the two would be safe from change. Personally, I would have been there making my case. From what I'd heard, straightening the road would cut through a section of woods on that property and part of a field.

I thought maybe there would be a vote right then, but the township supervisor announced that the board would take everything they'd heard under consideration and the meeting was adjourned.

"You can see how much of Leon's field would be messed up," Howard said as everyone stood to leave. "Those pictures in the back show it clear as day."

"What pictures?" I asked, turning to look behind us. A woman I recognized smiled, and I smiled back.

"The ones that lawyer fellah put up on the bulletin board."

There were too many people milling around for me to get a clear view of the bulletin board that took up a third of the back wall, but I could tell there were notices tacked along one side. Most of the people standing in front of the board were facing the opposite side. I guessed that was where the pictures were.

I caught a glimpse of Abby Warfield moving in that direction. Since I'd come to this meeting at her urging, I wanted to be sure she knew I was here. "I'm going to go take a look at them," I told Howard. "Not that it matters to me."

"It'll matter if your taxes go up," he said and gave a huff. "Road's been that way long as I've lived here. No reason to go and change it now."

I wanted to tell him things had changed since the horse-and-buggy days, that kids nowadays drove a lot faster than he probably ever did, and a person's life was more important than a farmer's field, but I didn't want to get into an argument with Howard. Our friendship was too tenuous. And maybe he was right. Maybe there was no reason to change things. Even though I rarely drove that direction, I had seen the speed limit signs posted before the curves. If people slowed down as they were supposed to, there wouldn't be a problem. No one would lose land, and Abby wouldn't have cars careening at her house and kennel.

I reached the back of the room and finally saw the pictures Howard had mentioned. Stunned, I stared at the five aerial photos pinned to the bulletin board. They were the same pictures I'd found in Donald Crane's briefcase. Or almost the same.

Abby was pointing at one, talking to a young couple. "You can see," she said, tracing a line along the curve of the road, "how a speeding car could go straight into my yard from here."

I stood beside the couple and looked at the photographs with new insight. No longer were these photos taken over unidentified farms. These were pictures of a local area. The major difference between these prints and the ones I'd looked at last Friday was the markings. Those pictures had dots and Xs designating certain areas. The ones in front of me had no dots or Xs, just dotted lines showing the route of the proposed road change.

I could see why Leon Lersten and Olivia Halsted were concerned. The dotted lines either eliminated or bisected huge chunks of their land.

I stepped closer to one of the photos. I presumed it was a view looking down on Olivia Halsted's house and property. As her lawyer had argued, the proposed roadway would almost reach her front porch and would take out several trees in the process. If I'd been her, I wouldn't have been happy with the plan.

The photo next to the one showing Olivia Halsted's house and property had been taken using a wider lens and included the northern edge of her property, the southern edge of Leon Lersten's, and the corporation's property between the two. The proposed new section of road would take out a dense area of trees, cut through a field, and eliminate what looked like an old shed. It also ran through a fenced area to the north.

77

"That's Leon Lersten's farm," Abby said, pointing at the fourth photo on the board. "And I don't see what his big gripe is. That section of the field he's so worried about doesn't produce enough to make it worth irrigating, even with the fertilizer he keeps adding. As for the part of that hill that will be leveled, big deal."

"You're talking about cutting down a part of Proctor's Hill," an elderly woman looking at the photos said, reverently touching a section of the photo with a fingertip. "I used to pick apples there before Leon bought the farm from Elgin Proctor." Her fingertips slid over to a body of water shown on the east side of the existing road. "When I was a child, my friends and I used to go swimming here." She laughed. "Proctor's Pond seemed bigger then. Not sure if it had more water or if I was just smaller."

Abby snorted. "Ever think it might be smaller because Leon pumps water out of that pond to irrigate his fields?"

The elderly woman glared at both of us. "Why don't you go back to the city where you belong."

The woman turned and stalked off, and I whispered to Abby, "I don't think you made any points with her."

Abby shrugged and pointed at the last photo. "This is my place."

Although I'd seen her house in the first print, this one showed less of the curved road and a more detailed view of her house and what I assumed was her kennel. "These must have been taken a month or more ago," she said. "See how the door on the lean-to at the end is almost off its hinges? I've fixed that. Fixed the hole in the roof, too." She pointed at an area on the kennel's roof that was darker than the rest of the shingles. "That's now my feed room. I've been doing a lot of work on the kennel. Probably why I've been so tired lately."

"Where did these pictures come from?" I asked.

"I asked Leon to bring them," a man answered, and I immediately recognized Neal Wager's smooth baritone. He and Leon Lersten were standing just behind Abby and me.

I moved slightly to the side, so I could see the lawyer's face. "I wonder why a man named Donald Crane would have had copies of these."

"Donald Crane was found dead yesterday," Grace said, joining her brother and Neal Wager. "It was on the news. Oh, P.J., I didn't realize it was you. What happened to your face?"

"I ran into a door." I didn't care if she believed me or not. "And I know he's dead. That's why I'm curious about the pictures." I edged back, away from the bulletin board and closer to Abby. "There were copies of these pictures in Crane's briefcase, along with some boxes of dirt, a map of some sort, and what looked like a lab report."

"There's nothing unusual about any of that," Leon said. "I hired Don to analyze the soil on my farm. To do that, he takes random samples. The report he gave me included a sketch of the field I fertilized this year." He looked at his sister. "Must be he kept copies of the photos he took, along with the original lab report."

"You had those tests done back in April, didn't you?" Grace said, then looked at me and frowned. "Why'd he still have the dirt in his briefcase? And why'd he show you the report?"

"He didn't show me anything. In fact, I never met the man. His aunt gave me the briefcase Friday, after my talk at the library."

"Why?" Both Grace and Leon asked.

"She seemed to think I could help her." A definite misconception on her part. "She said the briefcase contained something that might put her nephew's life in danger."

"Jeez, almighty," Abby gasped beside me. "And now he's dead? Do you still have the briefcase?"

"No. A guy came and took it Saturday."

"Looks like you didn't give it up willingly," Grace said, her gaze on my face.

"He took me by surprise." I smiled. "But he didn't get everything."

"What did he miss?" Abby asked, sounding like a little girl about to discover a secret.

"Some papers I'd spilled wine on. I'd put them in another room to dry."

"And you still have them?" Grace asked.

"I have copies. I gave the originals to the sheriff's department."

"And have you been able to figure anything out from those copies?" Abby asked.

"Not a thing," I admitted.

"If I were you," Grace said, "I'd get rid of those papers. Burn them."

For some reason, the fact that she wanted me to get rid of the papers made me wary. Grace had been at the library when Ida Delaney first tried to give me the briefcase. For all I knew, Grace may have seen my grandmother place the briefcase in the trunk of my car. And Grace would have had my business card. She could have told the bruiser who came to my house Saturday that I had the briefcase and where I lived.

"Maybe I will," I said. "After all, the sheriff's department has the originals."

"Doesn't make sense," Leon mumbled, shaking his head. "Why would Don carry around a lab report and samples taken last April?"

I couldn't answer that any more than I could understand why someone attacked me for what was in that briefcase. I looked back at the pictures on the bulletin board and pointed at the one that mostly showed the property between Leon Lersten's and Olivia Halsted's places. "Who owns this land?"

"A corporation," Neal Wager said, moving closer to the photo. "LRP Incorporated, otherwise known as Land Right Properties. They bought eighty acres from Mrs. Halsted several years ago, after her husband died."

"Thought they might send someone tonight," Leon said and glanced around the room. Most of the people who had come for the meeting had left. Those who remained were forming smaller groups. "If LRP had a representative here, he didn't speak up."

"Maybe they don't care if a road goes through their property," Abby said.

"The way they got 'No Trespassing' signs all around that place." Leon shook his head. "I don't see why they wouldn't care."

"Maybe they care more about the lives that would be saved," Abby countered.

Leon huffed. "Lives would be saved if people slowed down when they came to those curves. Or didn't drink and drive. You city folks and your need for straight roads. Next thing you'll want all the trees removed so cars don't run into them."

Leon Lersten sounded a lot like Howard. And I guess, in a way, both men were right. People trying to escape life in the cities moved to the country and then got upset because farm animals smelled, there weren't as many conveniences, or roads weren't straight. In my case, I was keeping Howard from hunting in a woods where he'd grown up hunting. More than once he'd told me I should move back to the city.

"Come on, Leon," Grace said, taking a step back from the rest of us. "It's getting late and I still need to drive back to Kalamazoo. We presented our case. We just have to hope the township board has the sense to leave things as they are."

"But they can't," Abby said, her voice raising an octave. "If that road stays the way it is, one of these days someone you care

81

about will get hurt."

"Maybe. Or maybe not," Grace said, sounding tired.

She and her brother left, but the lawyer stayed. "Mrs. Warfield, if you're so worried about someone ending up in your front yard," he said, "why don't you put up a barricade of some sort?"

"Oh sure." She glared at him. "I put up a barrier, someone hits it and is injured or dies, and the next thing I know, I'm being sued. You lawyers love those kinds of cases, don't you?"

"I don't handle injury cases."

I wondered what kind of cases he did handle. If he was representing Mrs. Halsted, I guessed his practice had something to do with real estate.

"You know what I mean," Abby said, still glaring at him.

Her evil-eye look didn't seem to bother the man. Voice calm, Neal said, "You're asking this township to pay hundreds of thousands of dollars to change something that has been in existence for decades. Leon's right. If you want straight roads, move back to the city."

"I've lived here for over seven years."

"And those curves were there when you bought your house. Why demand a change now?"

"Because I don't want cars ramming into my kennel."

"Then build a barricade," he repeated. "Sandbags cost a heck of a lot less than straightening a road."

"Lotta good that would do if one of those big trucks ends up in my yard."

"You mean the milk truck?" Sondra asked, and I realized both she and her husband Bill had joined our group.

"If Gordon is driving over the speed limit, his boss needs to know," Bill added.

"No." Abby looked at the two of them. "I'm not talking about the truck that picks up the milk from dairy farms. I don't know what kind of truck it is, but every so often one goes by my place. Always late at night. Really, really late. The sound of shifting gears and squealing brakes wakes me up. Trust me, one of these days he's not going to make the curve."

"Has this truck ever ended up in your yard?" Wager asked.

"Not yet."

"So you have a dream about a truck driving into your yard, and now you want to tear up my yard," another voice said, this one with a slight warble. "Take a sleeping pill."

Both Abby and I looked at the older woman who had come up next to Neal Wager. Decades of living and working outside had wrinkled and thinned Olivia Halsted's skin, and marred her complexion with age spots. She placed a hand on Neal's sleeve and smiled up at him. "The Martins have offered to drive me home."

He nodded, but Abby wasn't about to let the issue of the trucks drop. "It's not a dream, Mrs. Halsted. Those trucks are real. You must hear them. If they go by my place, they've got to go by yours."

"If they're real, they probably do," Mrs. Halsted said, her smile condescending. "But I sleep with ear plugs. Maybe you should, too, my dear."

"And if one of those trucks comes barreling into my yard, and I have earplugs in, will that make everything okay?"

"Oh my, you are upset." Olivia Halsted gave a deep sigh. "My dear, I just don't want to lose my front yard. If that road goes through, they'll cut down the blue spruce my husband and I planted the first year we were married. I just . . ."

The way Olivia Halsted looked, I thought she was going to cry, but then I heard someone near the front of the room call her name, and she took in a deep breath and smiled. "It's time for me to go." Again, she looked up at Neal Wager. "You take care, and give me a call in the morning, okay?"

"I will," he responded. "And don't worry. We'll save your tree."

"And you take care," she said, reaching over and giving my arm a pat. "Don't go running into any more doors."

Her gesture took me by surprise. "Me? No. No, I won't."

"Do stop in some time." She smiled. "I always have home-made cookies in my cookie jar."

"I'll . . . I'll do that," I stammered, not sure what else to say.

Abby glared at me, and I knew she felt I was taking the enemy's side. "They're going to vote against straightening the road just because of her," she said as Olivia Halsted toddled away to join a couple at the door. "It's the poor little old lady versus the relative newcomer."

Having lived in the area for seven years, Abby wasn't exactly a newcomer, but around Zenith, anyone who hadn't been born in the area was considered just that. The fact that my grand-parents had lived in the township all of their lives, and my father grew up and went to school in Zenith, made me an in-betweener.

"I don't know what the road commission will decide," I said. "You gave a good argument."

"I'm with you, Abby," Sondra said. "My kids play outside. If I lived where you do, I'd be demanding they straighten that curve." She stepped away from us. "And speaking of kids, we need to get home and make sure ours are getting ready for bed. See you, P.J. Abby. Mr. Wager."

Sondra and Bill nodded at each of us, then headed for the outside door. The other couple also said their goodbyes, leaving me with Abby and Neal Wager. I wanted to take a closer look at the photos on the bulletin board, but Abby was blocking them. "How did—" I started, only to be interrupted by Abby.

"So why is a big-city lawyer out here, defending an old lady?" she asked Wager. "Are you related or something?"

"Kalamazoo is hardly a big city," he said.

"It's a helluva lot bigger than the village of Zenith." Abby eyed him suspiciously. "Is she your aunt or something?"

"No relation," he said calmly and smiled at me.

"So why don't you just go away?"

"Why don't you move?"

Abby snorted. "Why don't you go jump in the lake."

I felt as if I were at a tennis match. First I'd look at Neal Wager, then at Abby, then back at Neal. My neck was getting exercise, which it probably needed, but my head was beginning to hurt.

"You're not going to win," he said, softening his voice.

"Fuck you."

I looked back at him, surprised at the strength of Abby's wording and wondering what he would say next. All he did was smile.

The argument seemed to take all of Abby's energy. With a sigh, she turned away and headed for the front of the room. I wasn't sure what to say or do. If I'd been in her place, I would have been frustrated. Besides having a sexy voice, Neal Wager had presented some pretty convincing arguments. If I were on the township board, I would vote against straightening the road.

"I think she's a little upset," Neal said.

"She's worried that people won't leave their dogs at her place if they think a car or truck might ram into the kennel."

"I take it you're a friend of hers."

"She's a client." I didn't see any need to tell him she'd just hired me.

"A client, huh?" He gave me a quick glance up and down. "You're a lawyer?"

"No. CPA."

"I see." He motioned toward my face. "When did that happen?"

"Saturday."

"Looks like it hurts."

"It's getting better." I glanced beyond him. The room was emptying out. "I, ah—"

He thrust out his hand. "I'm sorry. As you know by now, my name's Neal. Neal Wager. And you're . . . ?"

I shook his hand. "P.J. . . . P.J. Benson."

"Just the initials?"

"Just the initials."

"Well, P.J., how 'bout I buy you a drink?" He smiled. "The Pour House is just up the street."

In the village of Zenith, almost everything was "just up the street" . . . or just across it. A blinking red light hung above the main cross streets, a bank, post office, library, telephone company, and most of the town's other businesses flanking the sides of the two streets. The Pour House, which stood on the southeast corner, was the only bar and grill, and though it had changed hands multiple times over the years, it continued to be a meeting place for many of the locals.

"I don't know." I was hesitant about having a drink with Neal Wager. Not that I was worried about my safety. What I didn't want was Abby thinking I was consorting with the enemy.

She resolved that dilemma. "P.J., I'm going home," she called from the doorway. "See if you can convince him that loss of life is more important than loss of land. I don't have the energy."

"You have your orders," Neal said softly near my ear, sending a shiver of anticipation down my spine.

TWELVE

"So what is a nice girl like you doing in a town like this?" Neal asked after bringing two bottles of beer to the table and scooting his chair closer to mine.

We clinked bottles, then he took a long draught from his, before giving a sigh and licking his lips.

I watched him, saying nothing. I didn't feel that old clichéd line deserved a response.

"Really," he repeated, eyeing me as he set his bottle on the table. "Why are you living in Zenith and not Kalamazoo or Battle Creek?"

"You make this town sound like the pits."

"And you're saying it's not?" He glanced around the room, and so did I.

In a way, I could understand his attitude. Several of the bar's patrons were dressed in bib overalls, and looked like they hadn't made it past high school, if that far. But I knew better. Zenith High had one of the lowest dropout rates in the county, and eighty percent of its graduates went on to college. The slender, gray-haired man, deep in conversation with the bartender, had a PhD in chemistry and taught classes at Western Michigan University. While the gal and guy playing pool each held bachelor's degrees and were starting their own business. And one of the men at a table opposite ours had sailed across the Atlantic and spoke three languages.

"I like it here," I finally said. "You get to know people."

"Ah, but do you want to know them?"

"For the most part, yes." I took a sip of my beer. It was cold and sharp against my tongue.

"You've lived here less than a year. Maybe you'll change your mind."

"Maybe," I agreed, then put my bottle down and frowned. "How do you know how long I've lived here?"

"Olivia told me." He reached over and touched my hand. "I noticed you the moment you arrived at the meeting."

"Probably noticed my face." I pulled my fingers away from his and touched my cheek. I could feel the makeup I'd caked on. It was starting to crack. "I must look a sight."

"Not bad, really." He also touched my cheek, his fingertips gracefully sliding down my jawline, the pad of his thumb lightly brushing across my lips.

I pulled away from the contact and grabbed my beer bottle. This was moving too fast. I took a gulp, then choked and coughed as the liquid burned its way down my throat.

"You okay?" Neal asked, bringing his chair even closer and thumping my back.

"I'm fine. Fine," I managed between coughs. "It just went down the wrong way." *And you are way too smooth for me,* I thought, noting his pant leg was now touching mine.

Perhaps he realized I was uncomfortable with him being so close. With two scoots, he had his chair back to its original position, facing me. "So," he said, "how do we convince your buddy that the road shouldn't be straightened?"

"Abby is not my buddy. In truth, I just met her today."

"But you believe she's right about the road?"

"I don't know. I can see why she's worried about people driving too fast and ending up in her yard, but I can also understand why Mrs. Halsted doesn't want that tree removed or the road closer to her house."

88

"You could see from the pictures how much of her front yard she would lose. That tree she and her husband planted is very special to her."

"Putting up those pictures was a smart move. They really showed what would be lost."

Neal smiled. "As they say, 'A picture is worth a thousand words.' "

"I have a feeling you're a very good lawyer."

"I try to be." He sipped from his bottle of beer, glanced around the room, and then again scooted his chair closer and quietly said, "Did I hear right? You saw those same pictures in a briefcase owned by the man who was killed in Kalamazoo?"

I nodded. "They weren't quite the same. The ones I saw had dots and Xs on them, not lines showing the road change."

"And those pictures are the reason you have a black eye and bruised cheek?"

"I don't think those particular pictures are the reason, but I think the guy who came to my place thought there was something incriminating in that briefcase."

"But you didn't find anything?"

I shook my head. "All I found were a dozen aerial photos, five boxes of dirt, a map of some sort, a lab report, and a notebook—and that didn't have anything in it that could be used for blackmail."

"Blackmail? You're saying Crane was trying to blackmail someone?"

"That's what his aunt told me," I said, then remembered one more item. "Oh, there was a cell phone in the briefcase. One of those fancy ones that does everything but cook and wash dishes."

"The kind that takes pictures?"

"I assume so. You needed a password to see what was on the phone, and I never got past that."

"What did you do with the phone?"

"Put it back in the briefcase." Which, knowing what I knew now, was a mistake. "I wish I'd kept it out instead of those papers, but when I found the phone, I didn't think there was anything to Ida's story. I certainly didn't know her nephew was going to be killed, or that I was going to be attacked. If I had, I would have done a lot of things different." Like hidden the briefcase . . . or given it to Wade.

"Hmm." Neal slowly rotated his beer bottle between his hands. "Once you were attacked, I hope you reported all this to the police. Gave them a description of the guy who hit you."

"I called nine-one-one right away."

"Good." He nodded his approval. "So do they have any idea who the guy might be?"

"No, but a friend of mine is a detective with the sheriff's department. He wants me to stop by and look at mug shots. He thinks they might have the guy's picture on file. I'll probably stop by the station tomorrow. I didn't feel like doing much of anything today."

Once again, Neal reached over and touched the side of my face. "Looks like it hurts."

I didn't pull away this time. In fact, I rather liked the gentle touch of his fingertips on my skin. I grinned. "You're making it feel all better."

"Glad to hear that." He sat back in his chair and smiled. "You're too pretty to mess with people who would do this to you."

"I'm still not sure how I got involved. All I was doing was giving a talk on how to avoid scams. Next thing I know, an old lady gives me a briefcase and less than twenty-four hours later, I'm being slapped around and threatened."

"Well, hopefully you can put this all behind you and forget it ever happened."

I liked his attitude, so when he said, "Tell me more about

yourself," I did. Not everything right away. It took another beer and some nachos before I started talking about my schizophrenic mother, how my father, in essence, abandoned us, and how my energetic grandmother held us together when things got too crazy.

Between sips of beer and way too many nachos, I also learned a little about Neal Wager. He wasn't married. At least he said he wasn't, and I didn't see any tell-tale sign of a ring that had been recently removed from his left hand. He was thirty-four. Third in his class at the University of Michigan and passed the bar his first try. His specialty, as I'd guessed, was real estate. "Lately I've been handling a lot of foreclosures," he said. "Not something I enjoy."

"That's got to be rough." I'd seen way too many newscasts showing homeless families living in their cars.

"Whenever I can, I try to get my client and the mortgagee to work something out."

I liked this guy, and thinking of Nora, I said, "I might need your services. I have a neighbor who claims the woods behind my house became hers when my grandfather died."

"She has a quit claim deed?"

"No, a note. One she says he wrote and signed before he died."

"Is it notarized?"

"I don't think so." I tried to remember if there had been any sort of stamp, or another signature at the bottom of the page Nora had pressed against my car's window.

"We could fight it." He grinned. "And with me representing you, we'd win."

"You really think so?" I didn't realize how much Nora's threat had been bothering me until that moment. With Neal's assurance that we could win—cocky as he might sound—I felt as if a load had been lifted from my shoulders. "That's great."

He reached into his pocket and pulled out a business card. "Call me when you want to pursue this."

THIRTEEN

Baraka woke me early Tuesday morning, whining to go out. I stumbled to the door, sent him on his way, and started a pot of coffee before I truly had my eyes open or my mind working. Even after I'd fed Baraka and had a cup of coffee, my brain felt foggy. My punishment for having two beers the night before.

Over my second cup of coffee, I mentally reviewed the events of the previous night. I still wasn't sure how I felt about the road straightening issue, but the more time I'd spent with Neal Wager, the more I'd enjoyed his company. Enough so I actually felt guilty, as if I'd cheated on Wade by having a couple beers with Neal.

Those feelings of guilt had increased when I returned home and found a message from Wade on my answering machine. He didn't sound pleased that I wasn't available when he called. I could hear the question in his tone. He said, "Sorry I missed you. Call if you don't get in too late." What he really meant was, "Where the hell are you?"

Grandma had said I should give Wade a little competition. Maybe finding I wasn't at his beck and call would help our relationship. Or maybe it wouldn't. Who knew?

A telephone call interrupted my confused thoughts. It was one of the owners of Sporbach's Nursery. She said they were applying for a loan and needed a copy of this year's taxes. Could I send one?

I assured her I could, and as soon as I ended the call, I went to my office and pulled out their file. I made a copy of the tax form, grabbed a nine-by-twelve envelope, and headed for my dining room table. I started to move some of the papers scattered across the table out of the way so I'd have a clear spot to address the envelope, then stopped.

Beneath a piece of junk mail I'd received last Friday lay Donald Crane's cell phone.

I set Sporbach's tax form and envelope aside and picked up the phone.

I knew I needed to get the phone to the police, but I wasn't sure which law enforcement department to contact. Kalamazoo Sheriff's Department—specifically Deputy Chambers—or the Kalamazoo Public Safety detective handling Crane's murder. Chambers would probably accuse me of withholding evidence. Or comment on how I would have known the phone was there Saturday, when he came to the house, if I didn't have such a mess on my table.

I decided to call Kalamazoo Public Safety.

There'd been a number listed on the television for anyone with information about Ida Delaney or the Donald Crane murder to call, but I hadn't written it down, and I knew better than to dial nine-one-one. This wasn't an emergency. The non-emergency number listed in the phone book seemed my best bet, but after talking to the woman who answered, I wondered how long before anyone connected to the Donald Crane case would receive my message. Evidently everyone in Kalamazoo felt he—or she—had information about the killing.

I tried Wade next. I figured I owed him a call, and he should know about the phone. First I tried his apartment, then his office. He didn't answer either phone, so I left a message on his voice mail. "Hi," I said. "It's me. P.J. Sorry I missed your call last night. I went to a meeting about a road project here in Zenith, and I didn't get home until late. I . . ."

In spite of Grandma's suggestion that I give Wade a little competition, I decided not to mention Neal. I finished my message with, "I found Donald Crane's cell phone. I'm not sure what to do with it. Call me when you can."

First thing I did after leaving my message was hide Crane's phone. If that bruiser returned, he wouldn't find it sitting out in plain sight. Not like he had with the briefcase.

I dressed after that, prepared Sporbach's tax form for the mail, and then scrambled a couple of eggs for breakfast and had another cup of coffee. By nine o'clock, I was feeling half normal. "Come on, Baraka," I said, stirring my dog out of a morning nap. "Let's look at that chicken coop."

With a cat-like leap, Baraka was on his feet and at the door ahead of me. The first thing I noticed was in the hour since I'd gotten up, the temperature had risen at least ten degrees. I was glad I'd put on a T-shirt and shorts. It was going to be a hot one.

Cleaning my grandparents' old chicken coop involved more than removing soiled straw and laying boxes. Over the years, the building had become a Dumpster in itself. I set anything I could recycle aside, but most of the items I pulled out of the coop had been damaged by water or infested by rodents, insects, and spiders. The stench increased with each layer I removed and each degree the temperature outside increased. I wore a surgical mask to avoid contracting the Junta virus, and it helped filter the odor, but after a while having a layer of fabric over my nose and mouth began to bother me.

With broken glass everywhere, I kept Baraka out of the coop. Occasionally, as I traveled between the coop and the Dumpster, I'd stop and watch him chase a butterfly or dig a hole in the garden area, but by noon the humidity had increased to an unbearable degree, both for him and me. Rivulets of sweat poured from my scalp and dripped into my eyes. Baraka had found shade at the base of the Dumpster, but I'm sure he thought I was crazy as I traveled past him, going back and forth from the coop. Finally, I decided he was right.

"Enough for today," I said, wiping the moisture from my brow. "You ready to go in, boy?"

He beat me to the porch, his lips curled up in a smile and his tongue hanging out as he waited for me. I told him to stay, and he did, allowing me to enter the house first. I doubted I'd ever show him in obedience, but I had been working on the commands that make living with a dog a pleasure—sit, stay, come, and back up. I was training him to allow me to enter the house first, wait for my okay before going outside, and not to touch anything that dropped on the floor until I gave him permission. That was to keep him from gobbling down a pill or something that might harm him.

A quick check of my answering machine showed no messages from Wade or the Kalamazoo Criminal Investigation Department, and I knew I hadn't received any calls on my cell phone. While cleaning the chicken coop, I'd been listening for a call . . . and thinking about the cell phone hidden in my dining room. To see what was on it, I needed a password, but I had heard computer experts could find ways around password protection.

Back in April, when my computer stopped working, I'd found a computer expert. I hadn't been in contact with him since then, but I decided to give him a call. It took me a while to thumb through the Post-it notes I had stacked by my computer, but I finally found his name and number. He answered on the third ring.

"Ken Paget's Computer Repair," he said.

He sounded as young as the first time I'd talked to him. "Ken," I said. "This is P.J. Benson. I don't know if you remember me, but back in April you helped me so I could get a tax program running on my computer."

"Sure I remember you," he said, his voice warming. "P.J. The pajama girl." He chuckled at his joke. "I think you owe me a beer."

"I think I probably do," I agreed. "And if you can help me with my present problem, I'll definitely buy you that beer. Maybe two or three."

"Sounds good to me. What's the problem?"

"I have a cell phone. It's not mine. I want to know what's on the phone, but it's password protected. Is there any way to get around that?"

"I, ah . . ." He paused and cleared his throat. "P.J., what you're asking doesn't sound exactly legal. Do I want to ask who owns this cell phone?"

"A dead man," I said. "And I think he was killed for what's on this phone."

"Then you should give it to the police."

"I know, and I will, but somehow I've gotten involved in this, and I really would like to know why."

"Well, don't go trying different passwords. If you do, and keep failing, there's a good chance, at a certain point, everything will be erased off the phone."

"You're kidding." I wondered if Wade or the police would know that. Would they try different passwords and destroy whatever evidence might be on the phone? Wade's told me stories of goofs his fellow officers have made—how they've lost or messed up evidence, sometimes losing a case because of their errors. I didn't want that happening this time.

"I do know one guy," Ken said. "He might be able to get the password."

"But you don't think *you* can?" I was disappointed. Back in April he'd solved my problem over the telephone.

"I'd rather not chance it, but if you'll bring the phone to my shop, I'll take a look-see."

Curiosity or not, I wasn't eager to make the twenty-five mile drive into Kalamazoo. What I needed was a shower, and then a few hours of working on client accounts. No work, no money. "Let me think about it."

"Sure. Whatever. I should be around all day. Just give me a call if you're coming."

"I'll do that. And I will buy you that beer someday." I wanted to add, *When you're old enough to drink it,* but I thought I'd better not.

After hanging up the phone, I headed for the bathroom. My skin itched from the dirt and sweat I'd accumulated working in the chicken coop, and I felt like the spiders I'd seen lurking in the corners of the building were crawling all over me. A thick lather of shampoo and soap washed away the grime while a spray of water cooled my body. Baraka kept whining outside the bathroom door, begging to come in, but I ignored his pleas.

As I toweled my hair dry, I looked in the mirror. My hair was getting longer than I liked, the mass of brown curls that framed my face resembling a dust mop. *Time for a haircut,* I decided. The bruises on the sides of my face were still very visible, though the puffiness was gone and my skin was changing colors. Now some browns, almost the same shade as my eyes, had joined a combination of blues and purples. Not exactly a pretty picture, but I knew I was healing.

You're too pretty, Neal had said last night.

I hadn't thought much about his comment when he made it, but now I wondered if he'd been coming on to me. Wouldn't that be something if he had been? And what if he was?

I was pondering the possibility when the telephone rang. I grinned. It had to be Wade, finally answering my call. With only a towel wrapped around my body, I pushed my way past Baraka and picked up the receiver.

"So where have you been?" I asked before he had a chance to

say anything.

"Is this P.J. Benson?" a soft, wavering, female voice asked.

The lighthearted feeling I'd been experiencing disappeared, my senses going on alert. "This is P.J. What can I do for you?"

"I need help," the woman said. "Please help me."

FOURTEEN

"Who is this?" I said, although I already had an idea what the answer would be.

"Ida Delaney," she said, a hint of hysteria entering her voice. "I don't know what to do."

The anguish in her words sent a chill through me even though the temperature in my house was close to ninety. "Ida, where are you? You need to go to the police."

"No. No police. Can't go to the police. They killed Donald you know."

"The police killed your nephew?"

"I told them not to hurt him, and they told me to go to my room. I don't like Dr. Morgan. He's not a good man."

"Who is Dr. Morgan?"

Ida said nothing, but I knew she hadn't hung up. I could hear women talking in the background and a churning sound. "Ida," I said. "Where are you?"

"I don't know." The tremble in her voice increased. "I ran away. I heard Donald screaming, and then he stopped. I'm hungry. Can you bring me some food?"

"Call the police, Ida." It didn't sound like they had anything to do with her nephew's death, and I didn't want to get involved. "They'll bring you some food."

If the woman understood what I was saying, she chose to ignore me. "I've been hiding," she said, almost in a whisper. "For a long, long time. I'm so hungry. Please help me."

Why me? I silently asked. What in the universe made this woman think I could help her?

Considering how panicky she sounded, I tried to keep my voice calm. "Ida, I can't help you unless you tell me where you are."

"I'm not home." Again she stopped talking, her ragged breathing nearly obliterating the noises in the background. A rhythmic thumping stopped, and Ida called out. "Where am I?"

"Leaders' Laundry," I heard a woman say from somewhere in the distance.

"Leaders' Laundry," Ida repeated into the phone.

"On Portage Street?" If so, I knew the place. I'd even used the Laundromat a few times when I lived in Kalamazoo.

"Yes, on Portage. But don't let them find me. He's looking for me, you know. He scares me." She started to cry.

The soulful sound brought a memory of the guy who'd bashed me, and that tore at my resistance. I thought of my mother and how she acted when she went off her medicine, how lost and confused she'd be when either my grandmother and I or the police found her. The haunted look in her eyes.

"Ida, it's okay," I assured this woman. "Everything is going to be all right now. Let me talk to someone there. Let me talk to one of the women."

With a click, the line went dead.

I stared at my phone, unsure if Ida Delaney had hung up on me, or if someone else had disconnected us. I thought if I could talk to someone at the Laundromat, maybe they could get Ida to go to the police. And if I'd had caller ID, it would have been easy to call back. But I didn't have it, and I couldn't remember if the numbers to punch to get the last number that called were sixty-eight or sixty-nine. I set down the receiver and went to find my Kalamazoo phone book.

It took me a while to find the phone number for Leaders'

Laundry, and an eternity, it seemed, before someone answered the phone. When a woman said hello, I asked, "Is there an old lady there? She's short, plump, and has gray hair."

"You talkin' about the old, white lady who was on the phone a bit ago?" the woman who'd answered my call asked.

"That's the one."

"I don't know where she be."

"Did someone take her away?" I asked, praying Ida's call to me hadn't led to her demise. "A man? Maybe two?" She had said "they" several times.

"No. Ain't been no men 'round while I've been here."

That was a relief. "But you don't see her now."

"That's what I said, lady."

The woman sounded irritated, and certainly not in the mood to go looking for Ida Delaney. "Okay," I said. "Thank you."

I considered calling the police, but feared Ida would hide if she saw them. She might be old and somewhat senile, but if she'd avoided detection since Friday night, she could easily slip away again if spooked.

I looked down at Baraka, who'd stretched out near my feet. "Looks like I've got to drive into Kalamazoo," I said, and he lifted his head.

Baraka recognized certain words. *Walk. Food. Bath. Drive.* Whenever I said bath, he would slink out of the room. He wasn't fond of water. Walk, food, and drive all commanded his attention. He loved it when I took him in the car to my grandmother's house.

He rose, stretched, and went directly to the door.

"No, you can't go this time," I said. "I have no idea what I'm going to find." For all I knew, I might be headed out on a wild goose chase.

It didn't take me long to dress, and a doggie biscuit enticed Baraka into his crate, but the look in his eyes said he'd rather be going with me. I was almost out the door when I remembered Donald Crane's cell phone. As long as I was driving to Kalamazoo, I'd take it with me. I also grabbed my copies of the wine-soaked pages, the ones I planned on showing Wade. If I did manage to find Ida and get her to the police, I could turn both items over to them.

FIFTEEN

The Laundromat was exactly where I remembered, and I was pleased to find an empty parking spot near the entrance. Unlike downtown parking, I didn't have to worry about feeding a meter, but the spot did have a fifteen-minute time limit. I hoped finding Ida and talking her into going to the police wouldn't take any longer than that.

Midday traffic flowed steadily along Portage Street, and a few people occupied the sidewalk. I paused before stepping into the building, looking for any signs of the bruiser who'd hit me Saturday . . . or anyone who looked ominous.

Five women and three children were inside the Laundromat, the children running around, yelling. I skipped the women folding clothes or feeding them into washers and walked over to a middle-aged black woman watching a load of clothes going round and round in a dryer.

"Excuse me," I said, "but have you seen an elderly white woman, about my height, around here in the last hour?"

"You the one on the phone earlier?" the woman asked, turning toward me.

I nodded, recognizing her voice. "That was me."

She pointed toward the back of the building. "She's in there, in the bathroom. I went lookin' for her after you hung up. Told her you'd called, but she says she can't come out. Says it ain't safe for her."

I thanked her and headed for the bathroom. "Ida," I said,

tapping on the door. "It's me, P.J. Benson."

"P.J.?" I heard a click and saw the knob turn. The door opened a crack, revealing a sliver of Ida Delaney's face and body. "Do I know you?"

"You called me just a while ago," I said. "We met last Friday. You came to a talk I gave."

I kept waiting for some sign of recognition in her eyes. Nothing.

"You gave me a briefcase," I continued. "You said it belonged to your nephew. You were worried about him . . . said he'd threatened to blackmail someone."

"Blackmail." She shook her head and opened the door wider. "You should not blackmail people. I told Donald that. It can get you killed." Ida poked her head out of the bathroom and looked toward the street. "Did he come inside?"

I followed her gaze. "Did who come inside?"

"Dr. Morgan. He was out there." She pointed toward the sidewalk.

"What does this Dr. Morgan look like?" I asked, wondering if one of those seemingly innocuous pedestrians I'd seen might be the person who killed Donald Crane.

"Big." She held her hand high above our heads. "Dark hair. He's not a nice man. He cheats on his wife."

Her description could fit the bruiser who'd hit me Saturday, and I wouldn't be surprised if he cheated on his wife, if he had one. "I didn't see him," I said. "Not around here."

Ida Delaney took a hesitant step out of the bathroom. Although she still took up three times as much space as I did, her face looked gaunt, her cheeks sunken, and her eyes glassy. I wondered how much sleep she'd had since leaving her nephew's house.

"I'm hungry," she said.

"We need to get you somewhere safe, somewhere where you

can get some food and a good night's sleep." And a shower, I could have added, now that I'd gotten a good whiff of her body odor.

"I want to go home," she said, almost in tears. "My mother will feed me."

Considering Ida's advanced age, I was sure her mother was either dead or in a nursing home. However, from years of experience with my mother, I knew telling Ida that wouldn't help. "Before I take you home, we need to stop and talk to the police."

"No." She shook her head and took a step back. "I can't go to the police. They think I'm crazy."

"They won't think you're crazy this time. They want to talk to you. They're worried about you."

"Will they help me find my way home?"

"I'm sure they will. They've been looking for you, you know." The other women in the Laundromat stared at us as I slowly led Ida past washers and dryers. "The police want to help you, Ida. They're your friends."

She pulled back. "Dr. Morgan isn't my friend. I don't like Dr. Morgan."

"I don't either," I said as we neared the outside door. "It's all right, Ida. You'll be safe."

One of the children ran behind us, screaming as he passed, and Ida squeezed her eyes shut. "He screamed," she whispered. "But I knew I couldn't do anything to help him. I was so scared, I ran away."

"You had a right to be scared," I said, not entirely sure if Ida Delaney was remembering something from her childhood or what happened when her nephew was killed. "But we'll go see the police now, and you won't have to be scared anymore."

I opened the door and prayed she would step outside.

"They told me to stay in my room." She looked up and down the street. "Stay in my room and be quiet."

"There were two of them?" I gently pushed her through the doorway. "Dr. Morgan and someone else? Maybe a nurse?"

She sniffed the air, smiled, and looked at me. "It smells like bread."

Driving by the commercial bakery on Portage Street always made me hungry, the aroma of baking bread permeating the air for blocks around the building. "Yes, it does smell like bread. It smells really good," I said, wishing I'd taken time to fix a sandwich before driving into town.

"I'm very, very hungry." Ida gave me a plaintive look. "Can we get a hamburger? Please and pretty please." She looked back toward the Laundromat. "Some of the people who came here gave me money, but all they had in the machines were boxes of soap. One woman shared her lunch with me." Ida sighed. "I think that was yesterday."

"And no one called the police?"

"They were busy."

And people didn't want to get involved. I saw it on the news all the time: people ignoring a man hit by a car, crowds watching a woman being attacked and doing nothing, not even calling nine-one-one. I wasn't much better. Even now *I* wanted to walk away from Ida, pretend I'd never met her.

"Come on, get in the car," I urged, opening the passenger side door for her.

She reached into a pocket of her flowered cotton slacks. "I have money. See. Can we buy a loaf of bread?"

"Get in the car, and we'll go buy a hamburger."

I knew, the way she smelled, I wasn't going to take her into a restaurant, but there were a couple fast-food places nearby with drive-through windows.

The promise of food worked. Ida slid into my car.

"I like hamburgers," she said, pulling more quarters from her pocket.

Amid the coins, she had my business card, its edges frayed and one corner torn off. She studied it for a moment, then held the card up near my face. "This is you, isn't it? I didn't know who else to call. I tried calling Donald, but someone said the line was out of order. He'll have to get that fixed."

The look in her eyes had turned innocently childlike, and I knew she'd already forgotten that her nephew was dead. "Put on your seat belt," I said, resigned to the role of temporary guardian.

I put the air conditioner on high, both to combat the stifling heat outside and the smell that was quickly permeating my car, and our first stop was for food. I ordered two double cheeseburgers, a large fries, and a soda for Ida, and a chicken sandwich and coffee for me. Although I used the drive through, I pulled my car into a space on the lot. I left the engine running, along with the air conditioner. In the time it took me to eat my chicken sandwich, Ida scarfed down both burgers, all of the fries, and most of her soda. She was definitely hungry. Only when she let out a big belch and laughed did I try questioning her again.

"Tell me more about Dr. Morgan," I said. "Was he a friend of your nephew?"

She frowned. "I don't think so."

"Do you remember what happened last Friday, after you talked to me at the library?"

I could tell from the look she gave me that she didn't, so I tried prodding her memory. "You came to my talk, and you gave me a briefcase. Donald's briefcase. You put it in the trunk of my car. Then what did you do?"

"I guess I went home," she said.

"And your nephew was there?"

"I think so."

"And some men came?"

Ida stared at me. "You know about them?"

"Just what you've told me."

She nodded. "They yelled at Donald, and then they yelled at me. Even Donald yelled at me." She looked away, but I saw a tear slide down her cheek. "He yelled at me a lot that night."

I could imagine her nephew's frustration when he discovered his aunt had taken his briefcase. His fear when asked to turn over whatever was in that briefcase that he thought he could use as blackmail. At some point Morgan, or whatever his name was, must have found one of the business cards Ida took from my talk. A shiner and a few bruises seemed insignificant to what the guy evidently did to Donald Crane. I just hoped he now had what he was looking for, that it wasn't the cell phone I had in my possession. I didn't want the man paying me another visit.

"I've met Dr. Morgan," I told Ida. "He came to see me Saturday. He took the briefcase."

"Donald said I shouldn't have given it to you."

I wished she hadn't. "Can you describe the other man?" I asked. "The one with Dr. Morgan. Can you tell me what he looked like? His name?"

"He talked nice," she said.

"What was his name?" If we could tell the police the names of the two men, I'd feel a lot safer.

Ida frowned. "I don't remember."

"Was he tall? Short? Did he have dark hair or blonde?"

"I don't remember."

"Well, darn it, what do you remember?"

I didn't mean to get angry or raise my voice, but a morning of physical labor, along with the heat, had exhausted both my body and patience. Ida immediately shifted in her seat so she was looking away from me. Her entire being seemed to cave in on itself, and the submissive gesture made me feel terrible. I knew it was foolish to get upset with her, that it wasn't her fault her mind wasn't clear. I also knew I wasn't getting anywhere.

"I'm sorry," I apologized. "I didn't mean to yell at you."

Ida looked at me and sighed. "Donald's dead."

"I know." And I knew, for that moment, she also knew.

"Did you ever meet him?"

"No."

"They had his picture in the paper. A lady left the paper, and I saw Donald's picture on the front page. He had his arm around me."

She paused and swallowed hard, but I didn't say anything. I didn't want to interrupt her train of thought.

"He was a good-looking man," she continued. "Almost pretty, I'd say. Girls liked him, but he preferred men." She gave a slight smile. "He thought that would upset me, but I didn't care. He was always good to me . . . even when he yelled at me."

Ida turned back toward the window, and I saw the tears and heard her muffled sob.

Tears sprang to my eyes, and I blinked them away. I had no idea what her nephew's second attacker looked like, but I had a better picture of Donald Crane. I put my car in gear. I would leave it to the police to question Ida Delaney.

SIXTEEN

To my surprise, Ida didn't object when I told her I was going to take her to the police station. In fact, after another loud burp, she leaned back against the seat, and before I arrived at the large parking lot off East Crosstown Parkway, she was sound asleep.

I held Ida's hand as we walked under the blue awning that displayed the words Kalamazoo Public Safety. The outside doors opened to a spacious but austere room in which two chest-high tables dominated the center of the area, and a few chairs lined the side walls. An old man and a young boy seated on two of the chairs kept looking toward a set of double doors at the far end of the room. I led Ida to a window marked Records and told the woman standing on the other side of the glass that we needed to see the detective handling the Donald Crane murder.

She gave Ida a quick scan, looked at something on the counter in front of her, nodded, and picked up a phone.

"Someone will be down in a minute," she said, and sure enough, in no more than a minute an African American man and a Caucasian woman, both dressed in street clothes, came through the double doors at the end of the room. They stopped and stared at Ida and me. Behind them was a uniformed officer, his hand resting on his gun holster.

Tall and slender, and wearing a short-sleeved, flowered cotton shirt and khaki pants, the woman started toward us. "We've been looking for you, Ida."

Ida shrank back, closer to me, her fingers tightening around mine. The woman must have seen the panic in Ida's eyes because she stopped. That or Ida's body odor held her back. I saw her wrinkle her nose before she asked me, "And you're . . . ?"

"P.J. Benson." I gave Ida's hand a slight squeeze and told a small fib. "Ida asked me to bring her here. She's a little nervous . . . and very confused. I think she's going to need protection."

"That's what we're here for, Ida," the woman said softly, and then smiled at me. "I'm Detective Daley. And this is Detective Ferrell." She motioned toward the African American man behind her.

In size alone he made me think of a football tackle, his broad shoulders and thick girth presenting an imposing figure. " 'Bout time you showed up, Ida," he said and took a step toward the three of us.

Ida cringed and looked at me. "Can we go home now?"

"Not yet," I said, knowing there was no way these detectives would allow Ida to go home. "You need to tell them what happened. They need to know about those men who hurt Donald."

"No." She kept shaking her head. "I want to go home. I'm tired."

"I bet you are tired," Detective Daley said, holding out her hand as she came closer. "Let's go up to my office. You can rest up there." She placed a hand on Ida's arm. "We'll take care of you now."

Ida looked at the female detective, then at me. "Will you come with me?"

I wanted to turn Ida over to the police and forget I was ever involved in the death of her nephew, but I knew I couldn't. It would be like abandoning a child . . . or a lost puppy. "If they'll let me, I will," I assured her.

"Of course we'll let you," Detective Daley said, smiling at me. "We have some questions we want to ask you, too."

I should have known bringing Ida here would get me involved. I smiled and wondered how long this would take. Detective Daley led us through the double doors to an elevator; Detective Ferrell followed. Ida waddled along beside me, never letting go of my hand. Once out of the elevator, we made our way to a sterile-looking room with molded plastic chairs and a plain, rectangular table. A smoke alarm and a fire alarm were the only adornments on the beige-colored walls, but I was sure there was a monitoring device hidden somewhere. Wade told me law enforcement always recorded interviews.

"Would you like something to drink?" Detective Daley asked once Ida and I were seated. "Coffee? Iced tea? Water?"

"I like tea," Ida said. I shook my head.

Both detectives walked out, leaving us locked in the room. I'm sure they hoped we'd say something important while they were gone. I leaned back in my chair and closed my eyes. But if I'd thought I might get some rest while the detectives were gone, Ida had other ideas. "They don't have a TV."

"No, no TV." I yawned and opened my eyes.

"What time is it?" Ida tilted her head to look at my watch. "I wish they had a TV. They didn't have one at the Laundromat either, and I don't like missing my shows. Do you watch *General Hospital*? I've been watching that for years. Has anything happened to Claudia?"

I'm not an aficionado of soap operas and had no idea who Claudia was. "I don't know. I don't watch that show."

"The woman doesn't know when to keep her mouth shut." Ida sighed, and for the next five minutes, I learned not only about Claudia, but about a myriad of characters, the problems they'd had in the past and the troubles they were getting into when she last had a chance to watch. I tried to act interested, for Ida's sake, and I wondered how the person observing us was enjoying the conversation. I didn't think this was the sort of information Daley and Ferrell were hoping to glean from their absence.

When they returned, a glass of iced tea in hand, Detective Daley was grinning. Ferrell, however, had a scowl. *Good cop/bad cop?* I wondered. Detective Ferrell certainly didn't endear himself to me when he started out saying, "Okay, Ms. Benson, just exactly why are you here?"

I'd bet, during their absence, they learned everything they could about me. The Internet would have provided some information, along with records they had of encounters with my mother. More than once I'd had to bail her out of trouble when she went off her meds. They might even know about my relationship with Wade. The Kalamazoo County Sheriff's Department and Kalamazoo Public Safety might be separate entities, but they often worked together on cases and many were friends.

"I met Ida last Friday," I said. "She gave me a briefcase she said belonged to her nephew. She said he was trying to blackmail someone, and she was worried."

Ferrell's eyebrows rose. "Blackmail? Blackmail who?"

"I don't know." Though I was sure Dr. Morgan—or whatever the bruiser who hit me was named—was involved.

"And why did she give you the briefcase?" Ferrell asked. "Why didn't she contact us?"

"I don't know why she gave it to me," I admitted. "She said you—the police—wouldn't believe her, that you thought she was crazy."

"We have had a few encounters with Ida," Detective Daley said and smiled. "Haven't we, Ida?"

Ida wrinkled her brow and narrowed her eyes until they were blue slits. "Do I know you?"

"I helped pull you out of a window."

Ida's gaze drifted to the security card box by the door. "I don't remember."

"I do," Detective Daley mouthed toward me.

"Where were you Friday evening?" Ferrell asked me.

"At home."

"Can anyone verify that?"

"Yes. For most of the night Sheriff's Detective Wade Kingsley was with me."

Both Howard and Ferrell nodded. Neither asked where home was or why a sheriff's detective would be with me, confirming they already knew about my relationship with Wade and where I lived.

"Is he the one who gave you that shiner?" Ferrell asked.

"Wade? No way." I touched the side of my face. "I think the guy who did this to me is the one who killed her nephew."

That took him aback. "You know who killed Donald Crane?"

"Not for sure. All I know is the man who came to my house, who took Donald Crane's briefcase from my table and hit me, fits the description Ida gave me of the man who came to her nephew's house Friday night. She said his name is Morgan. Dr. Morgan."

The two detectives looked at Ida. Ferrell spoke first. "Is that right? Did a Dr. Morgan visit your nephew Friday night?"

"Dr. Morgan isn't a nice man." Ida shook her head. "He pretends he is, but I know better."

"Ida, can you tell us more about this Dr. Morgan?" Detective Daley said, her voice gently coaxing. "Has he come to your house more often than just last Friday?"

Ida gave the female detective a curious look. "He's on every day. Well, not Saturday or Sunday, but Monday through Friday." She pointed at the bare walls. "You could watch him if you had a TV."

Oh great, I realized. Dr. Morgan was one of the characters on a soap opera. I looked at Detective Daley and shrugged. "I thought he was real. I mean the man who hit me was real, and I thought . . ."

"He slapped Donald's face," Ida said, interrupting me. "And the other man said he'd been a bad boy. A very bad boy."

"Who had been a bad boy?" Ferrell asked.

Ida gave him a look of surprise. "Weren't we talking about Donald?"

"Yes. Of course." Ferrell made a grunting sound. "So a man came to your house Friday and hit your nephew? Two men?"

"That's what I said."

"And you're sure about that? It's not something you saw on television?"

She frowned at him. "Why would someone on the television hit Donald?"

"Why indeed," Ferrell grumbled, and glanced my way. "Do you know the other man's name?"

"It seems I don't know anyone's name."

Ida squeezed her lids shut, and I saw a tear slide over her wrinkled cheek. "Can I go now?"

"Not yet," Detective Daley said, gently patting Ida's arm. "What else can you tell us about these men? What did they say to your nephew?"

"They told him he made a big mistake, and he said he was sorry."

"Do you know what kind of mistake he made?" Daley asked. "Why he was sorry?"

"No." Ida shook her head, more tears sliding down her cheeks. "He said I was a stupid old lady who didn't know anything. He yelled at me." She pointed a finger at me. "I thought she would help me."

Both detectives looked my way.

"I never met her before Friday." I said. "I don't know why she thought that."

"Let's step outside for a few minutes," Detective Daley said to me.

Once outside of the interview room, she took a deep breath. "Jeez," she muttered on the exhale. "That lady needs a bath. We're going to have to fumigate the room when we're finished."

"She's been hiding in the bathroom of a Laundromat."

"Obviously one without a shower." Daley took me into the next room, a duplicate to the one we'd left. Once we were seated, she said, "Okay, from the beginning. How did you get involved in this?"

I summarized the events of the last few days, starting with my talk at the library and concluding with Ida's phone call earlier today, and how I'd found her hiding in the Laundromat. I was about to tell the detective about the cell phone I'd found just that morning when she interrupted me, the tone of her voice anything but cordial. "Why didn't you report any of this to us?" she demanded.

"I did," I said. "At least I tried. I called yesterday and again this morning. Each time I left my home and cell phone numbers. So far no one has called me back."

Detective Daley huffed. "We've been deluged with calls. I think every queer in town must have phoned."

"Ida more or less told me her nephew was gay."

"Gay?" Daley said. "Donald Crane was more than gay; he was a promoter of gay rights. He's participated in and led several rallies in the last few months. If he was blackmailing someone, we may have a motive for his murder, and an explanation for the missing computer and files. Could be he found out something about one of the church fathers opposing him. Or maybe this Dr. Morgan is more than a TV character. Although this city professes to be tolerant of alternative lifestyles, a doctor

might not want his sexual preferences known. We'll be checking—"

She must have remembered at that moment I was a civilian.
She stopped mid-sentence and smiled, once again Ms. Conge-
niality. "I'm sorry we didn't get back with you right away, Ms.
Benson," she said. "I'm afraid half our staff is either out sick or
on vacation. We're very glad you came in and that you brought
Ida to us. What you've told us should help solve this case. Is
there anything else you can think of?"

SEVENTEEN

Once Detectives Ferrell and Daley decided I'd related everything I knew about Donald Crane and his murder, they said I could leave. Back in my car, I'd just lowered all the windows to let out the heat and lingering body odor when my cell phone rang. I recognized Neal Wager's smooth baritone the moment he said hello. "I wanted to follow up on that question you asked last night," he said. "But I'll need the exact location of the property in dispute."

I explained I wasn't at home—though he probably already knew that since he'd called my cell—and that I couldn't give him the exact description, as it appeared on my tax papers. He said a general location—my address and the nearby streets—would be sufficient.

Once he had that information, I decided his call was fortuitous. "Remember how I told you Donald Crane's aunt gave me his briefcase?" I said. "Well, she called me today, and I just left her with the police. But I'm worried about her."

"I'm not a criminal lawyer, P.J."

"I know. And she's not a criminal." I proceeded to tell him how I'd found Ida hiding in the bathroom at the Laundromat, about her dementia, what she'd seen Friday night. "The detectives said they'll have her admitted to the hospital for evaluation, but I'm worried about her. From what I've learned, she has no one. I think she needs an advocate, someone who'll

119

make sure she's protected and doesn't end up wandering the streets."

"You say she knows the name of the men who killed her nephew?"

"She keeps calling one Dr. Morgan, but she's also said that's a character on a soap opera, and when the detectives checked the yellow pages, the only Dr. Morgan listed in the Kalamazoo/Battle Creek area is a woman."

"But she could describe the men who killed her nephew?"

"Sort of." I chuckled, remembering the vague description Ida had given the detectives. If I hadn't personally met one of the men, I wouldn't have known what he looked like from Ida's rambling, disconnected responses, and her description of the second man could have fit a lot of men, including Neal.

"Do you think she could identify them if she saw them?"

"Yeah, I think so. Those two men really scared her." Which might, in part, explain her mental escapes to the past.

"The way the detectives talked," I said, "I think they'll be questioning all of the known homosexuals in this area. They're pretty sure this has something to do with Crane's lifestyle. He probably had pictures of someone important in a compromising position and was threatening to blackmail him."

"Obviously not the wise thing to do." Neal said.

"The police can get Crane's phone records and trace his calls." I knew that for a fact. "Once they know who he contacted, they can bring them in, and his aunt will be able to identify the two who killed her nephew."

"In that case, she will need protection," Neal said. "I'll get back to you as soon as I find someone."

After ending my call with Neal, I rang Ken Paget's Computer Repair. "Great," Ken said when I told him I was in town and had the cell phone with me. "I'll put a fresh pot of coffee on, and we can take a look at it."

I didn't need any more coffee, but I was eager to hear what he had to say about the phone. While being questioned by Detective Daley, I'd decided I wanted to know what was on it—if anything—that was important enough to kill for. After that I would gladly turn it over to the police.

I stopped at a Quick-Stop gas station before heading for Ken's shop. Besides filling my car, I picked up a six-pack of Bell's Oberon. It's a popular beer, and I believe in supporting local businesses as well as paying my debts.

Ken Paget's Computer Repair was a little hole-in-the-wall stuck between a barbershop and a stairwell that led to upstairs offices. The small bell hanging over the door gave a jangle when I entered the shop, and I could smell fresh coffee brewing. A counter separated the narrow space at the front of the room from the larger portion behind it, a low, swinging gate giving access to the work area. Even farther back was a door I assumed led to a storeroom.

Computers and computer parts, DVD players, and GPS devices filled shelves and work areas, along with electronic measuring devices, tools, and electric tape. An array of manuals was stacked on one shelf, two more open on the work table beside a torn-apart computer, their schematic drawings marred with coffee stains. Styrofoam cups, scrunched-up fast-food wrappers and sacks, along with half-empty bags of potato chips and pretzels, filled the empty spaces between equipment. The place was a mess, even messier than my work area at home.

An air conditioner was noisily keeping the shop cool, and the contrast from the steamy outside air made me shiver. "Hello," I called out.

"Be just a minute," I heard from the area behind the back door.

The man who stepped through that doorway and into the main portion of the shop looked nothing like I'd imagined.

121

Instead of a teenager with peach-fuzz on his face, Ken Paget had a dark brown goatee, no hair on his head, tattoos up his arms, and was probably pushing forty. If I'd had to describe him to anyone, I'd say he looked like Howie Mandel.

He held two mugs in his hands. "You my pajama girl?" he asked as he neared the counter.

"That's me."

He set the mugs on the counter, steam rising from the coffee they held, and stuck out his right hand. "Glad to meet you, P.J. You're as pretty as you sound on the phone. 'Cept for that shiner, of course."

"It looks better than it did." I said and shook his hand. "And no, I'm not going to explain what happened."

"Ah, a lady of mystery." He grinned seductively. "That's what I like. Grab a mug—either one—and come on back here."

A quick glance at the two mugs showed no traces of dirt, so I grabbed the one with Canada geese on the side, leaving the one with pictures of fish for Ken. Mug in hand, I joined him on the other side of the counter. He pulled a wooden chair over near a stool and motioned for me to sit down, which I did.

"This is it," I said, pulling the cell phone out of my shoulder bag. "Think you can get around the password protection?"

He took the phone and turned it over in his hand, running a fingertip over the slender case. "This is one of the newer ones. Which means I'm not even going to touch it."

"Oh." Disappointed, I held out my hand for the phone.

Ken didn't hand it back. "I figured it might be one of the newer ones, so I called that friend I mentioned. He's pretty sure he can get it unlocked. He's one of those people who keeps the security guys busy."

Doing what? I wondered, but simply asked, "Do we take it to him or is he coming here?"

"He won't be able to look at it until after two, and I thought—"

Since it was already after two o'clock, I interrupted him. "That's perfect. I'm curious to see what's on it."

"Two in the morning," Ken said and smiled. "He sleeps during the day and plays in a band at night. He wasn't real pleased when I called him this morning."

"Two in the morning?" I considered the idea of driving back into Kalamazoo at that hour, to meet with two men I barely or didn't know, and immediately vetoed the thought. "Can't he come over here before he goes to work?"

"He might drop by, but I doubt it. He kinda likes to get a buzz on before he starts playing, if you know what I mean."

I understood and wasn't sure I wanted someone with a "buzz on" touching this cell phone.

"Oh, he'll be fine by two," Ken said, reading my thoughts. "And what I was thinking, is you and me could make it a date tonight. Get those beers you owe me and listen to the band until my friend is available."

"I, ah . . ." He'd taken me by surprise, and for a moment, I simply stared at him. Grandma had said I should date others, give Wade a little competition. The idea had sounded good when she mentioned it, but I wasn't sure I was up to two dates in two nights with two different guys.

"I can't," I finally said. "Not tonight. I cleaned my chicken coop this morning, and I'm absolutely beat. But—" I stood. "I do have something for you."

When I'd arrived at the computer shop, I still hadn't been sure if Ken was old enough to drink, so I'd left the six-pack in my car. The beer had been cold when I bought it, but sitting under the hot sun, it was probably rapidly heating up. I set my mug on the closest empty space on the work bench and headed for Ken's front door.

"Where are you going?" he called after me.

"Be right back," I said and hurried to my car.

Minutes later, I was back, carrying not only the six-pack I'd purchased earlier, but also the copies of the drawings I'd found in Ida's nephew's briefcase. I'd totally forgotten I was going to give those to the police. "This is for you," I said and handed Ken the six-pack. "I hope you like Oberon."

"Yeah, I do," he said, but I noticed he was frowning when he set the six-pack on the floor by his stool, and I heard him mumble, "Not exactly what I had in mind."

I didn't think so, but a date wasn't what I'd had in mind, either. I sat down again. "Okay. Back to the phone. Is there another time your friend could work on it?"

"Why don't you just leave it? I'll have my friend give it a look-see tonight. Then I'll call you in the morning and let you know if he was able to get into the system and change the password."

I didn't like the idea of leaving the cell phone. "Your friend couldn't, maybe, give the phone a 'look-see' and change that password tomorrow morning? I could bring it here early, before he goes to bed."

"By early, you mean three in the morning?"

Obviously my "early" and Ken's friend's weren't the same. "No, but . . ."

"Do you want to do this or not?"

I couldn't decide.

"My invitation's still open."

"Isn't there any other way?" The moment the words were out, I realized how that sounded. "I mean, I'd like to go out with you, but not tonight. And I just wanted to see what was on this. The police are going to be upset as it is that I haven't handed it over to them."

"And what do you think is on here?"

"I don't know. Maybe pictures of some city official or politician doing kinky things. Or a religious leader."

"Kinky, huh?" Ken ran his fingertip over the edge of the phone. "Now you have me curious."

"Yeah, well, don't get too curious. Whatever it is, it got one man killed." Once again, I held my hand out for the phone. "Maybe I should forget trying to see what's on it and just turn it over to the police."

"And if they screw up what's on it . . . ?"

Ken left the question open, but I knew he'd also heard stories of court cases lost because evidence was mishandled or went missing. Law enforcement wasn't perfect.

I drew my hand back. "Okay, see if your friend can change the password tonight. But don't let him do anything that will mess up the phone. I'll come back here in the morning, and you can either show me what you found, or I'll take the phone to the police." *Or maybe both.*

"Sounds like a plan."

"Meanwhile," I handed Ken the papers I'd brought in with me. "You're good at figuring things out. Look at these and tell me what you think."

He studied the pages for a few moments, then shrugged and handed them back. "The one looks like a map of some sort, and the others look like some sort of lab report. Are they supposed to mean something?"

"I don't know." But I wished I did. "They were also in Donald Crane's briefcase, along with aerial photographs of farms near where I live, and that cell phone. And since the guy who came to my house Saturday morning asked for the briefcase, not just a cell phone, I thought maybe something on these pages might also be important."

Ken's gaze locked on my bruise. "This 'guy' is the one who gave you that shiner?"

125

"Yes." I looked away, surprised by the tightening in my chest and the tears that sprang to my eyes.

"What are you trying to do, Pajama Girl, solve this case for the police?"

"No, but I don't like being attacked in my own house." I wiped away the tears.

"What you need is a man to protect you."

The way Ken said it, I had a feeling he was open for the job. I figured I'd better squelch that idea right away. "I already have one," I said. "Detective Sergeant Wade Kingsley. He's a homicide detective for the Kalamazoo Sheriff's Department."

"Well, let's hope it's not your homicide he's investigating next." Ken looked back at the cell phone on his work bench. "You say there were pictures of farms?"

"Aerial photos," I said. "Of farms not far from where I live."

"Maybe Crane discovered a meth lab." Ken pointed at the sheet of chemical formulas. "Farm's a perfect place to have one."

I hadn't considered that. "I gave the originals of these pages to the sheriff's department. I'll find out if they're considering that possibility."

"And we'll find out what's on this." He tapped a finger on the cell phone. "You're still welcome to join us tonight."

"Wish I could," I said, wondering how many more lies I'd tell today. "But I'll tell you what. I'll pick up your bar bill. Okay?"

"Sounds good to me."

I left after that, praying I wasn't making a mistake leaving Donald Crane's cell phone with Ken. I almost didn't notice the tan sedan parked two cars behind mine, and maybe it wouldn't have concerned me if it hadn't pulled out right behind me.

EIGHTEEN

I turned right on the first side street I came to. The tan sedan did the same. At the next corner, I made another right turn. So did the sedan. I repeated this maneuver three times, choosing different streets, turning left then right, and varying how far I traveled on each. It didn't matter. Every time I made a turn, so did the sedan.

And then it was gone.

I made two more turns, working my way back to Westnedge Avenue, but I didn't see the car again.

Was it merely a coincidence that I chose the same time to leave Ken's shop as that car pulled out? A coincidence that I turned down the same streets that driver intended to turn onto?

I didn't think so, but I wasn't sure if the experience had anything to do with Donald Crane's briefcase or not. Either way, even though I was only a short distance from my grandmother's house, I decided not to stop. I certainly didn't want to lead anyone there.

I checked my rearview mirror. As far as I could tell, no one was following me. Nevertheless, when I reached a strip mall, I pulled into the parking lot and grabbed my cell phone. Ken Paget answered on the third ring.

"Hey," I said. "Maybe I'm being paranoid, but I think someone followed me from your shop."

"You okay?"

"Yeah." I kept glancing around, looking for the tan sedan . . .

or anything that looked suspicious. "Either I lost them, or . . . or I am getting paranoid. Anyway—" I sighed. "I thought I should let you know."

"Gotcha. You take care. Okay?"

"Same for you."

I didn't relax until I was on I-94, heading east toward Zenith. Physically exhausted from the heat and clearing the rubbish from the chicken coop, and emotionally exhausted from dealing with Ida Delaney, the cell phone, and the possibility I was being tailed, all I wanted was solitude. A walk in the woods with Baraka sounded good, and I knew my dog would be ready to escape the confines of his crate.

Wade hadn't called my cell, so I hoped when I arrived home I would find a message on my answering machine. That I hadn't heard from him bothered me. The way Wade had been acting lately, something was wrong.

He's busy, I told myself. *Busy being a father to his son. Busy being a homicide detective.* Yet, in the back of my mind was always the question: Was he pulling away because he was afraid I would become a schizophrenic? I was probably one of the few women approaching thirty who actually wished she were closer to forty. By then the possibility of me contracting the disease should be over.

"Don't live in the past, or pine for the future," my grandmother often said, especially when I started lamenting about my chances of turning out like my mother. "Live for the moment."

Good advice, except the moment I pulled into my driveway and saw the shattered window next to my front door, I wished I could either go back in time or jump to the future.

I turned off my engine and got out of my car as quietly as possible. The crows that reside in my woods were cawing up a storm, but I couldn't hear any human voices. Cautiously I neared my house, my cell phone in hand, a finger on the speed dial that would connect me to the nine-one-one dispatch.

One of the rocks that usually lined the edge of the steps to my porch was missing. Living in the country, with my closest neighbor a quarter mile away, no one would have heard the window being broken, and whoever did it only had to wait until there were no cars on the road—which out here was often.

I stood near the broken window, looking inside. I could see papers on the floor by my dining room table, open buffet drawers, their contents also dumped on the floor, and that Baraka was still in his crate, seemingly unharmed. He was lying down, his head on his front paws. If anything, I'd say he looked guilty.

I listened for sounds: a creaking of stairs, a door opening or closing, steps, voices. I heard nothing. Only when I was sure there was no one in the house did I open my front door. It was no longer locked.

When I entered, Baraka rose to his feet, but he wasn't wagging his tail as he usually did when I returned. Head held low, he still looked as if he'd done something he was ashamed of.

"You okay?" I asked, nearing his crate.

A tentative wag of his tail was his answer.

"So what happened?" I unlatched the door to his crate and quickly grabbed his collar. I didn't want him stepping on the broken glass. A cut pad can bleed like crazy and takes forever to heal.

Baraka came out of his crate slowly, tail between his back legs.

"Did they hurt you?" I ran my hands over his head, back, and legs, but I couldn't feel any bumps, and he didn't flinch at my touch. He seemed perfectly all right, except for his behavior.

"It's all right," I said and went down on my knees and hugged him. "You couldn't do anything to stop them. I understand."

Baraka licked my cheek, and I would have sworn he sighed. I

had a feeling I knew what was wrong with him. Rhodesian Ridgebacks are sensitive dogs. Back two months ago, when my house was repeatedly invaded, Baraka was too young to consider himself my guardian. Lately, however, he'd been showing signs of territorial possession. Today someone had invaded his territory, and he hadn't been able to defend it.

"It's okay," I repeated. "It's okay."

Only when I felt him lift his head did I lead him to the front door, carefully avoiding the glass on the floor. Outside, I released my hold on Baraka's collar. He looked around, then trotted down the steps and over to the maple tree. As he cocked his leg, I sagged down on my front steps and called nine-one-one.

After reporting the break-in, I called Wade. To my surprise, he answered. "Hi," he said. "I just got in and heard your message. You found a cell phone?"

"Yes, but that's not why I'm calling. My house was broken into. Again."

"You're kidding."

"I wish." I proceeded to tell him what I'd found, ending with, "I haven't touched anything, but nothing valuable seems to be missing. My TV, computer, and all of my office equipment are still here."

"Your dog's okay?"

I appreciated him worrying about Baraka. "He's feeling guilty for not protecting the house, but otherwise, he seems to be all right."

Tears blurred my vision, and a lump in my throat made it difficult for me to talk. "I didn't think . . ." I started, then choked back a sob. "Damn it, Wade, why does this keep happening to me?"

"I don't know, honey." His voice softened. "Look, I'm swamped right now, but I'll try to get out there. Okay? Don't touch anything until the deputies arrive."

"I won't." I knew the drill. Keep the crime scene pristine. "At least there's no dead body." I glanced back at the house. "At least, I hope there isn't."

"Well, don't go checking. Let the deputies do that."

I wasn't about to go wandering through my house looking for bodies, and I was glad when two uniformed deputies arrived. First they checked every room in the house. There were no dead bodies, thank goodness, and once they were certain the intruder was no longer on the premise—their words, not mine—they asked me to go through the house with them so I could tell them what was missing. When we finished, as far as I could tell, nothing was missing. Nothing of value, at least. If any of my files were gone, I couldn't tell. Not with just a quick glance.

They took the rock that had been thrown through my window, but they didn't give me much hope that they'd be able to lift any fingerprints from its rough surface. They did dust the doorknob and anywhere they thought the intruder might have touched. I had a feeling any fingerprints they found would be mine.

I kept Baraka outside while the deputies and I went through the house, and they collected evidence. He seemed to be over his feelings of guilt and showed off for the deputies when they finished and came outside. I tried to tell them they were going to get dog hairs on their uniforms, but they each rubbed their hands along Baraka's ridge and felt his silky ears. And he, in turn, sniffed their crotches and rubbed against their pant legs, leaving reddish-brown hairs on the fabric.

The two men were about to leave when another vehicle—a black sedan—pulled into my yard. For a moment I thought it might be Wade, driving a car from the motor pool, but then I realized it was a BMW. Neal stepped out and asked, "What happened?"

"Ms. Benson's house was broken into," one of the deputies answered. "Would you happen to know anything about it?"

"Me?" Neal looked at me, then back at the officer asking the question. "No. This is the first time I've ever been out here. Ms. Benson and I met last night, and I thought I'd stop by and see if she wanted to go out to dinner."

The two deputies glanced my way, and I nodded. "He's a real estate lawyer," I said, and wondered if they would report back to Wade. Not all of the deputies know Wade and I had been dating. If these two did, maybe this would spark that bit of jealousy Grandma had suggested.

Finally, the deputies said goodbye and drove off, leaving me with Neal. He stepped back when Baraka moved toward him. "*That* is a big dog," he said. "What is he?"

"A Rhodesian Ridgeback." I quickly ran through my usual explanation of the ridge, and how it came from the European settlers' dogs breeding with the native African dogs that had a ridge.

"You say they used them for hunting lions?" he repeated when I finished my spiel.

"They used them as pack dogs with the lions. The dogs would keep the lion at bay until the hunter arrived. They're pretty good. I haven't had a lion around here since I got him."

For a moment Neal looked perplexed; then he grinned. "That's good." His attention left Baraka and turned to my house. "So what happened?"

"Someone broke in."

"Get anything of value?"

"Not that I could tell." I sighed. "My only guess is this has something to do with that briefcase I told you about. The one Donald Crane's aunt gave me. I thought once that guy got the briefcase, I'd be left alone. Looks like I was wrong."

"Was there something he didn't get? Something he might

have come back for?"

"Just some papers and the cell phone I thought he already had . . ." My attention shifted from Neal to the road. I could see a tan Jeep slowing as it neared my house. Even from a distance, I recognized it as Wade's.

Neal noticed and turned to look that direction. "Someone you know?" he asked.

"Yeah." A giddy sensation tickled my insides. "A friend."

Friend and lover, I silently added, glad that he'd come.

I could tell Wade wasn't pleased to see Neal with me. Dark glasses hid his eyes, but his body language relayed a stiffness that reminded me of how Baraka walked when he was wary of a situation. Wade nodded my way and said my name, but his attention focused on Neal. I decided I'd better defuse the situation immediately.

"Wade, this is Neal Wager. He's a real estate lawyer. Neal, Sergeant Wade Kingsley, a homicide detective with the Kalamazoo County Sheriff's Department."

"A real estate lawyer?" Wade's posture relaxed a bit, and he cocked his head as he looked at me. "Are you thinking of selling this place?"

"No, but Nora's been bugging me, claiming my grandfather signed a note giving her the woods upon his death."

"She's not supposed to call or come anywhere near you."

I forced a laugh. "Tell her that."

"I'm also representing Olivia Halsted," Neal said, extending his right hand. "They're threatening to put a road through her front yard."

Wade shook Neal's hand, then immediately moved closer to me. Talk about territorial. Grandma was right. A little competition was reigniting Wade's interest in me.

"So what did you find missing?" Wade asked, nodding toward my house.

133

"Nothing." I leaned against his side, taking comfort in his nearness. "At least nothing I noticed."

"What about those papers and that cell phone you mentioned," Neal said.

"I'd taken them with me to Kalamazoo."

"So you turned the phone over to the police?" Wade gave a slight nod of approval.

"Actually, no." I grimaced, knowing how he would react. "I left it with a computer guru I know. He's going to try and get around the password so we can see what's on the phone."

"You gave the phone—evidence in a murder investigation—to some computer guy?"

Wade's tone of voice reminded me that in his book procedure topped curiosity. I knew nothing I said now was going to please him; nevertheless, I tried to explain. "Detective Daley said half the staff was out sick or on vacation. And you've told me stories about evidence that was screwed up, how cases you thought were slam dunks were tossed out of court because of 'technical' errors. I was afraid the police might mess up whatever is on that phone. That or it would take weeks before they got around to it."

"P.J., you could be charged with withholding evidence."

He was right, but still I argued, "As soon as Ken's friend gets past the password, I'll turn the phone over to the police."

"No, you get it to them now."

"I'm sure she thought she was doing the right thing," Neal said in my defense.

Wade glared at him. "We don't need your input."

"Sorry." Neal raised his hands and stepped back. "I just . . ." Wade's look silenced him, and Neal shrugged. "Catch you later, P.J." Another step back, and he nodded at Wade. "Nice meeting you, Detective."

"Yeah," Wade said, his expression conveying the opposite.

"You were rude," I said as soon as Neal drove off.

"Yeah, well." He walked away from me, toward my front door. "What are you going to do about that window?"

"I don't know." I hadn't thought that far ahead, but something would have to be done. With a hole that big, every insect in the state of Michigan would head for the inside of my house, especially once the sun went down, and I turned on the lights.

"You have any plastic? For now you could tape a sheet of plastic over the opening." He shook his head as he neared the broken pane. "You're going to have to special order the glass. The windows in these old houses aren't standard."

As if I didn't know that.

Looking at the broken window, all I could think was Ida Delaney and her nephew's briefcase were costing me money. Which reminded me: "I delivered Ida Delaney to the detectives investigating her nephew's murder. I think they hoped they'd learn something from her, but half the time she doesn't know what's going on . . . other than they scared her."

"Who scared her?"

"The two guys who killed her nephew. She called one Dr. Morgan, but later she said Dr. Morgan was on a soap opera she watches, so I doubt that's really his name. However, the way she described him, I think he's the one who hit me Saturday and took the briefcase." I pointed at the window. "He's probably the one who broke into my house today. He came back for that cell phone. There's something on it he wants."

"Then you'd better get it to the police right away."

I sighed and gave in. "Yeah, you're right." Not that I was eager to drive back into Kalamazoo. A glance at my watch showed it was nearing five o'clock. I wasn't sure what time Ken closed his shop or where he lived. "I'll give him a call."

"Good." Wade glanced at his own watch. "I've got to go. I have a five-thirty appointment. Get that cell phone and turn it over to the police. Immediately if not sooner."

"Yes, master," I said, giving a slight bow.

As I watched him walk back to his Jeep, I realized he hadn't kissed me. Not when he arrived, and not when he left. He also hadn't said what kind of appointment he had, and hadn't offered to cover the broken window or clean up.

"So much for everlasting love," I said as I rubbed Baraka's head and watched Wade drive away.

Not that we'd ever pledged everlasting love. Neither one of us had used the word *love*. Lust. That was what we'd been enjoying.

I revised my statement. "So much for everlasting lust."

Maybe I should have gone out with Ken. Or maybe I still would. I pulled out my cell and scanned through my contacts until I found the number I'd entered for Ken. Five rings and his recorded voice told me to leave my name, number, and a short message.

"Hey, Ken, it's your pajama girl," I said, rather liking his nickname for me. "Give me a call. I need that phone."

NINETEEN

I looked for another phone number for Ken Paget but found none. I didn't even find a home address, just the one for his repair shop. Tired and hungry, I wasn't about to drive back into Kalamazoo, not until I had some idea where Ken might be. A wise decision I discovered when Ken finally did return my call.

By then I'd swept up the broken glass, fed Baraka, taped a sheet of plastic over the broken window, and grabbed a sandwich for myself. Stretched out on the couch, I was half asleep when my cell phone rang. Ken's youthful voice was barely audible over the sound of electric guitars and people talking in the background. "Just noticed you called," he said, a slight slur to his words.

Just noticed or ignoring me? I wondered. He hadn't acted happy when I mentioned Wade.

"I need that phone back," I said, raising my voice.

"Damn, you don't have to yell."

"Sorry." I spoke softer. "I wasn't sure you could hear me. You at a bar?"

"Yeah. The one where my friend is playing. He looked at the phone before he started his first set. Said he thinks it won't be hard to break into."

"I don't want him breaking the phone."

"You know what I mean. Hey, honey, bring me another one of these."

For a moment, I thought he was talking to me, then I realized that last bit must have been directed toward a waitress.

"I've been ordered to get that phone to the police," I said, still irritated that Wade had given such an order.

"Call me in the morning," Ken said. "I'll let you know how things went."

"No, I'll—"

Ken hung up. I immediately called him back, but his voice mail came on. I knew he wasn't going to answer.

"Men," I grumbled. One ordered me around, the other one ignored me. No, both of them ignored me.

I went back to the couch. Ken hadn't mentioned the name of the bar where his friend was playing, and I was too tired to drive around Kalamazoo checking out bars. He'd told me to call him in the morning, so that's what I would do. I would call him, go pick up the cell phone, and then I would turn it over to the police. They could even have the papers I had. I wanted nothing more to do with Ida Delaney, her dead nephew, or that damn briefcase.

Ken called me in the morning before I finished my first cup of coffee. "Hey," he said when I answered the phone. "Guess what happened last night."

"What?" I asked, hoping it would be good news, but fearing the worst.

"My place was broken into."

"You're kidding." Except, from the tone of his voice, I knew he wasn't. "Did they get the cell phone?"

"Nope, had it with me. But I'm guessing that's what they were after."

"Why do you say that?"

"The way they tossed the place. They were definitely looking for something, and the way they acted before they left, I don't think they found it."

"You saw how they acted? You were there?"

"No, after you called and said someone followed you, I got out of there as quick as I could. But before I left, I made sure my security cameras were working. I use two. One that's visible and one that's hidden. Kids knocked out the visible one right away. They didn't have a clue where the other one was set up. The officers who took my report recognized one of the boys."

"These were kids? Boys? Not men? Not a big guy with dark hair?"

"Three teenagers. Maybe fifteen or sixteen. Police said the one is in a gang. Others probably are, too. Could be pure coincidence they decided to hit my place last night. Cops said they've hit other places in the neighborhood, and they took several items that could be sold for drug money, along with a couple hundred I had in the back room."

"But you don't think it was a coincidence?"

"Don't know, but it sure looked like they were searching for something specific."

"Like a cell phone." Wade was right, I should have turned that phone over to the police when I found it. "Ken, my house was broken into yesterday, probably while I was at your shop."

"Jeez, what have you gotten yourself into, Pajama Girl?"

"I don't know, but I don't like it. Give me a half hour to finish up here, and I'll drive into Kalamazoo and pick up that damn phone."

"Don't have it," Ken said.

"What?"

"Last night, my friend and I sort of had a few too many beers. He tried a couple of things, when they didn't work, we decided he'd better wait until morning to tackle it. So I let him take it home."

I closed my eyes and sagged down onto one of my dining room chairs. Maybe whoever broke into Ken's shop didn't get the phone, but it was gone. "You're telling me your friend has the cell phone?"

"Hey, you wouldn't have wanted us messing up, would you? He was really buzzed last night, and I was feelin' no pain. He'll get on it today."

I said nothing.

"You'll have the phone by this afternoon. Okay?"

"I have a better idea. Tell me where your friend lives, and I'll go get the phone." I would get it and turn it over to the police.

"Not a good idea. My friend doesn't like to be disturbed while he's sleeping."

"What if whoever broke into your shop and into my house goes after your friend?"

"They'd be sorry."

The way Ken said it, I wasn't sure I ever wanted to meet his friend.

"Look, Pajama Girl, don't you worry about my friend and don't worry about me. We'll get that phone so you can see what's on it. After that, you can do whatever you'd like." He cleared his throat. "By the way, you did promise to pay my bar bill, didn't you?"

"Yeah." I had a feeling that might have been another mistake. "How much are we talking about?"

I cringed when he told me the amount. This entire fiasco with the briefcase was getting very expensive.

Ken repeated that I'd have the phone sometime in the afternoon. In truth I didn't think I'd ever see the phone again.

TWENTY

I sat staring at the plastic on my shattered window until Baraka came over and reminded me it was time for his breakfast. After he was fed, and I'd downed another cup of coffee, I decided to take him for a short walk. As I started along the pathway through the woods, I remembered Howard had said he'd seen Nora digging around some junk Sunday.

I loved being able to step out my back door and walk along a wooded path, but there were times I questioned why I was so gung-ho about keeping those woods. For years my grandfather used the area as his private junkyard. If he bought new car tires, the old ones were rolled out back of the house and left amid the trees. Same with car parts, metal burning barrels, household items, and stacks of wood.

"So, Grandpa, is there a buried treasure back here that Nora knows about?" If so, I would like to find it before Nora did.

Baraka chased after a squirrel, losing it when it went up a tree. He circled the tree several times, but never looked up. Watching him made me wonder how many things I miss because I wasn't looking in the right direction.

Back at the house, an almost empty refrigerator convinced me the first thing on my agenda needed to be a trip to the grocery store. This time I left Baraka loose in the house. Even if he chewed up my slippers—which I hoped he wouldn't—I didn't see that he'd make any bigger mess than the person who ransacked my house the day before. He might even scare someone away.

The drive to Zenith didn't take long. There I had two choices: a small stop-and-shop that primarily sold liquor, cigarettes, and snacking items or the locally owned grocery store, just a half-mile out from the main four corners. I chose the grocery store. It didn't have the variety of items the big chain stores in Battle Creek and Kalamazoo offered, and the prices were higher, but it was convenient, and it was a great place to meet neighbors and catch up on what was going on.

The first person who stopped me was Pat Yelton, the township treasurer. Pat was probably in her late forties, always wore color-coordinated outfits—usually pantsuits, even in the summer—and always looked as if she just stepped out of a beauty parlor, not a strand of her auburn—probably dyed—hair out of place. We were both looking for ripe—but not too ripe— bananas.

"I saw you at the meeting Monday night," she said. "Your face looks a lot better today."

That statement could, I guess, be translated: You looked terrible that night. I simply said, "Thanks" and started to move my cart away.

Pat placed a hand on my arm, stopping me. "What do you think about this road straightening issue?"

Since the resolution didn't involve me, and I had enough problems of my own, I hadn't been thinking about it at all. I said, "Quite a dilemma."

"I'm on the committee that has to decide." Pat sighed. Then she lowered her voice. "I think Leon doesn't want that road going through his property because he's growing pot."

"Marijuana?" I said, louder than I meant, then also lowered my voice. "You're saying Leon Lersten grows marijuana?"

Pat nodded, glanced around the store, and then edged closer to me, almost speaking directly into my ear. "Most of the farmers around here are complaining about how tight money is, how they're barely making a living. But not Leon and his wife. They took a trip to Europe last winter. Hired someone to take care of the farm and were gone for over a month. Even took his sister along with them. You tell me where he's getting the money to do that?"

Since Leon and his wife weren't clients of mine, and I wasn't privy to his financial affairs, I couldn't tell Pat anything. Not that I would have. I did find it interesting that she thought he might be growing pot. Monday night Leon had said Donald Crane took soil samples from his farm. Ken had thought those drawings and printouts might have something to do with a meth lab, but maybe he was wrong. Those Xs could indicate marijuana growing sites. It wasn't unusual for drug enforcement teams to find fields of marijuana and corn planted virtually side by side.

Some farmers were innocent. During the night, others invaded their fields, planting and tending a more lucrative crop. Unless the host farmer accidentally stumbled across the stash before it was harvested, they'd be none the wiser. Other farmers did the planting themselves, figuring they might as well reap some of the financial gains, especially if they didn't have to claim the money on their income taxes. Leon Lersten could be one of those farmers. It would explain why he wouldn't want a team of surveyors traipsing through his fields and discovering more than they should.

"Mrs. Halsted's the one I feel sorry for," Pat continued. "Olivia has had more than her share of problems. Her husband, bless his soul, was a gambler. That's why she had to sell that property between her house and Leon's farm. When Albert Halsted died, he left Olivia so far in debt, I'm amazed she didn't have to sell the house as well as that property."

"Neal said . . ." I started, and then quickly corrected myself.

"That is, her lawyer said a corporation bought the property. I was surprised they didn't have someone at the meeting representing their interests."

"Me, too," Pat agreed. "But you know, in the years I've been treasurer, I've never met anyone connected with that property. I send the tax bills to a post office box in Kalamazoo. Long before the due date, I get a certified check with the corporation's title and a signature I can't read mailed back to me. I keep thinking that land's going to be turned into a residential subdivision, that maybe this anonymous corporation is actually owned by Leon's sister, Grace. Or maybe Grace and Leon together. After all, she is in real estate."

"Abby said she hears trucks go by her place some nights. Do you think they might be bringing in building supplies?"

"Possibly. One of our local pilots said he flew over the area a couple weeks ago, and it looked to him like a big hole had been dug. I was sure that was going to be for a basement."

"But wouldn't you know?" I asked. "I mean, wouldn't someone—at least a representative of the corporation—have to get a building permit if they were going to build a house or houses on that land?"

"It's the law, but there are some people who think if they have something started, it will make it easier to convince us to give them a permit. In this case, we don't have to worry. Monday one of the DEQ guys walked the property. He said he could see where a hole had been dug, but it was filled back in. My guess is this road straightening business made them change their mind. That or the downturn in the housing market."

Pat gave my discount store T-shirt and ragged cut-offs a quick glance, and I wondered what she thought of my attire. I've never been particularly concerned with looking fashionable, but I didn't want her telling others I couldn't afford decent clothes. A CPA should look moderately successful.

Worried about how I looked, I wasn't prepared for her next question. "So what do you think of Mrs. Halsted's lawyer? He's pretty cute, isn't he?"

"I, ah . . ." I forced myself to stop stammering. "Yes. He is nice looking."

"Heard you two were seen at the Pour House Monday night."

I should have known word would spread. Nothing is sacred in Zenith. "I wanted to talk to him about a real estate problem I'm having. He's a real estate lawyer, you know."

"Um-huh. Right." Pat's smile said she wasn't buying my story. "You still seeing that sheriff's detective?"

"Saw him just yesterday," I said and decided Pat was getting a little too nosy.

"He stops at your house quite often, I hear."

I'd bet anything Howard told her that. For a man who says he likes his solitude, he sure is a gossip.

"Yesterday, that sheriff's detective was ordering me to get a cell phone to the police," I said, Wade's demand still irking me.

"So did you give it to him?" Pat asked, clearly curious.

"I didn't have it with me," I said. "I'd given it to a computer person I know in Kalamazoo."

Pat's expression brightened. "A computer person? Is he any good? You know, we need some work done on the township's computers, and we're looking for bids."

I didn't know that, but I was willing to throw some work Ken's way, especially since I was probably responsible for his shop being robbed. "His name's Ken Paget. Paget Computer Repair. Give him a call."

I'd called Ken so many times in the last two days, I'd memorized his number. She wrote it down on an envelope she had in her purse.

"Tell him I sent you," I said. I hoped, if he got the bid, he might forget the bar bill he wanted me to pay.

145

"I'll do that," she said, then pushed her cart away from mine.

I hurried through the rest of my shopping, and had half of my groceries loaded in the trunk of my car when Nora came up beside me. Immediately, I took a defensive stance. I did not trust the woman, but I figured there wasn't much she could do in a public place, with people going to and from their cars.

"That door really did a job on your face," she said, almost smirking.

"Took me by surprise."

"Better take care of yourself. Anything happens to you, those woods will definitely be mine."

"Over my dead body."

She grinned. "That's what I'm saying."

TWENTY-ONE

I watched Nora walk away, the reality of what she'd just said slowly sinking in. *She threatened me.* With me gone, there would be no one to contest that note she said my grandfather had written. No one to stop her from taking possession of those woods.

Twice she'd tried to kill me and had failed. What would she do next? My stomach churned at the thought of having to be on guard all the time, and I knew I had to do something about getting her put back in jail.

I waited until Nora entered the store before I finished loading my groceries. I'd just closed the trunk when another woman's voice stopped me from getting into my car. Leon Lersten's wife, Wilma, rolled her grocery cart up behind me.

"I heard you talking to Pat," she said, glaring at me. "We are not growing marijuana. And it's none of that woman's business how we can afford a trip to Europe. We pay our taxes. On time. That's all she needs to know."

I wasn't sure what to say, but I didn't need to worry. Wilma Lersten went on. "Also, that friend of yours, Abby Warfield, is nothing but a troublemaker. More than once I've seen her over on that land owned by the corporation. They've got 'No Trespassing' signs all around the property, but does that stop her? No. The day I found her poking around our barn, I confronted her. And you know what she said? That she was looking for her dog. Which she probably was. From the day she

147

and her husband brought that dog home, they've let it run loose."

Wilma Lersten barely paused for a breath. "Have you seen her dog? I know I wouldn't leave a dog with her. I—"

"She's not a friend," I finally managed. "Just a client."

Wilma Lersten snorted. "Then maybe you'd better be a little more selective in your clients."

With that, she pushed her grocery cart on down the row of cars until she reached a tan sedan—a sedan that looked very much like the one Morgan, or whatever the hulk who hit me was named, drove off in. Looked like the tan sedan that had followed me when I drove away from Ken's shop.

I slid into my car and started the engine, but I waited until Wilma Lersten drove off before I pulled out of my parking space. I wanted to see that sedan's license plate. Problem was, when I got close enough to read the plate, I couldn't. Mud spatter covered the back bumper, license plate, and part of the sedan's trunk. If there were two Ls or number ones, I couldn't tell, and I didn't think following her back to her farm, and asking her to clean her license plate, would go over too well. But I was curious. I wanted to know if the Lerstens had anyone named Morgan working for them, or anyone who might fit the description of the man who'd taken Donald Crane's briefcase and hit me. And I knew just who to ask. Howard Lowe.

I called Howard the moment I arrived home, but gave up after the sixth ring. He didn't have an answering machine, so I knew I'd have to try again later. I also called the sheriff's department and reported Nora's disregard of her restraining order. The woman I spoke to said she'd inform the judge. I hoped that would take care of Nora.

I'd just finished putting my groceries away when my cordless phone rang. I hoped it was Ken saying his friend had discovered what was on Donald Crane's cell phone. But it wasn't. To my surprise, Neal Wager said, "I've been thinking about you."

"Oh yeah?" His voice had such a relaxing, melodic sound, I eased myself onto one of my dining room chairs and smiled. "And what have you been thinking?"

"That you should go out to dinner with me tonight. That is, if your detective will let you."

I knew Neal was searching for how romantically involved I was with Wade. Since, at the moment, I wasn't sure, my answer was easy. "Who . . . or whom I go to dinner with is my decision, not Wade's."

"I just didn't want to step on any toes," Neal said, his tone still cautious.

"I thought you were asking me out to dinner. Are we going dancing, too?"

He chuckled. "Not tonight. I am a lousy dancer, and would never take anyone dancing on a first date."

So he considered this a date, not business. I liked that. "What time? And what should I wear?" I asked.

He said he'd pick me up at six-thirty and asked me what kind of food I liked . . . or didn't like. Then he blew the whole romantic angle when he said, "I've been doing some research on quit claim deeds, and claims on a deceased person's property. I thought you'd like to know what I learned."

"Definitely," I said and decided mixing business and pleasure wasn't totally bad, not if I could finally stop Nora from claiming my woods were hers.

Neal ended our conversation by repeating what time he'd pick me up. He never did tell me how to dress, but I wasn't overly worried. Nowadays most restaurants didn't have dress codes and just about anything was appropriate as long as the patron had money or a credit card to pay the bill. Since my selection of dresses was almost nonexistent, a pair of slacks and a nice top would have to do.

One thing I liked about working out of my house was I didn't have to wear business attire or fancy outfits to an office. Sweats and jeans in the winter, shorts and T-shirts in the summer. The other thing I liked was I could set my own hours. But I knew, if I wanted any income this month, I needed to finish a couple of the accounting jobs I'd been ignoring.

By mid-afternoon, I had one client's paperwork finished and ready to mail. I'd just started on another client's file when Baraka rose from where he'd been napping by my feet and went to the door. A tentative woof pulled my attention to my yard. I hadn't heard a car pull in or the gate open, but Abby Warfield was heading for my front door.

Both Baraka and I were on my porch by the time Abby reached the steps. She greeted my dog with a hug and a doggie biscuit—after asking my permission to give him one—and said yes when I asked if she'd like a glass of iced tea. "You won't believe what happened today," she said, following me into my house. "Leon Lersten came over and offered to buy my property. Everything. House. Kennel. Land. Not only that, he offered me more than I would ever get if I tried to sell it on the open market."

"So are you going to sell?" I asked as I dumped some ice in two glasses and poured tea out of a pitcher from the refrigerator.

"Hell no." Abby chuckled and accepted the glass I handed her. "Well, not for that price, at least."

"Do you think he'll offer more?" I motioned for her to take a chair at the table. As she did, I shoved some of the papers covering the surface to the side, making room for our glasses.

"Maybe." She grinned. "Let's put it this way. If he wants it, he'd better kick in a helluva lot more. That house and land are all I own. If I sell, I've got to make enough to buy another house and put money in the bank to live off of. At least until I find a decent-paying job, which, at my age, might take a long time."

"So are you going to wait and see if he raises his offer before you do anything about a bookkeeping system?" I hated the idea of losing a potential client, but it sounded like selling would be Abby's best option.

"Oh, I still need to set one up. Whether I sell or not, I've been boarding dogs since the first of the year. Not a lot of dogs, mind you, but a few. I have expenses I want to deduct from my income, and I can't do that if what I'm doing is just a hobby. Right?"

"Right," I agreed.

"So we need to make this look like a business. I need my paperwork in order so the IRS won't question my deductions."

"The IRS can always question your deductions," I said, hoping she didn't plan on including any outlandish items. "But you're right, if your records are in order so you can verify everything you deduct, and you can show how each item pertains to your business, you shouldn't have any problems. Also, if you do sell your place, I can help you with those taxes."

"I love it." Abby rubbed her palms together and grinned. "Leon thinks by buying me out he's going to win. But he's wrong. I might not be on his case about the road, but I'll be the one walking away with his money."

"Speaking of Lersten's money," I said, remembering my conversation with Pat Yelton that morning. "Do you think he's growing marijuana?"

"Marijuana?" Abby seemed to consider the idea as she took a sip of her tea. "I guess he might be." She set her glass back down and leaned toward me. "Personally, I think they have a meth lab in one of their barns. Lately, when the wind blows from that direction, you wouldn't believe the smell." She sat back and waved a hand in front of her face, as if pushing away the odor.

"You're the second person who's suggested that," I said. "Have you reported your suspicions to the sheriff's department?"

"I've thought about it, especially the other day when the smell was really bad. But from my experience, you can make all the reports you want, and nothing ever happens."

"Really? Whenever I've called the sheriff's department, they've responded right away."

"Well, I haven't actually ever called the sheriff's department," Abby said, giving a shrug. "But I sure haven't had any luck when I've reported the problems I've had with my water."

"What kind of problems?"

"Well, for one thing, it's loaded with rust and every so often it smells like rotten eggs."

"I had the same problem here." I pointed the direction of my well. "All my clothes were getting rust stains. I finally had to install a water conditioner."

"That's what they told me to do." She snorted. "I think they must get a kickback from these water softener companies. But I showed them. I buy bottled water. That and take my clothes to the Laundromat. Except now I swear I smell gasoline every so often."

"That doesn't sound good. I hope you reported that."

"I did, and I was really impressed when the county drain commissioner himself showed up at my door. But, of course, that day the water didn't have any odor, and now the man's disappeared."

"They still haven't found him?"

"Not a sign of the guy, according to the papers. And I've never gotten the results of the water sample he took. I don't think he ever sent it in. I think he skipped town, that's what I think. Whadaya wanna bet some of our hard-earned tax money is also missing? Do you know if they use gasoline to make meth?"

Abby's rapid switch back to the production of methamphetamine left me dazed. "No, I don't know."

"Betcha it is. Betcha that's why Leon wants to buy my place . . . so I'll stop complaining about the smell. Probably bought off that drain commissioner, and now he's trying to buy me off. Well, he'd better make it worth my while if he doesn't want me turning him in."

"I hope you didn't say that to his face?"

"Sure I did. It's called incentive."

Her blasé attitude worried me. Telling someone you might turn them in for growing or manufacturing drugs didn't seem like a good idea. "What did he say?"

"He told me I was crazy. He also threatened my dog." She reached down and gave Baraka's head a pat. "I don't know why he gets so upset over my dog being on his property. Dexter has been going over there ever since I got him. Dogs don't know property lines."

"Which is why I have a fence around this place," I said, only partially agreeing with Abby.

"My kennel runs are fenced in, but Dexter doesn't like to be confined. Howls like a baby." She motioned outdoors. "I see you ran the fence all around the house. Bet that cost a small fortune."

"It wasn't cheap." But I considered my dog's safety important.

"Well, even if I stay where I'm at, you won't see a fence around my place, not unless I win the lottery or get a really good-paying job. I doubt one would work with Dexter, anyhow. When he goes hunting, nothing stops him."

"Sounds like my neighbor's dog." Although we couldn't see Howard's farm, I pointed that direction. "He has a coon hound that's always slipping his collar and heading for my woods. At least that's what Howard tells me. Personally, I think he lets his dog loose so he'll have an excuse to hunt over here."

"Well, I don't hunt, other than for my dog." Abby stood and pushed her chair back from the table. "Guess I'd better get going. I just wanted to tell you about Leon's offer. Meanwhile, I'm getting my papers together. Would you have time tomorrow to stop by?"

"Sure. What time?"

"Give me until the afternoon." She grinned. "It'll probably take me that long to find all the bills and receipts you'll need."

I walked with her to her car. At the gate, I told Baraka to sit and stay. I emphasized the "stay" command by holding the flat of my hand in front of his face, then left the gate open and joined Abby by her car.

"Wow," she said, watching Baraka sit where I'd left him. "Dexter's slowed down, but he sure wouldn't do that. If I don't sell the place, maybe I'd better take some lessons from you on dog training."

"Takes time and repetition." *Along with luck,* I thought, praying nothing distracted Baraka. "But it's worth it."

Abby opened her car door, but before she slid in, she turned back toward me, the look on her face quizzical. "Do you think Leon would do something? To shut me up, I mean?"

"I don't know."

Her question, however, worried me. Donald Crane had done some work for Leon Lersten, and now Donald was dead. The briefcase connected with Crane's death held a lab report and soil samples from Leon Lersten's farm. And maybe pictures on a cell phone? Pictures of something Leon didn't want publicly known?

"Maybe I shouldn't have said anything to him about turning him in," Abby said.

"Maybe you shouldn't have," I agreed. "Do you know if he

154

has anyone working for him named Morgan? A tall guy." I held my hand above my head. "Dark hair. Maybe drives a tan sedan."

"Wilma drives a tan Chevy."

"I know. Would this guy drive it sometimes?"

"Can't tell you if he would or wouldn't." She shook her head. "I'm afraid I'm not buddy-buddy with my two neighbors. Leon and Wilma are always bitching about my dog, and Mrs. Halsted drives me nuts talking about how things used to be. And of course, ever since I proposed straightening those curves, all three of them have been on my case. So maybe they've got someone working for them who fits your description or maybe not. Seems like I've seen a dark-haired guy in a tan car drive by. But I wouldn't know his name. Why do you want to know?"

"Just curious." I decided to leave it at that.

TWENTY-TWO

I wore light-tan cotton slacks, a rose-colored, short-sleeved, scoop-necked silk shirt that set off my brown eyes and hair, and a pair of brown leather sandals that had low heels. For jewelry, I chose a handmade, beaded choker and dangling earrings. I figured I looked dressy enough for a fancy restaurant and casual enough for a fast-food place, though I didn't really think Neal would take me to one of those.

When he stepped out of his car to pick me up, I could see he'd chosen a similar combination: tan slacks, a pale-blue, short-sleeved shirt, loafers, and no tie. He wouldn't tell me where we were going, not until he turned off Columbia Avenue in Battle Creek and drove down to the parking lot of a lakeside restaurant. I'd eaten there once before, in the winter, and because it was already dark by the time my friend—another woman—and I sat down for dinner, I didn't appreciate the beauty of the site. Tonight the sun was a good three hours from setting, and I could see sailboats on the water, a gentle wind filling their sails.

"Beautiful," I said.

"Yes, you are."

I turned away from the view outside to find him staring at me and smiling. Mr. Silver Tongue was at it again. "I meant the lake."

"I know, and I know what I meant." Neal took the menu the waitress handed him. "You're not wearing as much makeup as you were the other night."

I touched my cheek. "Did I put on enough to cover the bruise?"

"It barely shows." He grinned and started to say something else, but we were interrupted by the waitress asking for our drink order. That given, we concentrated on the menu, then ordered. We were sipping our drinks before Neal brought up the topic of Nora and my woods. "I don't think you have to worry about a letter of intent that wasn't notarized or witnessed," he said. "Especially if you can produce witnesses who will testify that this was not your grandfather's desire."

"Will I have to go to court?" I didn't want court costs, lawyer fees, and the possibility of a judgment going against me.

"Maybe, but I really don't think it will come to that." He grinned. "You hire me, and I'm sure I can convince this woman she doesn't have a chance of winning."

"You are one self-assured—"

"Bastard?" he finished for me, grinning like a kid.

"I don't know your heritage, but consider yourself hired if Nora pushes this."

"Good." He took another sip of his drink. "Now that we have that out of the way, what exactly is your relationship with that detective?"

"We've been going out," I said, not wanting to go into details.

"Sleeping together?"

I raised my eyebrows. "I don't think that's any of your business."

"I'll take that as a yes." He gave a dramatic sigh. "So, do I have a chance?"

Considering Wade's recent behavior, and Mr. Neal Wager's good looks, I wasn't about to say no. "We'll have to wait and see."

"Good." He leaned back in his chair and smiled. "You'll

discover, I'm a very patient man . . . and I usually get what I want."

"You make me sound like a prize in a contest." I didn't like that.

"A very valuable prize, I'd say. By the way, did you get that cell phone to the police, as your detective ordered?"

Neal knew how to press my buttons. Being ordered around by Wade, or anyone, didn't go well with me. I was pleased to say, "No. My computer guru still has it. That is, a friend of his does. But you won't believe what happened yesterday."

I proceeded to tell him about Ken's shop being broken into. "Quite a coincidence, don't you think?" I said as the waitress set our salads in front of us. "Both my place *and* his being broken into. Obviously it's the cell phone they're after."

"You think the same people broke into your house and his shop?" Neal asked, his fork poised above his salad plate.

"I think there's some connection." But my theory was weakened by the fact that Ken's security tape showed three teenagers—not two grown men. "When Ken's friend figures out how to access what's on that phone, we should know what this is all about."

"He hasn't been able to do that?"

"Not so far." I sighed. "Ken called me this afternoon. He said I needed to be patient, that his friend is taking his time because he doesn't want to screw up the phone. I'm beginning to think this friend has already screwed up the phone, and whatever was on there is gone. That or he's decided to try a little blackmail on his own."

"Not exactly a good idea."

"Probably not, but the way Ken talks, this friend of his isn't exactly an upstanding citizen." I stabbed a bite of salad and smiled. "Could be the bruiser who hit me will meet his match."

"And you'd like that, I take it."

"What I'd like to see is the guy arrested and put in jail."

"Have you found out anything more about him?" Neal asked, digging into his own salad. "You said he was a doctor or something?"

"Ida called him Dr. Morgan, but I don't think that's his name."

"She still hasn't remembered the other one's name?"

"Not as far as I know." Of course, I'm not on the police department's need-to-know list. "I did call the hospital. I couldn't talk to Ida, but they did give me the name of her lawyer. I'm assuming he's the one you sent."

"Arthur Hicks?"

I nodded, and so did Neal. "I called him right after I talked to you yesterday. Art's a good man. I told him to let me know where she goes once she's released from the hospital."

"And you'll let me know?"

"Of course." He smiled and reached across the table to touch my hand. "You're a good person, P.J. Caring and considerate."

I wasn't sure about that. In truth, I simply wanted to know if Ida Delaney was out of my hair; however, I didn't think I'd better say that, so I smiled back and said, "She's a nice person."

"Who's gotten you punched in the face and in trouble with your boyfriend."

"Slapped, not punched," I corrected. "And I don't want to talk about Wade. How did your day go?"

I ate my salad while Neal told me about a class action suit being brought against a contractor who'd built substandard houses. Listening to his description of the contractor's shoddy workmanship, I decided my grandparents' old farmhouse—even without central air conditioning—wasn't all that bad. While eating our entrees, our conversations turned to our pasts: schools we went to, places we'd visited, likes and dislikes. I told him how my mother and dad gave me the name Priscilla Jayne, and how the kids at school always teased me, calling me names like Prissy and Sissy. "As soon as I could, I legally switched my name to P.J.," I said. "It usually throws people the first time they hear it, but, heck, it's better than Prissy, or Pris, or Cilla."

We didn't leave the restaurant until after eight o'clock. A few clouds were moving from west to east and the air was heavy with humidity. "They're saying it might rain tomorrow," Neal said. "We could use some."

I agreed. The temperatures had been higher than normal for four days. As much as I'd longed for warmer weather last winter, I was ready for a cool down.

At my house, Neal walked me to the front door. I could see Baraka on the other side of the plastic I'd put over the broken window. I still hadn't called anyone about fixing that.

I wasn't sure if I should invite Neal in for coffee or not. I didn't want him getting the wrong idea. Coffee would be all I was offering. Until it was clear that Wade was through with me, I wasn't about to sleep with another man.

Neal solved my dilemma. "I had a wonderful time, P.J.," he said. "But I've got to get back to my office. I have an eviction to deal with in the morning, and I want to make sure all the paperwork is in place."

He kissed me before I had a chance to react. A long, wet, tongue-probing kiss combined with a breath-stealing hug that should have set my heart pounding. Should of, but didn't. What did raise my blood pressure was when I heard a vehicle approach, slow, then rev its engine and speed away from my house.

It took me a moment to extract myself from Neal's embrace. By the time I turned and looked down the road, all I could see was the back end of a tan Jeep.

Even at a distance, I knew who it was.

Twenty-Three

As soon as Neal drove off, I called Wade's cell phone number. I hoped he'd either gotten his working again or had bought a new one. By the sixth ring, I didn't think he would answer. Then he did. A gruff: "What do you want, P.J.?"

"That wasn't what you think. He took me by surprise."

"Yeah, right."

"He did. We were saying goodnight, and then . . ." I didn't want to say what happened then.

"You went out with him?"

I wasn't about to lie, not to Wade. "We had dinner. We talked about Nora's claim on my woods and about the road they want to straighten."

"Well, I hope I didn't interrupt anything."

"He's gone."

Wade said nothing.

"Where are you now?"

"Heading home."

"Have time for a coffee?" I hoped he would come back. We needed to talk. I needed to understand what was going on.

"I'm tired."

"How about tomorrow then? Can you come for dinner?"

"I don't think it's a good idea. Not now."

His disconnect was so abrupt, I stared at my phone, tears forming in my eyes. Talk about screwing things up. Leave it to me to meet someone I liked, and then ruin everything.

My personal pity party didn't last long. About as long as it took Baraka to go outside, then come back in the house. Irritation supplanted my tears. Wade and I weren't engaged. He'd never said he loved me; never asked for a commitment on my part, or indicated one on his part. For the last two weeks he'd practically ignored me, didn't include me when he went fishing with his son, and accused me of bad mouthing him to his coworkers.

I had a right to go out with someone else if I wanted. I had a right to kiss another man . . . if I wanted.

I gave myself a slew of excuses why I was in the right and Wade was wrong; nevertheless, I ached inside, and a few more tears wet my pillow before I finally fell asleep.

That empty feeling was still there in the morning as I went through my usual routine of letting Baraka outside, fixing coffee, and feeding him. Food had no appeal for me, which wasn't all that bad considering how much I'd eaten the night before. But even my coffee didn't taste right. I hoped work would take my mind off Wade and our relationship, but more than once I realized I was staring at a page of figures, my thoughts somewhere else.

A few minutes before ten o'clock, my cordless phone rang. I grabbed the receiver, hoping it was Wade, apologizing for his behavior the night before. The voice on the other end was male, but it wasn't Wade. It wasn't anyone I recognized.

"Is this P.J. Benson?" the man asked.

"Yes," I said cautiously. "And you are . . . ?"

"Arthur Hicks. Neal Wager called me the other day, and—"

"You're the lawyer," I said, recognizing the name.

"Yes." He chuckled. "And please, no jokes about me being a hick lawyer."

"No problem as long as you lay off the pajama jokes."

"Pajama?" He paused. "Oh, P.J. Gotcha." He cleared his throat. "Anyway, I thought I should give you an update on your aunt's condition. I—"

I stopped him there. "She's not my aunt."

"She's not?" The phone went silent on his end, though I heard women's voices in the background. Then a muffled summons for a Doctor Patel.

Finally, Hicks cleared his throat and said, "That, ah . . . that creates somewhat of a problem."

"What kind of a problem?"

"Well, your aunt . . . that is, Mrs. Delaney, is about to be released from the hospital, and I assumed . . ."

Again he paused, and I could guess what he assumed—that I would be paying the hospital bill, along with his fees. "We're not related in any way," I said. "I barely know the woman."

"In that case, do you know if there's someone I should contact? A relative or person with power of attorney?"

"From what I've heard, there was just her nephew."

"Who is now dead." Hicks made a sound somewhere between a sigh and a grunt.

"What's going to happen to her?" I asked, realizing I did care. "She can't go back to her nephew's house, and you can't just put her out on the street. She saw the men who killed her nephew. She's afraid they're after her, and she may be right."

"She's not going to go out on the street," he assured me. "Or back to her nephew's house. The problem is, I'm not sure where she can go. That's why I was hoping you . . ."

"I can't take care of her," I said before he finished. "I live way out in the country. I'm not set up to—"

"How far out in the country?"

"About twenty-five miles southeast of where you are right now."

"And you live by yourself?"

"With a dog," I said, feeling my resolve give and wondering how Ida and Baraka would get along.

"Work outside of the home?"

"Only when I have to go to a client's house. I'm a CPA. Self-employed."

"You're right," he said. "Your place wouldn't work. Although her health is quite good, she does have dementia and would need more supervision than you could provide. Her evaluation summary suggests she be placed in a group home. Only problem is . . ."

"Is what?"

"One won't be available for at least four days."

"So you're looking for someone to watch her short term?"

"Four days to a week."

I had an idea. "Let me call my grandmother. In the past, when Grandma had to be out of town, she's hired people to watch my mother. She might know someone who could take Ida in for a short period of time."

"I have an eleven-thirty luncheon appointment on the other side of town," he said, but agreed he'd wait at the hospital until I had a chance to talk to my grandmother.

He gave me his cell phone number, clicked off, and I immediately called my grandmother. To my relief, she was home. I summarized what had been happening since I'd last seen and talked to her. Her response was simple. "Have him bring her here."

"To your house?" It wasn't a possibility I'd considered. "What about mother?"

"What about her? Most of the time she's at work or off with her new beau. This will give me some company."

"Ida gets things confused. Repeats herself."

"So I noticed when I talked to her at the library last week. Don't worry, P.J. I know what I'm getting into. After all, I've

164

had to deal with your mother a good part of the last thirty years. Consider this my good deed for the month."

"I don't think she smokes." I'd lived with my mother and grandmother off and on for years. Both were chain smokers and grandma's house reeked of smoke.

"So it will be an inconvenience for both of us."

"I'll see what the lawyer says."

I called Arthur Hicks back. "Sounds as good as anything," he said. "Give me the address, and I'll drive her over there."

I called my grandmother back, and told her Ida Delaney was on her way. I also promised I'd stop by in the evening. "I have a new client I'm meeting with this afternoon, and I'm not sure how long that's going to take, but there's a guy in Kalamazoo I need to see."

"Ah ha," Grandma said. "Someone new?"

"No." I thought about telling her about my date with Neal, then decided against the idea. Nice as Neal might be, I didn't see that relationship going anywhere. No sense in even bringing up his name. "This is strictly business."

"In that case, how are things going with your detective?"

My grandmother is just plain nosy. Even though she couldn't see my actions, I shook my head. "Not all that well right now."

"Want to talk about it?"

"Maybe tonight." I wouldn't mind hearing her opinion of Wade's recent behavior.

"Okay. See you then," she said and hung up.

The moment the line was clear, I called Ken. He sounded half asleep when he answered. "Yeah, whadaya want?" he asked, his youthful voice gravelly.

"It's P.J.," I said. "Were you asleep?"

He grunted, and cleared his throat a couple times. "Sort of," he said. "What time is it, anyway?"

I glanced at my clock. I'd been on the phone longer than I'd thought. "Almost eleven."

"We had a late night last night." I heard him chuckle. "Or maybe I should say an early morning."

"You and your friend?"

"Yeah." He sounded clearer, more awake. "Hey, I think maybe you're right about someone wanting that phone. I was followed yesterday."

"A tan sedan?"

"No, this was a white car, but I ditched it. You're hurting my business, you know."

"I'm sorry." I hadn't meant to involve him. I didn't want to be involved myself. "Call the Zenith township treasurer, Pat Yelton. I told her about you, and she wants you to bid on a job."

"Sweet."

I hoped so. "I'm driving into Ka'zoo this evening," I said. "I want the phone back. Where can I meet you?"

"Hmm, that might be a problem."

My stomach tightened. "What kind of problem?"

"We've kinda misplaced the phone."

"Misplaced it?" I sank onto a chair. "Ken, how could you do that?"

"Good question."

He belched, and I grimaced. I'd been an idiot to give the phone to him and not the police.

"But I think I know where it is," he said, once again sounding like a young kid. "Whadaya say I get it back to you tomorrow sometime?"

"Do I have a choice?"

"I promise, I'll call you tomorrow," he said, not really giving me an answer.

"Your friend's not using whatever is on that phone to blackmail someone, is he?" I asked, remembering my conversation with Neal. "Or are you?"

"No way."

"Don't forget, the last man who tried that is dead."

"Pajama Girl, stop worrying. We're not trying to blackmail anyone. I simply put the phone somewhere nice and safe last night." He chuckled. "And now I don't remember where that was. But I'll find it. I promise. Tomorrow you'll have that sweet little phone in your hand."

"And once I do, it's going to the police."

"Fair enough," he said. "Now I've got to go take a shower and about a dozen aspirin."

TWENTY-FOUR

I sure hoped I had that "sweet little phone" in my hand tomorrow. I hated to admit Wade was right. Curiosity be damned. I should have given the phone to the police as soon as I found it. If I had, they would probably have the men who killed Ida's nephew in jail, she wouldn't be in any danger, and I could stop worrying that I'd now put my grandmother and mother in danger. I could also get back to business as usual, which included doing payroll for several clients, and paying my own bills.

The first thing I did after my grandfather died and I discovered I'd inherited his house and a comfortable sum of money was quit my job at Quick Sums and start my own business. Being self-employed had its advantages, but it also required self-discipline. To make money, one had to work.

I actually made a profit in April, in spite of having to deal with dead people and a sheriff's detective who somehow managed to get into my bed. The media coverage provided the best publicity I could have imagined—or purchased—and led to several new year-round accounts as well as clients who simply wanted help with their taxes.

May, also, wasn't a bad month. Though nothing to brag about, my bank statement showed more income than out-go. The way things were going this month, however, I had little hope of breaking even, much less making a profit. The bills were adding up fast: first my visit to the ER, then a broken

As the Crow Flies

window, followed by Ken's bar bill—along with the beer I bought him—and now Hicks's lawyer fees. I needed to get to work.

I spent the next hour and a half preparing payroll checks for two local clients, which I would deliver in the morning, then I fixed myself some lunch. I waited until I'd eaten and had my dishes done before I called my grandmother. "Did he bring her?" I asked.

"He did. In fact, Ida and I are having a nice little chat right now. Aren't we, Ida?"

"Is that Donald?" I heard Ida ask in the background.

"No, it's my granddaughter," Grandma answered. "I'll let you know if your nephew calls." Grandma lowered her voice when she spoke to me. "She thinks he's still alive."

"You going to be able to handle this?" I really hated involving my grandmother. My mother presented enough problems.

"It'll work, for a while. Mr. Hicks, the lawyer, didn't stay long. I guess he had to be at a restaurant at a certain time. He did say he'd let the police know Ida was staying here for a few days, just in case they wanted to talk to her."

"Donald?" I heard Ida say, her voice somewhat muffled. "Is that Donald?"

"No, it's my granddaughter," Grandma Carter repeated, then chuckled. "I wonder if your mother's medicine would work on her. Not that I'm going to try, but . . ."

She let the sentence trail off, and I grinned. "I told you this wouldn't be easy."

"We'll manage."

I hoped Grandma was right. She sounded tired. "I'll give you a break this evening."

"Why don't you join us for dinner?"

"I think I'd better pass on that." I certainly didn't want to give Grandma additional work. "I'm meeting with a new client

169

this afternoon, and I have no idea how long it's going to take."

"Okay, see you when you get here."

"Was that Donald?" I heard Ida ask Grandma just before I ended the connection. "Is he coming?"

I waited until two o'clock before I prepared to go to Abby's. The moment Baraka saw me pick up my shoulder bag and briefcase, he headed for the door. I often took him with me when I visited clients, but I didn't want to do so this time. Until Abby knew why her dog was losing weight, I didn't want Baraka anywhere around her place.

"Sorry," I told him. "You've got to stay and guard the house," I decided not to crate him. So far he hadn't chewed anything he shouldn't.

Abby had said, "As the crow flies it's only a mile to my place," but I'm no crow, and a large pond and swampy area made walking or driving straight to her house impossible. After backing out of my yard, I headed west for a half mile to the main road that connected Zenith to a small village about ten miles south. I turned left on that road and traveled another eight-tenth of a mile before I hit the curves that the township was now deciding whether to straighten or not.

I rarely traveled this direction, which partially explained why I hadn't recognized the aerial photos of the area. The first curve swung to the east, the road working its way around a fairly steep hill—steep, at least, for this area. Then the road swung right, this time to avoid a large pond and swampy area. The next curve again swung toward the left, but on my right I could see a long, gravel driveway, farmhouse, barn, and silos. That, I realized, had to be Leon Lersten's farm.

Abby's house and kennel appeared as the road again curved to the right, and I could see, if I'd been traveling at a high rate of speed, how my car might end up in her front yard. I pulled into her drive and parked. She came out of the house—a one-story ranch—as I was grabbing my briefcase and shoulder bag. A yellow Labrador retriever followed her, his body swaying slightly with each step he took. Once he reached me, he gave a half-hearted wag of his tail and sniffed my bare legs and sneakers.

The dog was terribly thin. I could almost count his ribs. His coat lacked luster, and his eyes had a cloudy appearance. The Lab looked much older than seven. Something was definitely wrong with him.

"P.J., this is Dexter," Abby said. "Dexter, sit. Shake."

Dexter gave a grunting sound as he sat and extended his right paw. I shifted my briefcase to my left hand and took his paw. Considering the milky coloring of his eyes, I wondered if he could truly see me, but he looked like he was smiling, his tongue lolling out the side of his mouth as he panted in the afternoon heat.

"Have you taken him back to the vet's?" I asked, straightening back up.

"No. Haven't had a chance." Abby pushed a lock of damp hair back from her face. "Damn, it's hot. I sure hope that weatherman's right, and we get some rain tonight."

I looked up at the sky. Steel-gray clouds blocked out the sun, and the air felt like a steamy, wet blanket, but nothing indicated it might rain in the next few hours. "Let's hope," I agreed.

"Come on inside." She pointed toward her side door. "I don't have air conditioning, but I do have fans."

She also had the windows open, and with the help of the fans and a cross breeze, the temperature in her kitchen was tolerable. A shoebox of papers sat near the middle of a square wooden table. "Want something to drink?" Abby asked, pulling the refrigerator door open. "Iced tea? Lemonade? Soda?"

"Water's fine," I said and picked a spot to sit.

"Flavored or regular?" Abby held up two bottles.

Normally tap water would have been fine, but I remembered she'd said her water tasted terrible and had an odor. "Regular," I said and snapped open my briefcase.

I pulled out a legal pad and two pencils, set them on the table, then leaned back in my chair and looked around. I had a feeling the décor—at least in this room—hadn't been changed in half a century. The wallpaper was an orange-and-green stripe, the gas stove, refrigerator, and dishwasher were harvest gold, and a faded and worn pale-gold linoleum covered the floor. Definitely retro-seventies.

"You've lived here how long?" I asked.

"A little over seven years." Abby brought a bottle of raspberry-flavored iced tea for herself and a bottle of water for me to the table. "Warren always wanted to live in the country. We came across this place almost by accident. I guess it had been for sale for a long time." She motioned toward the appliances. "As you can see, it's not exactly fashionably chic. But the price was right, and Warren said we could fix it up real cute." She sighed. "He did remodel the bathroom, but two years after we moved in, he got sick. Six months after that, he was gone."

"Cancer?" I asked.

She nodded. "It happened so fast." Again, she sighed. "I thought about selling back then, but we owned it free and clear, and this was his dream house. For me to leave would be like abandoning his dream. Which is why I'm still not sure I want to sell."

"Even if they don't straighten the road?"

"Yeah, well . . ." She gave me a conspiratorial look. "I'll get it straightened. You wait and see."

I liked her confidence, but looking at the shoebox on the table, I didn't think I was going to like her bookkeeping skills. "You have all of your income and expense receipts in here?"

"I know, I know. Not the best way to keep records." Abby

grinned. "Now you know why I'm hiring you. Oh, and I know I'll have another bill in a couple of days. Yesterday, after talking to you, I decided I'd once again try to get my well checked. This time I was connected with Kalamazoo County's Environmental Health Division. Seems I didn't need the drain commissioner to submit a sample. All I have to do is fill out a form, pay a fee, send in a sample of my water, and the Environmental Health Division will test it. Of course, there's no telling how long it will take them once I submit a sample."

She tapped her bottle of flavored iced tea. "I don't really want to have to put in another well, but buying this stuff is expensive. Also, I want to put automatic water dishes in each kennel, and run hot water to the feed shed, but I'm not going to do any of that until I know what's up." She gave me a quizzical look. "Can I deduct the cost of a new well?"

"A portion of it. You, or I, would need to figure what portion of your water consumption was involved in your business."

"How about grass seed? I didn't include it." She pointed at the shoebox. "But I had to buy ten pounds of grass seed to cover the tire marks that pickup made last month, skidding to a stop in front of the kennel." Abby rolled her eyes and snorted. "Damn teenagers. Bet you anything the driver had been drinking."

For the next two hours, we went through the papers she'd stuffed in the box. Coffee-stained bills lay on top of bank deposit slips. I asked questions, made notes and suggestions. By the time we walked back outside, Abby carrying the shoebox for me, I had some idea of how to set up a simple accounting system that she could handle on her own. "I'll pick up the software," I told her as I stuffed shoebox, briefcase, and my shoulder bag into my car. "Then we can find a time when we're both available, and I'll show you how to use it. By then I'll have these papers sorted into different accounts, and it shouldn't take you long to get everything organized."

"This is great." A smile brightened her face. "Let me show you the kennel . . . just in case you ever want to board your dog."

I followed her back to her kennel. Cement blocks had been used to create a rectangular building roughly four feet high in front and slightly lower in the back. The area had been divided into five sections, each with an opening to an individual run and a hinged, insulated roof. The hinges, Abby explained, were so she could lift the roof and extract a dog from above, if necessary. Five runs with cement floors and drains extended out from the dog houses. They were enclosed with galvanized-steel fencing, a front gate, and wiring over the top. "That's to keep other dogs or animals from climbing in from above." She smiled. "If someone leaves a bitch in heat, I don't want to send her home expecting puppies."

A portion of each kennel had also been covered with wood to provide a shaded area below and included a slightly raised platform where the dog could lay. The only thing missing was a dog.

"I didn't book any boarders for the month of June. I thought I'd have the automatic water bowls in by July." Abby shrugged. "Nothing's been going as planned."

She led me to the lean-to at the end of the block building. "My husband used this as a potting shed."

Abby opened the door and ushered me inside the small, wood-frame, storage-size building. "He loved flowers, and after he died, I stopped coming out here. Just too many memories. But then, a few months ago, when I decided to board dogs, I realized if I fixed the hole in the roof and repaired the door, it would be perfect as a feed room. And, as long as I was putting in those automatic water dishes, I decided I'd also run hot water out here. That way I can also use this as a grooming room. It will be perfect for small dogs, especially in the winter.'

She pointed at capped-off water pipes. "I'm learning a lot about plumbing. It's not as easy as I thought it would be. But once I know what's up with the water, I can get everything connected in a day or two."

I was amazed by how well she'd utilized the space available. She might not be organized in her bookkeeping, but her feed room was immaculate. First aid salves and lotions, along with dog shampoo, nail trimmers, and grooming brushes, sat on shelves above a metal food preparation table. Next to a deep sink, she'd stacked several feed dishes of varying sizes. In one corner sat a metal bin, its lid securely latched, while the shelf above it held bottles of vitamins and supplements.

"So what do you think?" she asked, closing the door behind us as we left, "Would you board your dog here?"

I wasn't quite sure how to answer. The kennels looked clean and solid, and her feed area was well organized and sanitary, but I didn't sense a love of dogs in Abby's attitude. No way would I allow Baraka to get as thin as her Lab. Not without doing everything I could possibly do to figure out what was wrong. No way would I put the straightening of a road ahead of my dog's health.

Before I could come up with a response, Abby added, "I know you wouldn't even consider it until they get the road straightened."

I took the easy way out and used a question to avoid giving an answer. "If it's straightened, how will anyone get here?"

At the moment, her drive connected to the road, but if the curve was removed the new stretch of road would be some distance to the west of her house. Between the existing road and where the new road would be located was a dense stand of woods. Woods that belonged to the LRP Corporation.

"Oh, they'll have to give me some sort of right away, either from Mrs. Halsted's or that corporation's property."

Mrs. Halsted's house, I assumed, was the one on the opposite side of the existing road, about a football field south of Abby's place. If the road was straightened, Grace Halsted would lose a good portion of her front yard.

"Sure you don't want to take Leon's offer?"

Abby smirked. "Only if he sweetens it big time."

TWENTY-FIVE

I was about to pull out of Abby's yard when I noticed Olivia Halsted standing by the mailbox of the house south of Abby's. She was waving an arm, signaling for me to come to her, so I turned that direction. As I neared, she motioned for me to pull into her driveway.

I didn't turn off my engine—or the air conditioning—but I rolled down my window and asked, "Is there a problem?"

"You taking her side?"

"Abby's?" I glanced back toward Abby's house. "No. I'm not taking anyone's side. She's a client."

Olivia Halsted *harrumph*ed. "She's a troublemaker, that's what she is."

"You mean because of the road?"

"See that tree?" She pointed at the gigantic spruce growing about ten feet in front of her house. "My husband and I planted it the year we were married. They straighten this road, it will have to go."

"That would be a shame."

Olivia Halsted's expression softened. "Indeed it would be." She smiled. "I knew your grandparents. I liked your grandmother. Your grandfather, however . . ." She shook her head. "They don't make them any more stubborn than that man."

"My mom says the same thing."

"Sorry to hear about your dad."

"Yeah, well . . ." I didn't want to talk about that.

"Your other grandparents still living?"

"Just my grandmother. Grandma Carter and my mother live together in Kalamazoo."

Olivia Halsted nodded and reached inside the car and patted my arm. "I hope you go see her often. We old folks enjoy visits from you young ones."

"I'm going there this evening, as a matter of fact. I talked her into taking care of an old lady with dementia, and I think Ida's already driving my grandmother crazy."

"Well, that's not good." Olivia Halsted again looked toward Abby's house. "Speaking of crazy. I heard Leon offered her a fair price for that house and land, and she turned him down. Is that true?"

"That's what she said."

"So she's not going to sell?"

"She says she will if he ups the price enough." I hesitated, then asked the question that had been bothering me. "Mrs. Halsted, do you have any idea how Leon Lersten can afford to offer Abby so much for her little farm? From what Abby said, the offer is way above market price."

"Not all farmers are poor."

"I know, but . . . ? Well . . . do you think one of his crops is drugs?"

"Drugs? You mean like marijuana?"

"Or meth?"

"Oh my." She took a step back and glanced toward Leon Lersten's farm. "Well, of course, I wouldn't know. My knees don't work like they used to, and I don't walk as far as I once did."

"Abby says every so often she smells a strong odor coming from his place. Meth labs produce strong odors."

Olivia Halsted chuckled. "So do farm animals."

"Do they make the well water taste and smell funny? Does

your water have a strange taste or smell?"

"My water?" She frowned. "No. I mean, I have a water softener because of the rust, and every so often I notice a sulfa smell, but it's been that way for years."

"Abby says lately hers sometimes smells like gasoline. She's going to get it checked."

Olivia Halsted shook her head. "Gasoline. That woman is crazy. If she knows what's good for her, she'll sell to Leon and go back to the city where she can have chlorine-sanitized water and all of the nice, straight roads she wants."

She moved away from my car, each step painstakingly slow. Before she reached her porch, I thought of one more question. "Do you know if there's a man named Morgan who works for the Lerstens? Either a Mister or Doctor Morgan, or Morgan something?"

Olivia didn't even look back, simply once again shook her head.

I waited until she reached her front door before I drove off. I was halfway home when my cell phone rang. Not wanting to drive and talk, I pulled over to the side of the road. It was Detective Ferrell.

"I understand Ida Delaney is staying with your grandmother," he said.

"Is that all right?" So far none of my efforts seemed to be working out right.

"Mr. Hicks seemed to think so."

"Anything new regarding her nephew's murder?"

"Interesting you should ask. We now have the papers you turned over to the sheriff's department, but I understand there was a cell phone in that briefcase, and that you still have it. I want that phone, Miss Benson."

"I don't have . . . that is . . ." The more I tried to think of an excuse, the more I realized I had none. "I'll make sure it gets to you," I said.

"Good. The sooner the better."

He ended the conversation, and I called Ken, who didn't answer, so I left a message. "The gig is up," I said. "The police know about the phone and want it. The detective who called sounded a bit hostile, so call me. I'm coming into town this afternoon, and you and I are going to find that phone."

Within minutes, I returned home. I figured a quick potty break for both Baraka and me, and then we would head for Kalamazoo. Those plans changed the moment I opened my front door.

TWENTY-SIX

Before I bought Baraka, I read dozens of books on raising dogs. Most stressed one thing: when leaving your puppy alone, put him in a crate. Using a crate is not punishment, it's salvation. It helps with housebreaking, and it prevents the dog from chewing valuable or harmful objects. Not that I put any great value on the fuzzy, blue slippers my mother gave me for Christmas, but they were warm and comfortable . . . and so easy to slip on in the morning.

They were now a multitude of blue scraps.

One of those scraps clung to the side of Baraka's mouth as he looked up at me with those big, brown eyes of his, his tail tucked between his legs. He knew he'd done something wrong, and I knew who was at fault—me. I hadn't put those slippers away this morning, and I hadn't put him in his crate when I went to see Abby. The temptation was simply too much for a six-month-old Rhodesian Ridgeback to ignore.

"Bad," I said, and placed Abby's shoebox and my briefcase on the dining room table, amid all the other papers I had piled there. "Bad, bad, bad." I repeated as I picked up the scraps of my slippers. I wasn't about to physically punish Baraka, but I wanted him to know I wasn't happy with what he'd done. He's a sensitive dog and would get the message.

I'm also trainable. Since leaving the slippers out was my fault, once I had that mess taken care of, I put Baraka outside and started picking up and putting away all of the other items

I'd left out. Then, since I had everything up off the floor—everything except tiny bits of fuzzy, blue slippers—I decided to vacuum.

I knew, subconsciously, I was putting off, as long as possible, the drive into Kalamazoo. I didn't want to face Detective Ferrell again. I wasn't even sure I wanted to see Ida Delaney.

My burst of house cleaning didn't last long. Even with my air conditioner on, and fans blowing, perspiration trickled down my back and between my breasts. Though it was barely four o'clock, the sky had grown dark, oppressive clouds threatening rain. In the distance, I heard a rumble of thunder.

I turned off the vacuum and stepped outside. We needed rain, but I didn't want Baraka outside during a storm.

For a moment I stood on my porch, watching my pup. An array of chew toys of various shapes and sizes dotted my front yard. Near the corner of the house, Baraka pounced on a large piece of braided rope, grabbed it in his mouth, gave it a violent shake, and tossed it in the air. Had it been a living creature, its neck or spine would certainly have been broken.

In many ways his actions reminded me of a lioness—lithe, quick, and deadly—and I wondered if the correlation between the Ridgeback's looks and the prey they were bred to corner was intentional. To hold a lion at bay, the dogs would have to be as agile as one. Tenacious and courageous.

Another rumble of thunder—still far away but coming closer—reminded me of why I'd come outside. I called to Baraka, "Come on, boy. Time to come in."

The rope forgotten, he trotted toward me, tongue lolling out the side of his mouth and tail wagging. A gust of wind rattled the plastic on the window next to me, and I looked that way. I was staring at the window when a quiver of fear ran down my spine, a tingly sensation causing the hairs on the back of my neck to rise. I felt a change of pressure in my ears, sensed rather than heard the stillness—the lack of sound.

Before I could grasp what was happening, it came. A loud, ground-shaking, ear-numbing blast.

Beneath my feet, the porch shook, and the plastic covering the shattered window snapped. I grabbed for the stair railing, and Baraka stopped his forward motion. He turned to face the road, and I looked the same direction. In the distance, somewhere south of my house, a plume of dark smoke rose to the sky to blend with the clouds.

I stared at the smoke, a jumble of thoughts racing through my mind. I knew something had exploded, but what? And where?

Within seconds I heard a siren in the distance. Either someone had called the Zenith fire department or they automatically responded to loud blasts. Closer by, I heard another siren. Then another, and another. The cavalry was coming.

Zenith, I've discovered, has a wonderful volunteer fire department. They'll be at the scene of a fire or emergency within minutes. They fight fires, and they save lives. Trained as paramedics, they can administer CPR or stabilize a victim within those fleeting "golden" minutes between life and death. I've even considered signing up for training.

I looked at my car, but before I had a chance to decide if I wanted to drive over to see what had happened, I noticed Howard Lowe's blue Ford pulling out of his drive and onto the road. He stopped along the shoulder in front of my place, and his passenger side window rolled down. "Did you hear that?" he yelled to me.

"Something blew up," I called back.

"Wanna go see what it was?"

"Yeah," I shouted back. "But let me put Baraka up."

I quickly crated Baraka, closed my front door, made sure I

shut the gate behind me, and dashed for Howard's car.

Large drops of rain started falling. Howard flipped a fast-food sack onto the back seat and gave the upholstery a quick brush with his hand. His effort did little to remove a matting of dog hairs. A nod on his part, and I scooted in, my T-shirt already rain-splotched, and my bare arms dotted with dollops of water. I pulled the door closed and rolled up the window.

The inside of Howard's car smelled of old hamburger wrappers, onions, mud, dog, and something I wasn't sure I wanted to identify. A multitude of sacks littered the back seat and floor, along with boxes of shotgun shells, tools, and a faded denim jacket. I started to put on my seatbelt, then realized the strap had been cut in half. Howard shrugged, and I decided it would be his problem if we got a ticket, not mine.

He floored his Ford the half mile to the corner, but waited before turning as two volunteer firemen's cars flew by, their sirens blaring and lights flashing. We followed close behind, heading for the S-curves. Smoke continued to billow upward, the initial dark plume now a light gray, and I could see flames.

"It's gotta be the meth lab," I said, as much to myself as to Howard.

He glanced my way. "What meth lab?"

"Leon's. Abby's sure he has one in his barn. Sometimes they blow up."

"Leon Lersten?"

"Yeah. Don't you ever wonder where he gets all his money? How he can afford to take his wife and sister along with him to Europe?"

Before Howard could respond, we both knew it wasn't Leon's barn that had exploded. Or his house. Or any of the farm buildings on his property. The moment we rounded Proctor's Hill, I had a clear view of the Lersten farm. Several cars and trucks were parked on Leon's property, but people were leaving their vehicles—some with umbrellas, some simply ignoring the rain—heading south on foot. Trees blocked our view, but the smoke and flames were coming from just beyond those trees.

Howard drove on by Proctor's Pond and Leon's farm, but as the road curved west again, a car blocked our progress. One of the volunteer firemen stood on the pavement, signaling for us to turn around. Howard stopped almost in front of him and rolled down his window. "What happened?" he called to the volunteer.

"Explosion," the man yelled back. "You'll have to go back. Find another route."

A sickening sensation twisted in my gut. Just out of sight were two houses: Abby's and Olivia Halsted's. The direction of the smoke narrowed the site down to one—Abby's. "Oh, my God," I murmured, and Howard looked at me.

He put his car in reverse, and we parked near the others on Leon's farm and joined the group hurrying toward the site of the explosion. Howard had no umbrella, but offered an old newspaper to use over my head. I declined. Other than making it curl tighter, the rain wasn't going to hurt my hairdo.

The temperature had dropped considerably once the rain started, and I shivered and wished I had more clothes on. I was glad I'd at least worn a bra under what was quickly becoming a very wet T-shirt.

We passed the volunteer fireman stopping traffic and wove our way through the parked cars of other volunteers. My first view of Abby's house made me stop and grab Howard's arm. It was now a shell of burning timbers, charred wood, and twisted metal.

Neither Howard nor I said a word. We simply stared, as did dozens of other onlookers standing around us. Unbidden tears formed in my eyes, along with a lump in my throat. From left to right, I scanned the area, hoping to see Abby. In my mind I kept praying she was all right. Finally, Howard voiced my fears.

"I sure hope she weren't in there when it blew."

"I was sitting in her kitchen less than two hours ago," I said, no longer able to tell where that kitchen once stood.

"I think that's part of a fridge over there," Howard said, pointing at a twisted, gold-colored piece of metal.

TWENTY-SEVEN

Streams of water mixed with the rain and slowly quenched the fire, the smell of charred wood permeating the air. Multitudes of hot spots continued to sputter, giving off a white steam. I heard more sirens and turned to watch two Kalamazoo County Sheriff's Department cars arrive. Four uniformed deputies stepped out and slipped into rain gear before walking over to talk to the fire chief. For a moment I thought one might be Wade, but as the man neared, I realized it wasn't.

I still hadn't caught sight of Abby, and I held my breath as the fire chief led the deputies to a spot about fifteen feet west of the now-smoldering site. Two volunteer firemen standing near that site stepped back, and the fire chief and deputies stopped.

"Don't think she made it," Howard said, barely above a whisper.

I closed my eyes, but I couldn't stop the tears. I remembered Abby's smile, her voice, and her determination. She and her husband had bought this small farm to fulfill a dream. She didn't pack up and leave when he died. She stayed and was about fulfill a dream of her own—to run a boarding kennel. Except now she was dead.

I opened my eyes again and looked for Leon Lersten. Rain mixed with the tears streaming down my cheeks, and I blinked to clear my vision. I saw one deputy walk back to his patrol car. His easy stride indicated there was no need to rush.

Leon and his wife stood off to my right. I stared at them, the

187

thought running through my head destroying the image of innocent bystander. "She shouldn't have threatened him," I muttered.

"Threatened who?" Howard followed my gaze. "Leon?"

I tried to remember exactly what Abby had said. "He wanted to buy her place. She said he offered far more than she expected or than she could get on the open market. But she told him she wasn't selling unless he offered a lot more. And then she threatened to turn him in."

"Turn him in for what?"

"For having a meth lab in his barn."

"And you think he did this?" Howard motioned toward the ruined house.

"I don't know. Maybe he just meant to scare her."

Howard snorted. He wasn't buying my theory. I watched the deputy slowly return from his car. He said something to one of the other deputies, who nodded, then headed off to talk to each of the volunteer firemen at the scene.

"Maybe it's not Abby," I said, doubting my words even as I spoke them.

"Did she have anyone else living with her?"

"Not that I'm aware of. Just her dog." I looked back at the site where the deputies had stopped. "Maybe that's what they found. Her dog."

"If her dog's one of those golden Labs, it's over there." Howard pointed to our left.

I saw Dexter and one of the volunteer firemen standing under a maple tree, slightly shielded from the rain. The volunteer wore the customary firefighter's protective gear, rain drops glistening on his tan jacket and trousers. A large hat covered most of his face. He held Dexter in place with a piece of binder twine attached to the dog's collar.

"That's him," I said. "He must have been outside when the

explosion occurred."

"Good thing he weren't in her kennel." Howard motioned that direction. "Least not that end run."

Although most of the kennel was undamaged, the feed room's roof had caught on fire—smoke now curling up from a gaping hole at one end—and the run closest to the house was a twisted mass of wood and fencing. Parts of the house being hurled against the structure had snapped posts and bowed wire.

"Dog looks in bad shape," Howard said, bringing my attention back to Dexter. "How old is he?"

"Not that old. She said seven."

"Thin as a rail. They'll probably put him down."

"They can't," I started, but knew they could. Dexter was sickly looking. His owner was dead. Dexter didn't have a chance.

I stepped away from Howard and started toward Abby's dog. I couldn't explain why. I wasn't one of those animal lovers who thought every stray should be rescued. I certainly didn't need another dog. I could come up with a dozen reasons why Abby's Lab should be put down, yet I knew I couldn't let that happen. He didn't deserve it.

"Hey, Dexter," I called as I neared the volunteer fireman and the Lab. "How you doing, old boy?"

Dexter gave a feeble wag of his tail. The volunteer looked my way, and I recognized him. "Bill. I didn't realize you were a volunteer fireman."

Bill Sommers, my dairy farmer neighbor, smiled. "Finished my paramedic training last month. Sondra figured with our four boys, and the accidents they get into, it was a good thing to know. This is my first fire." He nodded at the Lab. "So they have me babysitting a dog."

"Is she dead?" I'd seen the deputy stop and say something to Bill.

Bill hesitated. I had a feeling he wasn't supposed to say

anything, and his answer was ambiguous. "They found a body. From what I hear, they can't tell who it is. Not yet."

If they couldn't tell, it meant Abby must have been inside when the explosion occurred. Burns could destroy facial features and fingerprints. It might take dental records to identify her. Until then, no official announcement would be made, but I didn't have any doubts. "That's her dog," I said. "What's going to happen to him?"

Bill shrugged. "They'll probably call animal control."

Which meant Abby's Lab would be taken to the shelter. At best he might be kept alive for a week, but considering his condition, I doubted it. "Can I take him?" I asked. "If Abby's not dead, I'll bring him back."

"You want this dog?" Bill looked down at Dexter. "You sure, P.J.?"

Dexter was watching me, his tail slowly wagging. I had no choice. "Yeah, I'm sure."

"Then take him." Bill handed the rope to me. "Doesn't look like she ever fed him."

"She said he kept losing weight."

"Knowing you," Bill said, "this boy will be fat and sassy in no time."

"Are you saying Baraka's fat and sassy?" I hoped I hadn't been feeding my dog too much.

"Just big." Bill gave a nod and stepped away. "Thanks for taking him."

He headed for a group of volunteers, and I led Dexter back toward Howard. The rain hadn't let up and rivulets slid down my face. Dexter kept shaking, spraying more water over my legs. "I'm going to take him home," I told Howard. "I'll walk back. No sense getting your car all wet."

"Don't be silly." Howard joined the dog and me. "I'll take you—both of you—to your place. But you sure you know what you're doing?"

"No," I admitted. "But it seems like the right thing to do."

"You are crazy, you know." He strode out ahead of me, heading for his car. His take-charge attitude reminded me he'd once been a member of Special Forces. Age had slowed him some, but I was sure he could still hold his own in a fight.

"Get in," he ordered, pushing the seat forward so Dexter could get in the back. "Won't be the first time this car has hauled a wet dog . . . or person."

I appreciated Howard's offer of a ride, but Dexter wasn't eager to leave his home. Howard finally had to shove the dog into the back, but even before he had the car started, Dexter wiggled his way to the front seat and onto my lap. The car now smelled of wet dog hair, as well as onions, hamburger wrappers, and other aromas. The windows kept steaming up, and it took forever for Howard to work his car free from the other vehicles clogging the Lerstens' driveway.

I looked for Wade's tan Jeep as we drove away. If the deputy at the scene reported Abby's death as suspicious, Wade might be assigned the case. Although I'd heard some of the onlookers call the explosion a terrible accident, I didn't believe it was. Abby had threatened Leon. With her gone, he wouldn't have to buy her place to stop the straightening of the road. With her gone, the three parties opposed to straightening the road would have no opposition.

"What are you thinking?" Howard asked.

"That this wasn't an accident."

"Shoulda guessed." He snorted. "You know how many murders we had out here before you moved into your grandfather's place?"

"No." But I had a feeling Howard would tell me.

"None. Deaths, yes. Heart attacks. Farming accidents. Old age. But murders?"

"This is not my fault," I argued.

"Didn't say it was, but trouble sure seems to find you." He pulled into my driveway. "You be careful, girl."

"I will," I said and opened my door. "Thanks for the ride."

Dexter weighed so little, I easily lowered him to the ground. The rain had turned into a fine spray, the worst of the storm having passed. For a moment I stood where I was and watched Howard pull out of my yard. He didn't head for his farm but drove back the direction we'd come. I had a feeling he was going back to Abby's place. Blame it on his training in Special Forces or blame it on curiosity. Howard liked to know what was going on.

Dexter gave a small tug on the rope I held, his tail wagging hesitantly. I heard Baraka barking from inside the house. My ridgeback didn't like seeing me with another dog.

I wasn't about to bring the two dogs together. Not the way Dexter looked. Until I knew why the Lab was so thin, I wasn't going to chance contaminating my dog.

I led Dexter to the woodshed behind my house. Although one of my neighbors had brought over a load of wood in April, I'd burned about half since then and there was ample space in the shed for Dexter. The door was a good one, and I could open a couple of windows. A large black walnut tree shaded the shed, and the roof didn't leak. Dexter would be protected from the rain and sun, and an old blanket would give him a comfortable bed. I wanted to get him into a vet, but that could wait until morning. Right now I needed to call my grandmother and explain why I wouldn't be driving into Kalamazoo. She wasn't going to be happy.

TWENTY-EIGHT

"An explosion?" Grandma repeated. "This doesn't have anything to do with my house guest, does it?"

"No. If anything it's related to the straightening of a road, and—" I stopped myself. "Except . . ."

"Except what?"

"Except Ida Delaney's nephew took pictures that were used to show where that road would go. I saw copies in his briefcase and again at a meeting last Monday. And the wife of the farmer who hired Ida's nephew drives a tan sedan like the one I saw drive away from my place last Saturday." And like the one that followed me from Ken's, I remembered.

"Priscilla Jayne, how do you get yourself into these messes?"

That my grandmother was using my birth name meant she was upset. "I'm sorry," I said. "Look, I'm sure this woman's house exploding had nothing to do with Donald Crane's murder, but I'll see if I can find someone to take Ida. I certainly don't want to put you or Mom in danger."

"I'm not worried about any danger to us," Grandma said. "It's you I'm concerned about. Are you sure this wasn't an accident? Maybe she committed suicide. Did your friend have a gas stove?"

"Yes, she had a gas stove, but I'm sure she didn't commit suicide. Why would she? She and I were working on a bookkeeping system for her. She'd started her own business."

"Maybe the pilot light went out, and she didn't realize it,

didn't smell the gas . . . and then kaboom."

I remembered the explosion. Kaboom didn't describe the sound. And even though Abby hadn't struck me as an organized person, I doubted she'd turn on the stove and not notice it hadn't lit. Besides, when I was there, Abby's windows were open. Gas fumes wouldn't have had an opportunity to build up enough to cause a massive explosion.

But what would have caused the blast?

"I don't know," I finally said.

"Well, let's hope it was an accident." Grandma paused. "I mean, that sounds terrible, but it's better than the alternative, isn't it? And don't worry about not driving into Kalamazoo. Ida is watching TV. When the talk show is over, she can help me fix supper. And once your mother's home, we'll keep Ida entertained until bedtime. We can manage until your lawyer finds a place for her. Meanwhile, you take care of yourself."

I was hearing that a lot today. I promised I would and hung up.

Since I hadn't heard from Ken, I tried his cell again. No luck. Then I called Detective Ferrell. He'd gone home for the day, so I tried Detective Daley's number. No luck there, either. I ended up leaving messages on both of their phones, telling them I'd get Donald Crane's cell phone to them Friday.

Next I tried Arthur Hicks's number. Although my grand-mother had said she wasn't worried about having Ida at her house, I was concerned. I hoped the lawyer could find a permanent place for Ida before Monday.

Once again, I ended up leaving a voice-mail message.

Finally, I tried calling Wade. By the time I'd gone through his cell, office, and home phone numbers with no answers, I was ready to scream. "Dammit all," I snapped after the beep indicated I was being recorded. "Stop avoiding my calls. I need advice."

I'd fed Baraka before I made my phone calls. Now he wanted out. I watched him go down the steps and head directly for the edge of the fence that faced the spot where Howard let me and Dexter out of the car. Baraka sniffed the air, and I wondered what he could smell, if anything. Finally, he left that spot and trotted over to his preferred "potty" area of the yard.

I waited until my dog was back in the house before I gathered a couple of old blankets from upstairs and mixed together what I hoped would be an appetizing meal for Dexter. Although the Lab looked like he needed a lot of food, I decided to start with a cup of dry kibble mixed with warm water and a little raw hamburger. If he ate that, I'd give him more.

Baraka watched my every move and looked very disappointed when I didn't put the dish down on the floor. Food was the driving force in Baraka's life. It made training him easy, but I knew I was going to have to be careful I didn't overfeed him.

Dexter was lying down when I opened the door to the woodshed. He rose to his feet like an old man, and with clouded eyes watched me place the blankets I'd brought with me on the wood floor. I didn't want to touch him, but he looked so sad and confused, I patted his head before I placed the dish of dog food in front of him.

I expected him to gobble up the food, the way Baraka does, but Dexter merely sniffed it, then ambled over to the blankets, moved them about a bit, and collapsed onto them with a sigh.

There was something definitely wrong with the dog, and as soon as I was back in the house and had washed my hands, I called my vet.

He stayed open late on Thursday nights, and when his receptionist answered, I quickly explained my situation. She asked several questions about the dog's condition, then put me on hold.

"He can't see you tonight," she said when she returned. "But he said to bring the dog in as soon as you can tomorrow morning. He'll work you in."

The rain continued through the night, as did my tears for Abby, but by morning the downpour had diminished to a drizzle, and I knew the best thing I could do to honor Abby's death was take care of her dog. The weatherman predicted clear skies by Saturday morning, warm temperatures, and lower humidity. That would please Michigan's tourists and anyone who had the weekend off.

Now that I was working for myself, weekends no longer had the importance they once did. If I had work to do, I tackled it, whether it was a weekday or weekend. But since my vet didn't work on weekends, I was glad it was Friday.

I covered the back seat of my car with an old sheet before I let Dexter out of the woodshed. I wasn't worried about him running away. He could barely wobble much less run. From what I could tell, he was starving to death. Earlier that morning, I'd skipped the dry dog food and simply fed him raw hamburger. He downed a few bites, but before I left the woodshed, he threw it up.

I talked to Dexter as I made the fifteen-minute drive to Galesburg, but I wasn't sure it mattered. As far as I could tell, he slept most of the way. I'd chosen Rick Caselli as my vet when I bought Baraka for two reasons: his office was fairly close, and even before he became a vet, he'd had experience with Rhodesian Ridgebacks. A school chum's parents had raised them.

Rick's office was an old house on a side street in Galesburg, not far from the stoplight in the middle of town. The front entrance had been redesigned so I stepped directly into a waiting area. Rick's plump, gray-haired receptionist sat behind a counter. I'd been in often enough that she nodded in recognition when she saw me, but her eyebrows rose the moment she noticed Dexter. "I'll tell Doctor Caselli you're here," she said and stepped away from her desk.

Two other dog owners were seated in the waiting area, one on each side of the room. The way they looked at Dexter, and then me, I wanted to explain that this wasn't my dog, and I would never let a dog get this thin. I would have spoken up if Rick hadn't stepped into the waiting area and said, "Morning, P.J. That's the dog?"

"This is the one."

"Bring him right in."

He turned to the others. "Sorry, this is an emergency. I'll be with you as soon as I can."

Rick's behavior worried me. "What do you think is wrong with him?" I asked, concerned that I'd exposed Baraka to something deadly.

"I won't know until I examine him," Rick said, "but he looks terrible."

I told him all I knew about the dog, and explained how he hadn't eaten what I'd given him the night before and threw up the little bit he had eaten that morning. I had brought a stool sample from the woodshed, and Rick gave that to an assistant to check. Rick listened to Dexter's heart, checked his eyes, ears, and mouth, and then drew blood. Dexter didn't complain. "You say he's only seven?"

"That's what his owner told me."

"And she's now dead."

"Did you see the news last night?" I'd watched both the six o'clock and the eleven o'clock news. "That house that exploded south of Zenith?"

"This morning they said the explosion was caused by a gas leak."

"That's what I heard." I'd also heard the incident was being investigated, which meant it could have been an accident . . . or maybe not.

"Let me take a look at this blood sample," Rick said and left me with Dexter.

The Lab put his head on his paws and closed his eyes. I rubbed his head and thought about Abby. Less than twenty-four hours had passed since I'd sat in her kitchen, and we'd talked about setting up a bookkeeping system. Now she was gone. Dead.

Tears burned my eyes, and I blinked several times. I'd tried calling Wade again before I went to bed last night, then again this morning. No luck. I wanted to know if Abby's death was due to a terrible accident, or if they were investigating it as a murder. The second possibility scared me.

Rick's expression also scared me when he returned. "There's something wrong with this dog," he said. "Seriously wrong. His white blood count is dangerously low, and so is his red blood count. It's a good thing he didn't get cut in that explosion or he might have bled to death."

"Have I exposed Baraka to something bad?" I would never forgive myself if I made my dog sick.

"I don't know," Rick said, looking at Dexter who hadn't opened his eyes, much less raised his head. "Question is, what do you want to do now?"

Go back to the moment I decided to take this dog home, I thought. But, of course, that wasn't possible.

"I can give him a transfusion," Rick said, perhaps sensing my indecision. "Build up his red and white blood count. Meanwhile, I'll send a blood sample up to Lansing and ask them to analyze it. You'd be better off if you knew exactly what was wrong with this dog."

I understood what he was saying. Baraka would be better off. "Do it," I said.

"I'll keep him here. That way we can monitor his response to the transfusion. I'm also going to put him on antibiotics. I'm sure with that low a white blood count his immune system has been compromised."

I sighed in relief. I didn't want to take Dexter back to my house and chance exposing Baraka even more to whatever the Lab had. I didn't ask Rick what this would cost. I'd foolishly taken on the responsibility of the dog. Now I would pay for it.

I gave Dexter one last pat on the head before Rick's assistant carried the dog out of the room. "I'll call you if anything happens or when I hear something," Rick said, and I thanked him.

He was spraying down his examining table when I stepped out of the room. The two dog owners were still waiting. They looked first at my face, then at my side. Their expressions changed from curiosity to sympathy when they saw Dexter was gone.

I might have said something to them, but I recognized the blonde at the counter, talking to Rick's receptionist. I also recognized the miniature poodle cradled in her arms. "Ginny," I said. "Is something wrong with Spike?"

Wade's sister looked my way and grinned. "No, just time for his nails to be trimmed. He puts up such a fuss, I let them do it." She handed Spike to the receptionist, who carried the yapping, wiggling poodle into a back room.

Dogless, Ginny turned to me. "What about you? Is Baraka sick?"

"No, a neighbor's dog." Ginny's presence at the vet's office seemed preordained. "Do you have time for a coffee?"

"Sure."

We waited until Rick's receptionist returned. I expected a bill for this office visit, the fecal exam, and bloodwork. She waved me off. "Rick said he'd catch you later."

I wasn't sure what that meant, but I nodded my agreement.

Ginny drove to the coffee shop; I walked. It was less than a block from the vet's office, but Ginny was an interior decorator and probably had an appointment to go to either later in the morning or that afternoon. Her blonde hair was teased into a stylish do, that I was sure she didn't want ruined by the rain, and the spiked heels she had on could have easily slipped on the wet sidewalk. Her raincoat would have probably kept her pin-striped pantsuit dry, but why take a chance?

She was already seated at a booth, two cups of black coffee on the table, when I arrived. I told her I wanted to wash my hands before I joined her. Until I had some idea what was wrong with Dexter, I didn't want to chance spreading a disease . . . or catching it myself.

We hugged when I returned, and she asked how I'd been. I loved listening to her talk. She had a low, Marilyn Monroe voice. A near whisper I wished I could emulate.

I told her what had been happening. She made the appropriate responses. Finally, I brought up the subject that had been bothering me. "What's up with your brother?"

"What do you mean?"

"For almost two weeks now, he's been . . ." I wasn't sure how to explain Wade's behavior. "Like a different person. He doesn't answer my calls. Doesn't call back. Practically ignores me one minute, then gets all huffy and jealous the next."

"Whoa." Ginny sat back in the booth and blinked. "What happened between you two?"

"That's what I want to know."

"You say this started a couple weeks ago?"

"The week before he took Jason fishing. That's when he stopped calling, stopped coming by. He didn't even ask if I wanted to go fishing with them that weekend."

Damn, I could feel the tears forming in my eyes. I clenched my lips and took a deep breath, trying to control my emotions.

I would not start bawling in front of Wade's sister.

"You two didn't have an argument or anything like that?"

I shook my head, not quite ready to trust my voice.

Ginny glanced around the coffee shop. It was late enough in the morning that most of the patrons were gone, but a handful of men remained, their voices mingling with the clatter of dishes in the kitchen. "I don't know what to tell you, P.J.," she said and gave me a wan smile. "I haven't seen him for over two weeks myself, but that's not unusual. I do know sometimes he really gets wrapped up in his work. That always irritated Linda."

I didn't want to be like Wade's ex-wife, demanding more of his time and attention than he could give, but I didn't think asking a man to return a phone call was unreasonable. "This isn't just about me. I need his advice, as a law officer."

"I'll give him a call," Ginny said and reached over and placed her hand on mine. "P.J., I know he loves you. Something must be going on, something neither you nor I know about. I'll see what I can find out. Okay? Then I'll call you."

"Okay." Just hearing her say Wade loved me was reassuring. Maybe not a guarantee, but hope-giving.

We talked about her cats after that. "The boys," as she called them, had gotten into trouble again. Her two Siamese cats were characters, and she had me laughing by the time she glanced at her watch and said it was time to pick up her poodle.

I drove home feeling better about life. That feeling disappeared when I arrived home.

TWENTY-NINE

The car parked in my driveway didn't look familiar, but I recognized the man stepping away from my front door. A month earlier, Detective Dario Gespardo and his wife had been leaving a restaurant just as Wade and I arrived. Introductions were made—Wade presenting me as the woman who saved his life—and the men briefly talked about work while Gespardo's wife and I silently listened. Then we parted company. I probably wouldn't have remembered the man if not for the scar on his left cheek. Even from a distance, it was visible.

Wade said Gespardo had been with the Kalamazoo Sheriff's Department for close to thirty years, and that the scar came from trying to stop a woman from killing her husband. Time—and probable too many visits to restaurants—had given the detective a potbelly that his brown tweed sports jacket, light tan polo shirt, and brown slacks didn't disguise. His serious expression caused my stomach to knot.

"Has something happened to Wade?" I asked the moment I slid out of my car.

Gespardo stopped a few feet back from the gate and frowned. "Wade? No. He's on vacation, but far as I know, he's fine."

"Vacation?" Wade hadn't said anything to me about taking a vacation.

"It's you I need to talk to."

"Me?" I glanced toward my house. I'd locked my front door before I left, and as far as I could tell, the plastic covering the broken window was still in place, but Baraka wasn't barking. That worried me. "Did he break in again? Is my dog all right?"

Detective Gespardo also looked toward my house. "Your dog?" He shook his head. "I guess he's all right. He barked when I knocked on your door." He motioned that direction. "Can we go inside and talk?"

The way he asked made me uneasy, but I couldn't think of any reason not to let him inside my house. I hadn't done anything wrong, and I had no drugs or bodies lying around. Besides, even though it wasn't raining hard, I didn't relish standing in a drizzle.

"Sure," I said and motioned for him to go ahead while I closed the gate behind me.

Baraka started barking when I opened the door, but stopped the moment he saw me. "Could you unlatch his crate and let him outside?" I asked, heading for my bathroom. "I'm probably being overly concerned, but I don't want to touch him until I wash up."

"That's a Lab?" Gespardo said. "He . . . he looks mean."

I paused and looked back at Gespardo. He stood halfway between the front door and Baraka's crate, staring at my dog. "He's a Rhodesian Ridgeback, and he's just a puppy. He might lick you to death, but that's about the worse he'll do."

I didn't wait to see what the detective did. I closed the bathroom door and proceeded to wash every inch of my body that Dexter had touched. I even changed my T-shirt and shorts, and dumped the ones I'd had on directly in the washer. Detective Gespardo was standing in my dining room when I stepped out of the bathroom . . . and Baraka was in his crate.

"You didn't have to put him back in there."

"I never let him out. I figured you'd better do that." Gespardo moved farther away from the crate.

"He won't hurt you." I unlatched the crate, and Baraka came

out with a bound. First thing he did was head for the detective.

"Put him outside," Gespardo ordered, a note of panic in his voice.

"Baraka, come," I ordered and opened the front door.

There were days when Baraka did everything I asked. This wasn't one. He had his nose pressed against the detective's crotch when I pulled him away and scooted him outside. Even then, he barely went off the porch. He cocked his leg at the first bush, and was back at the door before Gespardo had a chance to refuse my offer of coffee.

"Could you leave him outside?" the detective said as I moved toward the door. "That or put him back in his cage."

"It's a crate, not a cage," I explained, but decided to leave Baraka outside. Gespardo was obviously afraid of dogs, and I didn't see any reason to upset him. I did, however, need to do one thing first. "Give me a minute," I said and grabbed the fly spray I use on Baraka.

Once I knew my dog wouldn't be chewed up by flies, I cleared space at my dining room table, we sat, and I gave the detective my full attention.

"How long have you known Mrs. Warfield?" he asked, pencil poised over a small notebook he'd removed from his jacket's inner pocket.

"Less than a week."

That seemed to surprise him. "But you were in her house yesterday."

"Yes. Less than two hours before the explosion." Which now seemed like a bad dream. "This morning, on the news, they still weren't releasing the name of the victim. It was Abby, wasn't it?"

"Is that important?"

The way he phrased the question seemed strange. "It would be for her."

A nod was his response. "Why were you at her house?"

"Because she asked me to set up a bookkeeping system for her. I was there to pick up her bills and receipts." I pointed at the shoebox on my table. "That's what she gave me."

He looked at the shoebox, then pulled it closer and opened the lid. I watched him paw through the papers inside, pausing at one or two. Finally, he replaced the lid. "There's nothing in there but bills and a couple of handwritten receipts for when someone evidently had her watch a dog."

"My job was to set up a computer program so she could keep track of her income and expenses. Once I finished with what's here, she would have had the first half of the year's information in place and simply could have added any income and expenses that occurred after that date."

"I'll want to take this with me," Gespardo said, touching the lid of the box.

"Sure." I certainly didn't need it now.

"So tell me, Miss Benson, did you and Mrs. Warfield get into an argument yesterday? Disagree over something?"

His formal use of my name, along with his very stiff attitude, bothered me. Maybe we weren't buddy-buddy, but Wade had introduced us. Gespardo should be a little friendlier than he was acting.

Something was up.

"Abby and I got along fine yesterday. Have since we met. Why do you ask?"

"After the explosion, you took her dog."

"Yeah. I didn't want animal control taking him."

"And why is that?"

"Because I was sure they'd put him down."

"And he was too valuable for that to happen?"

"Valuable?" I almost laughed. "No. Because he looked so bad."

Gespardo glanced around. "Where do you have him now?"

"I took him to the vet's, and Dr. Caselli wanted to keep him there, which was fine with me. There's something wrong with that dog. His blood count was way down. Rick's giving him antibiotics."

"Rick being . . . ?"

"Dr. Rick Caselli. He's a veterinarian in Galesburg. The vet I use for Baraka." I pointed toward my plastic-covered window where Baraka stood, his nose pressed against the plastic. "Why all these questions about Dexter?"

"And who's Dexter?"

"Abby's dog." I leaned toward Gespardo. "Why are you here? What do you want to know?"

"Miss Benson, you were the last person to see Mrs. Warfield alive."

"Yeah. So . . . ?"

"We're trying to find out exactly what happened yesterday."

"Do they know what caused the explosion?" That, it seemed, would help them determine what happened.

"It's still under investigation." He rubbed his left cheek, one fingertip running down the length of his scar. "It was hot yesterday afternoon. Was it you or was it Mrs. Warfield who closed the windows?"

"Closed the windows? No way." I laughed at the thought. "It wasn't just hot yesterday, it was steamy. And Abby doesn't . . . that is, didn't have air conditioning. Even with all of her windows open and a floor fan going, her kitchen was like an oven. She—" I stopped myself, realizing what Gespardo meant by his question. "You're saying her windows were closed?"

"The initial investigation indicates so."

"Why would she close her windows?"

"That's what we'd like to know."

I may be slow, but I finally figured out why he was at my

house. "You think I had something to do with that explosion, don't you?"

"I'm simply trying to understand what happened yesterday." He leaned back in his chair, looked me directly in the face, and said nothing.

Damn. It was obvious he thought I'd killed Abby.

"I don't know what happened," I said. "She was fine when I left. Her windows were wide open."

"Did she mention anyone who might have threatened her?"

"No. I mean . . ."

Gespardo leaned toward me. "You mean what?"

"There's a farmer. The one across the road just north of her house. He offered to buy her place, but she turned him down."

"And you think he might have killed her?"

"I don't know." But I remembered what Abby had said the day she came to my house. *"Do you think Leon would do something? To shut me up, I mean?"*

Would he?

"I think you might want to talk to him. Abby thought he might have something in his barn he didn't want anyone to know about. She even threatened to report him to the police."

"For what?"

"For having a meth lab." I wondered how Gespardo had lasted almost thirty years if he was this slow.

"So you think this farmer killed her?"

"I said I don't know. I just know Abby didn't hesitate to speak her mind. Besides threatening to call the police, she'd upset him and others with her insistence that the road be straightened."

"And these 'others' were?"

"The three property owners who would be affected by the change, if it occurred." He could have looked up their names, but I told him. "Leon Lersten, the farmer I mentioned; a land management corporation that owns the acreage directly across the road from her farm; and Olivia Halsted, the old lady who lives southwest of Abby's place."

Gespardo wrote everything down in his notebook, but I had a feeling he hadn't eliminated me from his list of suspects.

"Maybe someone else had a motive, I don't know," I said. "But I can assure you, it was to my advantage to keep her alive. At least until after she paid me for setting up her accounts."

The way he raised his eyebrows, I knew I hadn't said that right. "What I mean is . . . that is . . ."

"You took her dog."

"Oh, jeez." I rolled my eyes. "Her dog is sick. I took pity on him. Dexter isn't a show dog. He's been neutered, so he can't even be used for stud fees. Taking him is going to cost me money. I hate to think what the vet bill will be. Do you honestly think that's a motive for murder?"

Detective Gespardo again rubbed a finger over his scar, his mouth moving as if he were chewing on the idea. He didn't give me an answer, merely pushed back his chair and stood. "You shouldn't have taken the dog."

"Sorry," I said, though I wasn't.

He picked up Abby's box of papers. "You said your vet has the dog."

"Dr. Caselli. His office is in Galesburg."

"I'll have one of the deputies pick him up."

"Dr. Caselli?"

"No, the dog."

"And then you'll have him put down." It didn't seem fair.

"We'll see." He nodded and started for my front door, but paused the moment he opened it. Baraka had moved directly in front of the door, on the opposite side of the screen.

My dog's look was expectant; Gespardo's was panicky. "He won't hurt you," I said, though, at the moment, I wouldn't mind Baraka taking a bite out of the man's leg. However, that would only give the detective reason to put my dog down.

I nudged Gespardo aside, told Baraka to back up, and opened the screen door. I held Baraka in place as Gespardo left. "Make sure you latch that gate," I called after him, and watched to make sure he did.

THIRTY

I removed the sheet I'd placed over my back seat, but I didn't take Baraka with me when I drove into Kalamazoo. A good decision, I discovered when my mother answered the door. She likes to tease Baraka. "What are you doing home?" I asked, hoping Mom hadn't lost another job. A lost job usually meant she was off her meds.

"It's my day off. I have to work tomorrow."

That sounded reasonable.

"Come on in. Your grandma and her new friend are out shopping." Mom held up her hands and rolled her eyes. "That woman is something else."

"Pretty bad?"

"Let's say she makes me look sane."

Considering it was almost noon and my mother was wearing a fuchsia, baby doll nightgown and pink bunny slippers, that was saying something. At least it wasn't a see-through nightgown.

I followed her into the living room. She lit up a cigarette and plopped onto a corner of the couch. I took the opposite corner.

"So how's life?" Mom asked. "Been getting any lately?"

"Mother." It was my turn to roll my eyes.

She grinned. "I have. One of these days you'll have to meet Ben. He's not much to look at, but he's a sweety."

"This is the guy from work?" Grandma hadn't told me much about my mother's new boyfriend, other than he was older and seemed nice.

"The one and only." She sighed and took a long drag on her cigarette before blowing the smoke out in a series of rings.

I tried smoking once, when I was thirteen, just to see if I could blow rings like my mother did. I ended up swallowing most of the smoke and had a hacking fit. I think that was when I decided I was never, ever going to take up smoking. A vow I'd yet to break.

"Your grandma said some woman you knew died yesterday. Should we have a séance? See if we can bring her back?"

Even on medication, my mother was sure she could communicate with dead people. "It would be handy if you could," I said. "Just this morning, I had a homicide detective accusing me of killing her."

"Not your homicide detective, I hope."

"No chance of that. He won't even answer or return my calls."

"The cad." Mom tapped out her cigarette stub and lit another. "Men. Why do we let them get under our skin? I remember a time back when your dad and I were still dating, and he suddenly went south on me."

"Went south?" I didn't understand what she meant.

"Stopped calling. Didn't ask me out." She visibly shuddered. "And you want to know why? Because of some neighbor girl."

This was a story I'd never heard. "What neighbor girl? What happened?"

"Oh, I don't remember her name. Something like Norma or Lola."

"Could it have been Nora?" I knew Nora had lived in the neighborhood when my dad was growing up.

"Maybe. As for what happened, I'm not really sure. She was going through some sort of crisis, I guess, because later, when he started coming around here again, he said he'd been trying to bring her to her senses."

Keep her from turning into a lesbian? I wondered. If so, he'd failed.

"He never told you what happened?"

"Never. You know your father and his secrets."

I certainly did. "There's a Nora who keeps insisting Grandpa Benson promised her the woods behind the house. What's worse, I think she may have even killed him to get those woods."

"I thought your grandfather died of a heart attack."

"Maybe. Or maybe Nora gave him an overdose of sleeping pills. They didn't do an autopsy, and Wade doesn't think we could get an order to have the body exhumed, not without more evidence."

"Maybe we should have a séance for him."

"If you can call up his spirit, ask him why Nora wants those woods so badly."

Mom screwed up her nose. "Are we talking about the woods where he dumped all his junk?"

"That's the one. I guess Grandpa Benson bought those acres from Nora's uncle way back during the Depression. For some reason, she wants them back."

"I guess they might be valuable. My friend Ben says scrap metal is bringing a good price nowadays, and from what I remember, your grandfather dumped everything back there. And I mean everything. There's bound to be some aluminum. Copper tubing. Who knows what?"

"Considering the time and labor it would take to get everything out of those woods, I doubt selling the scrap would cover the cost."

"Then sell the woods to her. That'll make her happy, and you'll make a profit."

I shook my head. "I do not want that woman wandering around that close to my house. You may not remember . . ." My mother didn't always remember what happened when she was off her meds. "but Nora tried to kill me. Tried twice. And she's already creeped me out once this week, popping up behind the chicken coop. Even my neighbor said he saw her digging back there."

"Ah ha. Maybe there's buried treasure in those woods."

"You think so?" The image of a map flashed through my mind, its lines and markings faded, a large X barely visible. *Could there be something buried in the woods behind my house? A treasure Nora knew about but couldn't find? A chest filled with gold . . . or silver?*

Naw.

I might have said more, but my cell phone rang. I grabbed it out of my shoulder bag and looked at the number, my stomach doing an immediate flip-flop. A tap of my thumb completed the connection. With a nod toward my mother, I rose from the couch and made my way to the kitchen. I had no idea how this conversation was going to progress, and I didn't need an audience.

"You there?" Wade asked, his gruff tone telling me this wasn't going to be a romantic tête-à-tête.

"I'm at my grandmother's," I said, keeping my voice low and hoping he'd understand.

"My sister called and said to call you."

I leaned against the kitchen counter and closed my eyes. I'd hoped Ginny would tell me what was going on, not tattle to her brother. "You haven't been answering my calls."

He grunted, the sound derisive. "I've been busy."

My level of irritation skyrocketed. "Not from what I hear. Detective Gespardo said you're on vacation."

"Why are you bothering him?"

"I haven't been. He's been bothering me. Just this morning, he as much as accused me of killing Abby Warfield."

"Who's Abby Warfield?"

"The woman who died in that explosion yesterday evening. Your Detective Gespardo also acted all huffy because I'd taken Abby's dog."

"You stole a dog?"

"Took, not stole. Took it to my vet's because it's sick. Now I've probably exposed Baraka to something deadly, and I'm going to have a horrendous vet bill, and no one ever answers my calls, especially you." My voice cracked, the pressure of everything that had been going on bringing tears to my eyes.

"I've been . . ." He stopped himself, which was good, because if he'd said busy again I would have ended the conversation. "Distracted," he admitted after a second. "Dealing with a personal problem."

He'd lowered his own voice, and I had a feeling others were around, and he didn't want to go into detail. I also had a good idea what that "personal problem" might be. "About the other night," I started.

"Forget the other night," he said, way too quickly.

"I can, but can you?"

Again, a grunt on his part.

"Wade, I'm not like Linda, but you can't completely shut me out of your life and expect me to sit around twiddling my thumbs."

"What did my sister tell you about Linda?"

His sharp response sent a warning. I already knew how Wade's ex-wife expected him to change after they were married, nagged him about his devotion to duty, and divorced him when she realized he wasn't Prince Charming. But not before they had a child, a son she didn't hesitate to use to make Wade's life miserable.

"Your sister didn't say anything about your ex. She said she didn't know why you'd stopped coming to see me and wouldn't take my calls. Look, if you want to end whatever this relationship we have is, just say so. I'm a big girl. I didn't think this was going to work in the first place."

"I don't want to end anything," he said, barely above a whisper. "I just . . ." I heard him sigh. "I can't explain right now."

Maybe I'd said I didn't think whatever Wade and I had would work out, but deep down, I guess I wanted it to because his words eased the tension in my body. "Okay," I said, wiping tears away from my cheeks. "But when you can, we need to talk."

"Agreed." He cleared his throat. "In one of your calls, you said you needed advice."

"Help. Advice. Wade, I don't know what I've gotten myself into, or how, but way too much has happened in the last few days."

I proceeded to tell him about Abby, her suspicions about Lersten, his offer to buy her place, and her fear that he might do something if she didn't. "She thought he had a meth lab in his barn," I told Wade. "That alone might be motive for him to kill her."

"You told Detective Gespardo that?"

"Yes. But I'm not sure Gespardo cared what I said about Abby's neighbor. He was focused on the fact that I took her dog." I squeezed my eyes closed, thinking about Dexter. "Wade, there's something very wrong with that dog. I took him to my vet, and he had no idea why Dexter's red and white cell counts were so low. I'm afraid I've exposed Baraka to something deadly, and now that your department's taken Abby's dog away from Rick's care, how will I know if antibiotics will cure whatever it is?"

"Why would the sheriff's department want the dog?"

"Ask Gespardo."

"I will."

As if that would help. "Oh, and that cell phone I found in the briefcase, the one I should have given to the police but didn't . . . I did screw up on that." Telling all seemed a good idea, or maybe I just wanted to vent my frustration. "That guy I gave the phone to keeps giving me excuses why he can't give it back."

Wade sighed. "Give me the guy's name, and I'll check into that, too."

I told him Ken's name, and gave him a description. I also mentioned the break-in at Ken's shop, and that Ken had thought he was being followed. "He said it was a white car."

"Anything else?"

I wasn't sure if I should mention Ida, but what the heck. As long as I was dumping on him, I'd give him the full load. "You know the guy who was killed here in Kalamazoo? Donald Crane. Well, his aunt is now living here, with my grandmother and mother. Somehow I've gotten involved with her welfare."

"P.J., how do you get yourself in these messes?" Wade grumbled, but I sensed a level of amusement.

"I don't know, but I couldn't leave her in that Laundromat, could I?"

"One of these days you're going to have to trust us to do our job."

By "us" I knew he meant law enforcement—sheriff's deputies and the police. "I do trust you," I insisted, even though I knew that wasn't entirely true.

Someone in the background yelled Wade's name. "I've got to go," he said, his voice once again very formal. "I'll look into these things you've told me."

"And we'll talk? Soon?" I didn't want to spend any more hours second-guessing his motives.

"As soon as I can."

He clicked off before I could say anything more. He'd given me hope. An emotional respite. I must have been smiling when

I strolled back into the living room. My mother lifted an eyebrow as she lit another cigarette. "Was that lover boy?"

"That was Wade," I admitted.

"So all's forgiven? You kissed and made up?"

"Kissing over a cell phone is a bit difficult, Mom." And I wasn't sure about the "forgiven" part. "He did say he'd look into a couple of things for me."

"Just remember what I said about men." She took a deep drag on her cigarette. "They can't be trusted. Your father proved that."

I closed my eyes. The truth about my father had destroyed my childhood fantasies. Even now I found it difficult to accept the reality of what he was. "Wade's different," I said, and hoped that was true.

THIRTY-ONE

Grandma and Ida burst through the door just before one o'clock. Arms laden with brown paper sacks, both laughing, they waltzed into the living room. "We cleaned them out, Flo," Grandma said, looking at my mother. "You were right about great bargains. From now on, I'm buying all my clothes at Goodwill."

"Got this there," Mom said, flipping up an edge of her baby dolls.

Grandma dropped her sacks on the floor near my feet and leaned over to kiss my forehead. "You're looking better, honey."

"So's she," I said, watching Ida grab the remote control and plop down on the easy chair near the TV. A click and a soap opera came on.

"We had to get back in time for her shows." Grandma chuckled. "She's even getting me hooked." Grandma turned toward the television. "Ida, you want a sandwich or something?"

"Whatever you're having," Ida said, barely glancing away from the screen.

Grandma looked back at me. "What about you two?"

"I fixed us something a while ago," I said. "But I'll help you." I wanted to talk to my grandmother alone.

In the kitchen, I watched rather than helped. Grandma grabbed a can of tuna fish from the shelf and a jar of mayonnaise from the refrigerator. I hadn't thought about the added burden of feeding and clothing Ida when Grandma suggested bringing her there. "Ida looks really good, but you shouldn't be spending your money buying her clothes."

"Didn't cost all that much," Grandma said, after snagging the cigarette from between her lips so she could talk. "Besides, she needed a couple more outfits and underwear. She couldn't remember what happened to the clothes she had on when you found her."

I remembered how Ida smelled the day I picked her up at the Laundromat. "My guess is either the police kept them or they were dumped."

"She wanted me to take her home, but she couldn't remember where she lived."

"She probably couldn't have gotten in, anyway. I imagine her nephew's house is still off limits, still a crime scene."

"I feel so sorry for her." Grandma slapped the tuna fish mixture onto slices of white bread, added a leaf of lettuce and a couple slices of tomato. "Most of the time she thinks her nephew is still alive, but every so often her mind clears, and she remembers."

"Has she ever mentioned the names of the men who killed her nephew?"

"It's hard to tell." Grandma laughed. "She gets talking about this person and that, and what happened to them, and I think the people are real, but most of the time it's a soap opera she's remembering." A final puff and Grandma stubbed out the cigarette. "By the way, that lawyer you got for her called early this morning. He said Ida might be able to move into a home as early as Sunday evening."

"That's good." Ida might not remember who killed her nephew, but the killers didn't know that. Until those men were behind bars, she wouldn't truly be safe . . . and neither would my mother or grandmother.

"I'm thinking of driving her out your way tomorrow,"

219

Grandma said, placing a handful of chips on the plate, next to the sandwich. "Get Ida out of the house and show her where you live. Will you be around?"

"As far as I know, I will be." As long as I'm not arrested for Abby's murder, I thought.

"Hope the weather's good."

She headed for the living room, plates in hand. I heard Ida say, "Did you fix one for Donald?"

Grandma answered, "He won't be here for lunch."

By the time I stepped into the room, both Ida and my grandmother were focused on the television screen. Mom no longer occupied the couch. I guessed she'd gone upstairs. To change out of her sleepwear, I hoped. I stood in the doorway for a while, totally ignored. So much for a visit, but I'd see them tomorrow . . . without the distraction of soap operas. And I'd learned what I needed to know. Grandma, Mom, and Ida were getting along just fine, and Mr. Hicks would soon have Ida in a home. I said my goodbyes, yelling one upstairs to my mother and getting a shouted response back. From Ida and Grandma I received nods.

I drove by Ken's shop. The window was boarded up, a closed sign on the door. The saying, "No good deed goes unpunished" flashed through my head. If I'd known someone would break into Ken's shop to get that cell phone, I never would have left it with him.

If I'd known he'd disappear with the phone, I never would have left it with him.

I tried calling his cell. No voice mail this time, just a message that the number was not available. I didn't want to tell Detectives Ferrell or Daley I couldn't deliver Donald's cell phone because I had no idea where it was, so I didn't call either of them.

Halfway home, my cell rang. I'd taken the back roads to

Zenith, avoiding the summer construction on I-94. Several other drivers seemed to have the same idea, traffic along the two-laner heavy. Rather than chance an accident, I pulled onto the shoulder before answering.

"Dog's safe," Wade said, skipping any pleasantries. "Your vet scared our poor deputy. Told him what the dog has might be contagious, and he'd probably be dead by morning, so the deputy had better just leave him where he was. The man's washed his hands five times since he returned to the station."

"Oh that's encouraging." I'd petted Dexter. Let him rub up against my legs. Hugged him.

Wade chuckled. "I called the vet. Talked to him. Nice guy. I can see why you like him. He said, as far as he can tell, whatever is wrong with that dog isn't anything that can pass to humans . . . or to other dogs. But it is serious, he said, and he didn't want the dog moved. He wants you to call him."

"I will." Just as soon as I arrived home and looked up his number.

"You still at your grandmother's?"

"No I'm heading home."

"Be around this evening, or do you have a date?"

I could tell he was testing the waters. "No date."

"If I can, I'll stop by. We do need to talk."

"Sounds good."

I smiled as I ended the connection and pulled back onto the road. Wade had sounded more like his old self—gruff and to the point, but friendly. And he was right, we did need to talk, but I was hoping for a bit more than just talk. Blame it on my age . . . or too many years without, but I was getting as bad as a bitch in heat.

THIRTY-TWO

"Think you can get a sample of this dog's food and water?" Rick asked, after reassuring me that I hadn't exposed Baraka to any deadly virus.

"You think it's something he's been eating?" I remembered the thousands of dogs and cats that sickened and died after being fed pet food contaminated with melamine.

"Ate or drank. But that's just a guess. Until I have samples, I won't know for sure."

"I'll get those samples." Even as I spoke, I started looking for glass containers to take to Abby's.

"If I've already left the office, bring them to my house. I'm taking the dog home with me."

"Wow." I stopped rummaging through my cupboards. Rick's commitment to saving Dexter surprised me. "Thanks for scaring off that deputy."

He chuckled. "He came in all full of himself, demanding the dog. I just stretched the truth a bit." I could almost see Rick smile. "After all, we really don't know what's wrong with Dexter. It could be lethal."

"Would have been to Dexter if he was taken to the shelter."

Rick gave me his home number and address, and I promised to get the samples he needed to him as soon as possible. Finding suitable containers for those samples proved more difficult than I'd imagined. In the future I needed to save glass jars. I did discover two Mason jars in the cellar, and a good washing with soap and water removed the dust and cobwebs that had gathered in them. A box of lids, left over from the days when Grandma Benson canned, provided sanitary tops. Once again, I left Baraka loose in the house. He'd been in his crate while I visited my mother and grandmother, and I didn't feel it was fair to ask him to go in there again.

Yellow crime scene tape cordoned off most of Abby's yard and all of her house and kennel. I looked around for a sheriff's deputy, ready with my plea for permission to gather the samples my vet had requested. The acrid smell of charred wood lingered in the air, and the burnt timbers still standing created a silhouette of the house's frame. How anyone could tell if Abby's windows had been open or closed was beyond my comprehension. What the explosion hadn't destroyed had been consumed by the fire or ruined by a torrent of water.

"Anyone here?" I yelled, standing outside the tape barrier.

I knew I shouldn't cross that barrier, not without permission, but when no one answered my call, I ducked under the tape and headed for the lean-to next to the kennel. For all I knew, while working on installing an automatic watering system, Abby might have kept Dexter's dog food in the house. If so, it would be a miracle if I found a sample to take to Rick. Considering the damage the explosion and fire had caused, I wasn't sure what I'd find in the feed room.

The lean-to's roof had a gaping hole in one end, its edges rimmed with charred timber. I cautiously opened the door, wary of how stable the building might be. The floor and walls were water-soaked, both from the rain that had come through the hole and what the firemen had hosed in to quench the fire. Abby's metal feed bin, however, seemed intact, its lid covered with shingles, torn sections of roofing felt, and plywood. A half-burned rafter beam angled from the roof to the top of the bin, its end having dented but not punctured the metal.

I cautiously entered the room. The bottles and tubes that had sat on the shelves the last time I'd been there now lay in shattered and damaged piles on the wooden floor, along with feed dishes and grooming paraphernalia. Liquid medicinal lotions and a variety of dog shampoos had spilled onto the floor, mixing with puddles of water to create a sweet-smelling substance I wanted to avoid.

I knew I wouldn't get any water out of the capped-off faucet, but I hoped I would find some dog food in the bin. Although pinned down by the rafter, I managed to lift one corner of the lid high enough to see inside. Two bags of dog food were stacked against the far side, the top of one torn open. I tried, but I couldn't slide my arm in far enough to grab a sample.

I set the two mason jars on a nearby counter and began removing debris from the top of the bin. A wet mixture of soot and grime clung to my hands and within minutes I'd transferred some to my face and clothes. Not that I cared. All I wanted to do was nab a sample and return to my house. I could wash up later.

The rain had stopped while I was in Kalamazoo, a south wind scattering the clouds and raising the temperature. Ladies might perspire, but as I wrestled with the rafter pinning down the lid, sweat beaded on my forehead and slid down the side of my face. I'm sure I looked a mess when a familiar male voice demanded, "What are you doing?"

Startled, I jerked back.

Wade stood in the open doorway, a frown creasing his brow. He wore his usual brown cowboy boots and chinos, but the bomber jacket and white turtleneck he'd had on the first time I met him had been traded for a lightweight brown sports jacket and cotton shirt. The sight of him caused a flutter in my stomach, but the tone of his voice had me ready for a battle.

"What's it look like I'm doing? I'm trying to get into this feed bin."

"And what's in the feed bin?" He took a step toward me, still frowning, his posture stiff.

"Dog food." I tugged on the rafter.

"Stop," he ordered.

I glared at him. "Wade, I need to get a sample of this feed to the vet."

"Fine, but if you keep pulling on that rafter, you're going to have the other half of the roof on your head."

I looked up, and saw what he meant. Simply lifting the rafter had precariously moved the section of roof directly above my head. Relaxing my hold, I stepped back, clear of the area. "What do I do then? I need to get in there. I need some of that dog food."

"Your vet thinks there's something wrong with the dog food?"

"He's not sure."

Wade moved past me. "I'll lift, you get the dog food," he ordered. "But if I say get out of the way, you get out of the way fast. Do you understand?"

"Yes." Lordy, he could be irritating. I rubbed the palm of my right hand as clean as I could on my shorts, and then positioned myself to raise the lid and reach into the feed bin the moment Wade lifted the rafter.

"Ready?" he asked.

"Ready," I answered.

I heard him grunt and saw a space form between the rafter and the feed bin. Quickly I lifted the lid, slid my arm in, grabbed as much of the dog food as I could hold in my fist, and pulled my arm out.

Wade let the rafter down, and we heard a crunch above our heads. In unison we stepped back and watched a scattering of debris rain down on the lid. I deposited the dog food I'd grabbed into one of the Mason jars. It barely covered the bottom.

"I suppose you want more," Wade said, reading my mind.

I looked up at the weakened roof. "Think we dare?"

"Same routine," he said. "I'll lift, you grab. If I yell, you run."

We repeated the sequence. I added more feed to the jar, and more debris fell on the lid. A third time, and I didn't argue when Wade said, "Enough."

I placed the lid on the jar, grabbed the second jar off the shelf, and scooted out of the shed, Wade right behind me. We both stopped when we heard the clatter of falling shingles and wood. When the last ping sounded, I turned to Wade. "Thanks."

"You shouldn't be here."

"I know. I was going to ask permission, but there was no one to ask."

"You could have been injured if one of those boards had fallen on you. That tape's up there for a reason."

I knew he was right, but I argued anyway. "I needed these samples."

He shook his head. "You've got two jars. What else are you after?"

"Water. Drinking water. Whatever her dog would have drunk."

Wade turned toward the charred shell of Abby's house. "You're not going to get anything out of there. Probably nothing from any of the outside faucets, either."

"All I need is a little." Just enough for Rick to run his tests. "I'm hoping there's some left in one of the faucets."

I started wandering around the perimeter of the house, Wade following me. It didn't take long before I realized Wade was right. The explosion and fire, along with what the firefighters had done to put out the fire, had damaged the outside faucets as well as those inside the house. I was ready to give up when he put a hand on my arm and turned me so I was looking inside

Abby's house. "What about that?"

Standing toward the back, the outside and side walls around it severely damaged but still upright, sat a toilet and a small wash basin. I could tell the pipes under the wash basin were broken, but it appeared as if the toilet might still be functional.

"Give me the jar," Wade said.

I looked at the section of floor that would have to be traversed to get to the toilet. Broken glass and debris covered water-soaked wood and carpeting, a portion of the floor totally missing. "Let me go," I said. "I weigh less than you, and that floor doesn't look stable."

"P.J.," he growled, but I ignored him and stepped past charred studs into the house.

Wade started to follow me, grumbling something about me being stubborn, but halfway to the bathroom, I heard a crunching sound. Wade swore, and I stopped and looked back. He pulled his foot up from where it had gone through the flooring, stepped back, and lifted his pant leg. "You okay?" I asked.

"Yeah." He ran his hands over his ankle and calf muscle, then looked at me. "You be careful."

No need to tell me that. With each step I took, I gave a silent prayer that I wouldn't end up in Abby's cellar. By the time I reached the toilet, my breathing was shallow, my muscles tense. Carefully I set the jar down and lifted the lid to the toilet's tank. My efforts could have been for nothing if the pipes had cracked or the porcelain leaked.

I looked in . . . and smiled.

I returned to Wade's side with a full jar of water.

"Now what?" Wade asked.

"I get these to my vet."

"And that's all?"

The way he asked the question bothered me. "What do you mean, 'and that's all'? It's what I came here to do."

He didn't say anything, simply stared at me with those gorgeous blue eyes of his. I've learned this was a technique he used to get someone to keep talking. From what he'd said, it worked for him, at least some of the time. But not this time. I merely stared back and smiled.

Finally, he broke the standoff. "P.J., you shouldn't have come here at all. Right now, you're the prime suspect in this woman's death."

"Why? Just because I was here that day? As I told your buddy, Gespardo, I have no motive to kill Abby."

"Well, she certainly didn't commit suicide."

"I never thought she did, but why are you so certain she didn't?"

The way Wade averted his eyes I didn't think he'd tell me. I knew how he felt about civilians getting involved in police business. To my surprise, he said, "She was dead before that explosion occurred."

"Shot?"

"No, she was hit on the head. Several times."

I thought of the bruiser who'd hit me, how the slap of his hand had slammed my head against the door. If he'd hit me with his fist, hit me several times, would I still be alive?

"The preliminary autopsy report states the weapon could have been a frying pan," Wade said, changing my vision of the attack.

"She had one. I saw it on her stove." I also had one. A heavy, cast iron frying pan that I'd inherited from Grandpa Benson.

Wade looked toward the front of the house, where Abby's kitchen had once stood. "A deputy came out earlier and picked it up. He also stopped by your place."

"To get my fry pan?"

"No, he was looking for gasoline cans. Empty ones."

The only reason he'd be doing that was if gasoline had been

used to cause the explosion or spread the fire. I thought of the pile of rusted, empty gas cans my grandfather had left stacked out behind the woodshed. They were on my list of things to dump. "Did he find any?"

"He came back with pictures of a pile of cans. My guess is you'll be served with a warrant, and they'll be confiscated."

The deputy had to have come while I was in Kalamazoo, and I didn't like the idea of someone snooping around my place, but the thought of the sheriff's department removing those old gas cans made me grin. "Wade, you guys are wasting your time. Those cans were dumped there by my grandfather. They haven't had anything in them for years. The only one I use I keep near my lawnmower."

"I've told them they're focusing on the wrong person, that it couldn't have been you, but it seems they received an anonymous tip that you were seen over here not long before the explosion."

"You're kidding." Except, I could tell from his expression he wasn't. "Wade, I left at least two hours before this house exploded."

"I'm just reporting what I was told."

"Was this 'anonymous tip' from a man or a woman?"

"You know I can't tell you that."

"I'll bet it was Leon Lersten's wife." I pointed across the way toward the Lersten farm. "She jumped all over me the other day at the store. She thought I was taking Abby's side in the road straightening issue."

"P.J., come on. That's not a reason to implicate a person in a murder."

"Maybe not, but implicating me might keep the police from considering her husband."

"And why would her husband want to murder Mrs. Warfield?"

"Look." I pointed toward the road. "If Abby succeeded in getting that road straightened, Leon would have had to come up with a new irrigation system. He'd lose good farm land. And even if she didn't report her suspicions about a meth lab to your department, in the process of straightening the road, someone might have discovered it."

Wade shook his head. "Calling out the fire department and sheriff's department would increase the chances someone would notice."

"Okay." I wasn't convinced Leon was innocent. "You said your department is looking for a source of gasoline. Abby thought Leon was polluting her water with gasoline."

Again Wade shook his head. "I'm not sure how this farmer could get gasoline into Mrs. Warfield's water, but even if we assume he could, the gasoline wouldn't have reached all of the locations where the fire marshal found traces of an accelerant."

"All right, so maybe he brought it over. Maybe . . ."

Wade held up a hand. "Enough, P.J. Let *us* do the investigating."

"Yeah, well . . ." I glared at him. "So far *your* 'investigating' has led to Gespardo thinking I caused this, and I don't find that particularly comforting."

"If you're innocent, he'll work it out."

"If?" I poked a finger at his chest. "You're saying 'If I'm innocent'?"

He captured my hand in his. "Wrong choice of words."

I pulled my fingers free. "You'd better believe it." Frustrated, I gestured toward Olivia Halsted's place. "Talk to her. I stopped by her place right after I left here. She can tell you what time I drove off. She can also tell you I didn't come back here, not until after the explosion."

"And took the dog."

"Because he was sick . . . is sick." Another of those good

deeds that wasn't going to go unpunished. "Is that why you're here, to catch me returning to the scene of the crime?"

"No, I came out here because on the phone, you said you thought the farmer across the road had a meth lab. I thought I'd take a ride out here, talk to him, and maybe look around. But no one's home."

"Did you look in Leon's barn?"

Wade smiled. "Now, you know I couldn't do that, not without his permission."

"But if you just happened to be looking for Leon and the barn door was open . . . ?"

"Why then I'd have to check and see if he was there, wouldn't I? Which I did, and the only thing I found, P.J., was what you would expect to find in a barn."

"Really?" Considering both Abby's and Pat Yelton's suspicions, that surprised me.

"But there is a smaller building just off to the side of the barn. It's locked tight and the windows are all covered."

The way he said it gave me hope. "Did you check it out?"

"As much as I could. I did smell meth . . . methane gas. Something is decomposing in there."

"Maybe a dead body?" Perhaps Abby wasn't the first person Leon Lersten had killed.

"I don't think so, but that's something *I'll* check into."

He emphasized the personal pronoun, which didn't bother me. I wanted out of this mess. "Wade, why would someone try to frame me for Abby's murder?"

"Good question."

"Do you think her death might be tied to Donald Crane's briefcase? I did find aerial pictures of these farms in it, and Crane took soil samples from Lersten's farm. Maybe he discovered more than he should have. Maybe Abby did, too, and when Lersten saw me over here, he may have figured having me blamed for her death would eliminate me as a threat."

Once again, Wade was shaking his head. "From what I've heard, everything in the Donald Crane murder is pointing toward someone in the gay community. So, unless your farmer is gay, I don't think he's involved with that case."

I was pretty sure Leon Lersten was not gay, but I still felt there was a connection. "What if—"

Wade stopped me. "No. No 'what ifs.' You keep your nose out of this." He tapped me on the tip of my nose. "Stay away from here. Take your samples to your vet, and don't come back here."

I didn't like being bossed around and wanted to object, but with Abby dead, there really wasn't any reason for me to return to her place, and I did need to get the dog food and water samples to Rick.

THIRTY-THREE

On the drive back to my house, I thought about Wade's behavior. He'd said "If I was innocent." How could he think I would do such a thing. Where was the Wade Kingsley who'd sat beside me on my porch steps only a couple of weeks ago, shared stories of his childhood, and made love with me? His tap on my nose was affectionate, but not overly so. And he didn't kiss me before I left. What happened in such a short time to turn him into a stranger?

Once inside my house, I understood why Wade hadn't kissed me. Soot, dirt, and sweat covered my face and hands, and my hair felt like straw. A shower took care of the grime, and I called Rick as soon as I'd donned a clean T-shirt and shorts. He said to bring the samples to his house not the clinic. He'd be there by the time I arrived.

I hated leaving Baraka alone again, but I wasn't taking him in my car. Even though Rick didn't think Dexter had anything contagious, I wasn't taking a chance until I knew for sure. I did take a few minutes to play a form of tag with my dog. I'd run after him, and he'd tear off, heading around to the back of the house and returning to the front at a dead run. I'd tap him on the shoulder as he passed close to me, then I'd take off and he'd run after me, the side of his body just barely grazing my hip as he ran by. The challenge was to avoid being "tapped," and there were times when Baraka misjudged the distance and actually ran into me. I'd ended up on the ground more than once, and I knew this probably wasn't a good game to play, but it did give both of us some exercise.

Finally, with both of us panting, I gave Baraka a rawhide bone to chew on, and I took off.

The drive to Rick's place took twenty minutes, and as he'd promised, he was there. "Your dog's looking better," he said, taking me out to a kennel behind his house. "The transfusion definitely helped."

Dexter was lying on a carpeted, raised platform, head between his paws. He looked up when Rick called his name, gave a weak thump with his tail, but didn't rise to his feet. As far as I could see, he was still a very sick dog. "You're sure he doesn't have anything contagious?"

"Pretty sure." Rick cradled the two Mason jars I'd given him. "I have a friend who teaches chemistry at Western. I talked to him earlier, and he said I could meet him at the college around eight o'clock and he'd run some tests to see if there's something in the dog's food or water that could be causing his symptoms."

"So you'll know tonight?"

"I hope. I'll give you a call when I do." He walked me back to my car. "Don't worry, P.J., we'll figure this out."

I wished I could stop worrying, but too many scary things had happened in the last week for me to ignore the possibility I'd exposed my dog and maybe myself to something deadly. Back at my place, I sprayed the inside of my car with a disinfectant; nevertheless, I kept thinking my actions were too little too late.

The blinking message indicator on my answering machine caught my attention the moment I stepped into the house. Two calls were from clients, each with a request. The third call surprised me. "I saw you and a man across the road at that poor woman's house," a quavering voice that I recognized as Olivia Halsted's said. "Do they know anything more about what happened?"

She left her number, so I assumed she wanted me to call, but I was too tired to explain why I'd been at Abby's house. Maybe tomorrow, especially if Rick managed to figure out what was making Abby's dog so sick.

I did need to response to my clients' calls, but before I picked up the phone, I poured myself a glass of tea and found their file folders. I was about to punch in the first client's number when the phone rang. Startled, I almost dropped the handset.

The moment he said hello, I recognized Neal's smooth baritone. "I've been thinking about you," he said. "Ever since the other night. That was nice."

I wasn't sure if he was referring to the dinner or the kiss, so I kept my response neutral . . . and honest. "Best dinner I've had all week."

"Heard there was a little excitement out your way last night."

I assumed he meant the explosion. "That's an understatement."

"Mrs. Halsted's quite upset. She's called me three times today."

"She called me once," I said, not sure what he was getting at.

"You know how these older people are. Anything that disrupts their routine upsets them. Which, in this case, I can't say I blame her. Did you know the explosion broke two of her windows?"

"No I didn't." I glanced at my plastic-covered window. One of these days I needed to get that repaired.

"She wants to know everything that's going on over there. What caused the explosion. If Mrs. Warfield suffered. What's going to be done with the property. Everything." He paused and cleared his throat. "Anyway, I thought maybe I'd stop by this evening. I would like to see you again."

A part of me was flattered that Neal wanted to see me again, but I knew, sure as anything, if he did stop by, Wade would also show up. And I didn't really want to see Neal again. Not romantically. Dinner with him had been nice. He was nice. But Wade was the man I cared for. I might be upset with the lunk-head, but I still wanted to see him, wanted to be with him. "I'm afraid I'm going to be busy tonight," I said.

"That policeman of yours?"

"He's a sheriff's deputy," I corrected. And since I didn't want to lie, I changed the subject. "Did Mrs. Halsted see anything before Abby's house exploded? See another car or truck over there? Maybe see Leon Lersten walk over?"

"Not that she mentioned. Why?"

I didn't think it was confidential information, so I told him. "Because Abby's windows were open when I was at her place, but evidently they were closed when the explosion occurred."

"Maybe Mrs. Warfield . . . that is, Abby, closed them herself."

"The sheriff's department doesn't seem to think so. They think Abby was murdered."

"Murdered?" He sounded surprised. "Any idea who killed her?"

"No, which is why I'd like to know if Mrs. Halsted saw anyone else go over there before the explosion. As it is, I'm the last known person to have seen Abby alive."

"Do you need a lawyer? I know a good criminal lawyer," Neal said.

"No, I—"

I'd left Baraka outside when I arrived home, and he'd been sitting on the porch, nose pressed against the screen door, wait-ing for me to let him in. Suddenly he'd gone off the porch, trot-ting toward my driveway. Cordless phone in hand, I moved over to the doorway to see what had caught his attention. I smiled at the sight of a tan Jeep.

"I've got to go," I told Neal. "My date's arrived."

I think he said something before I disconnected the call, but I didn't care. From inside the house I watched Wade come into the yard and greet Baraka. Tail wagging, my dog crow-hopped around Wade, made a mock attempt to grab his hand in his mouth, then raced away and up the steps, skidding to a stop in front of the door. Eyes bright, Baraka looked at me through the screen, and I'd swear both of us were smiling.

"I think he's missed you," I said as I opened the screen door and let both Wade and Baraka inside.

"I've missed him." Wade gave Baraka's head a pat. "And you." Wade placed a hand on the top of my head, pressing down on curls that refused to be tamed. "Have you gotten shorter?"

"I hope not." I looked up, and he was smiling as he lowered his head to kiss me.

I stepped back and flattened the palm of my hand against his chest. "Just one minute, Mr. Sergeant Detective Kingsley. You can't be suspecting me of murder one minute and all lovey dovey the next."

He straightened, the look of surprise on his face amusing. "I never suspected you of murder," he said, and then gave a shrug. "Well, not lately. I said Gespardo thinks you're involved."

"No." I remembered his words clearly. "You said, 'If you're innocent.' If!"

"Well, you know what I mean." He blew out a frustrated breath. "Jeez, I don't need this, P.J. I came here hoping for . . . hoping you . . ." He shook his head and turned away. "Maybe I'd just better go."

"No." I grabbed his arm. "Don't go."

For a moment I thought he would leave. I could feel the tension in his arm through my fingers, read his irritation in the rigidness of his body. And then he turned and wrapped his arms around me. "Damn, I've missed you," he murmured and sighed.

We should have talked, should have cleared up our misunderstandings and doubts, but talk was the last thing on my mind at the moment. Our journey from the dining room to my bedroom was a series of mind-boggling kisses, items of clothing being discarded along the way. Baraka followed us until Wade closed the door on him. Some things aren't meant for a dog to see.

An hour later, I did hear Baraka whining and realized it was way past his dinner time. "Hungry?" I asked Wade.

He rolled to his side and smiled. "Not anymore."

"For food, I meant."

"Ah. Food." He kissed the tip of my nose. "I suppose we should eat, to keep up our strength."

"You're insatiable." I laughed and slid off the bed, the mirror on my dresser reflecting my nakedness. Reddened skin indicated where a day's growth of stubble on Wade's chin had irritated rarely kissed areas of my body.

I faced him and marveled at the tone of his body. Even relaxed, he projected strength and power. That I'd even considered Neal a substitute made me smile. Whether my relationship with Wade lasted or not, he'd spoiled me for other men.

"Come on, you sex machine," I said. "Let's see what I have in the refrigerator."

Thirty-Four

I fed Baraka, and together Wade and I found enough food in my freezer and cupboards to put together a tasty meal. He'd even brought a bottle of wine with him. "A peace offering," he said after getting it from his vehicle.

With my sexual needs satisfied, food in my stomach, and two glasses of wine giving me a hazy glow, I was at peace. In truth, I really didn't want to ruin the evening with talk. Wade was the one who brought up the subject of the last two weeks. "About my not answering your calls," he started, and I took in a deep breath, afraid of what he was going to say.

"I've just . . ." He looked away and sighed. "It's Linda."

I wasn't sure I wanted to hear about his ex-wife. "What about Linda?"

"She's getting married."

"And that's bothering you?" I'd always wondered if Wade still loved his ex.

He nodded and looked at me. "The man she's marrying is being transferred to another state. She's moving, taking Jason."

Wade's love for his son was something I knew and understood. Suddenly his desire to spend the weekend alone with Jason made sense. "What are you going to do?"

"There's not much I can do. The courts gave her full custody. The legal system doesn't seem to think an unmarried homicide detective could provide a stable home for a six-year-old boy. Even if I married, it wouldn't change things. Basically the courts

239

feel a child should be with his biological mother unless there are circumstances to the contrary. Well, there are no circumstances. Linda is a good mother."

A good mother, maybe, but she certainly hadn't been a good wife to Wade, and she wasn't being fair to him now. "How far away will Jason be?"

"California."

"Oh, Wade." I scooted my chair closer to his and wrapped my arms around his shoulders. I wanted to tell him everything would be all right, but I knew things weren't right in his world. "How can she do this to you? To Jason? That boy loves you, needs you."

"It's been tearing me apart," he said, choking back tears. "I've been talking to lawyers, friends of the court, everyone I can think of. I've taken days off to be with him, have been ignoring my job, ignoring everything . . ." He looked at me. "Including you."

"You should have told me. I would have understood."

"I think . . ." He looked away. "I think I haven't wanted to talk about it because I hoped she would change her mind, hoped this guy she's marrying would find a job here in Michigan. But every time I talk to her . . ." He snorted and shook his head. "She's such a bitch."

"Don't you have visitation rights?"

Wade scoffed. "You think I can afford to fly out to California every other weekend?" He shook his head. "Oh, I'll get him for a couple weeks in the summer and every other major holiday, but you know how that's going to go. She already comes up with excuses why I can't see him on my weekends, I'm sure she'll find reasons why he can't fly back here for visits. Bad weather. A school performance he can't miss. And my job will probably screw things up. You know how it is when I'm on a case. I can't just up and leave when I feel like it."

He leaned his head on my shoulder, and I held him closer. I felt him shudder and knew he was crying. I didn't know what to say, so I remained silent, but my thoughts bounced back through the last couple weeks. I'd selfishly thought his withdrawal was all about me. When he could have used my emotional support, he'd seen me kissing Neal. What a fine girlfriend I was turning out to be.

I'm not sure how long we remained in that position, but after a while he took in a deep breath, and I could sense he'd regained control of his emotions. When he raised his head, he kissed me. "Thank you," he said and kissed me again. Then again and again.

We ended up back in my bedroom. This time our lovemaking was less frantic, his touch tender and loving, each arousing step in the journey of reaching a climax as important as the release. A deep sigh and a kiss expressed his final satisfaction. For me knowing his lack of attention lately hadn't been due to questions about our relationship was as gratifying as the sex. He fell asleep; I was invigorated.

I slipped out of bed and did our dishes, swept floors, played with Baraka, and even straightened the papers on my table before crawling back in bed beside Wade. A grunt was his only indication that he knew I'd returned, and I wondered how many sleepless nights he'd experienced since his ex announced her intentions. Snuggling close, I slowly drifted off to sleep.

The smell of coffee and frying bacon greeted me when I opened my eyes. Wade was no longer beside me, but the scent of his body—and of our lovemaking—remained. I resisted getting out of bed and facing reality until Wade stepped into the room and asked, "You want one or two eggs?"

"Two," I said, realizing I was ravenous. "What time is it?"

"Almost ten. I fed Baraka. Shake a leg. I'm cooking those

eggs in five minutes."

Hardly enough time to take a shower and slip into shorts and a tank top, but I managed. My hair was still wet when I sat down at the table, and Wade handed me a cup of hot coffee. The sun was out, and so was Baraka, his nose pressed against the plastic covering my broken window. "When are you getting that fixed?" Wade asked, noticing the direction of my gaze.

"I haven't had time to call anyone," I said. "I'll do that today."

"I made a couple of calls," he said from the kitchen. "Found out what happened to your computer guy."

"What?" I started to get up from my chair, but Wade came back carrying two plates of food and sat down beside me.

"He's in the hospital. Thursday night, he and another guy were beaten up pretty badly. The police figure it was drug related. They found traces of marijuana in the apartment, along with some drug paraphernalia."

That Ken might do drugs didn't surprise me, but I wasn't convinced that was the reason for the attack. "How badly was he hurt?"

"Bad enough. His jaw, several ribs, and a leg were broken. His buddy is in a coma."

"It wasn't drugs," I said. "They were attacked because of that damn cell phone."

"You don't know that for sure. According to the detective I talked to, the other guy, the one in a coma, is a known druggy. This wasn't the first time he's been involved in trouble."

"Maybe not, but Ken's shop was broken into right after I gave him that cell phone, and last Thursday he told me he'd been followed the day before. It's just too much of a co-incidence. I'm sure they were attacked because of that cell phone."

I could tell from the look Wade gave me that he wasn't convinced, but he didn't completely blow off my theory. "I'll dig a little deeper," he said and dug into his bacon and eggs.

I stared at my plate. The thought of Ken with a broken jaw made my face ache, and I remembered the pain of being slapped by Morgan. Had that happened just last week? Within a span of seven days, two people I knew or knew about had died, I'd been hit, and two men who were helping me had been beaten up. "What is going on?"

"Huh?" Wade grunted, his mouth full of food.

"Thinking aloud," I said and made a decision. "What hospital is Ken in?"

Wade finished chewing his bacon before he answered. "Bronson. Why? You thinking of going to see him?"

"I think I should. I think I'm the reason he's there." And now I felt guilty for being upset with him for not answering my calls . . . for all the trouble I'd caused him.

Wade shook his head. "They have his jaw wired shut. From what I was told, he can talk, but he's hard to understand. Wasn't all that cooperative, either. Didn't give them anything solid to go on. You want my suggestion?" He went on before I could respond. "Stay away from the guy."

"Wade, I can't. Maybe you and the police think what happened to Ken is drug related, but I don't."

"Honey, the man admitted he and his friend had drugs on them when they were jumped."

"And all of this bad stuff just happened to happen after I gave Ken that cell phone?" I shook my head.

"Bad things happen to people who do drugs. Trust me, the man brought it on himself."

Trust me? I tried not to grin. Wade had made up his mind, and there was no use arguing with him. "Okay, if you say it's drugs, it's drugs. But I still want to go see him." I picked up my fork. "If what happened to Ken had nothing to do with the cell phone, maybe he still has it."

THIRTY-FIVE

Wade stayed and helped with the dishes, but I could tell his mind was somewhere else, especially the way he kept glancing at the clock. "What's up?" I finally asked.

He chuckled and hugged me. "You're getting to know me too well."

"So?"

"So I'm picking Jason up in an hour. We're going to a ball game."

"I thought you had him last weekend."

"I did. Linda's allowing me extra time with my son." Sarcasm laced his words. "As if a few days during the week and a couple extra weekends will balance months of not seeing him."

His pain was palpable, and I rubbed my palms over his back, wishing I could ease the tension in his body. "When is she moving to California?"

"Six weeks. Maybe sooner." He sighed and stepped back. "I'm sorry, P.J. I hate to eat and run, but my mind is focused on Jason right now. Try to stay out of trouble. Okay?"

"Gladly," I promised. "You just do what you've got to do. Don't worry about me."

I took Baraka out for playtime after Wade drove off. The Dumpster beckoned me to continue cleaning the chicken coop, and I had bookkeeping to do, but I wanted to see Ken. Wade might think the mugging was due to a drug deal gone bad, but I had my own theory.

An hour later, I parked in the lot off John Street in Kalamazoo and walked into Bronson Hospital. An elderly woman seated behind the information desk instructed me on how to find Ken's room, and I headed that direction. Although Wade had told me the extent of Ken's injuries, seeing him lying on a hospital bed, tubes connected to his body and a stack of pillows elevating his right leg, shocked me.

Cartoons played on the television mounted on the wall opposite the bed, the sound coming from a device lying near his head. I rapped on the doorjamb, and Ken turned slightly to the side so he could see me. A flicker of pain crossed his eyes, but he smiled.

"Hi," I said softly and entered the room. "I just heard what happened."

His face was swollen and mottled with dark bruises, but it wasn't until he parted his lips that I saw the tangle of wires holding his jaw in place. For an instant, I thought of Hannibal Lecter.

"Glad you came," he said through the pins and wires, his words muffled.

"Are you in a lot of pain?"

" 'appy juice," he said and gestured toward an IV attached to his arm.

I understood. "They're giving you pain killers."

A nod.

"I'm so sorry."

"Caught us off guard."

"It was the phone, wasn't it?"

"They took it. Took all our phones. Computer. CDs. Jerry's stash."

I assumed Jerry was Ken's friend, and the stash was the drugs the police were focused on. "I heard your friend's in a coma."

Again Ken gave a slight nod. "Big bruiser slam Jer's head

against table. Guy was crazy. Kept hittin' us."

"Did he have dark hair? Wear dark glasses?"

"Wore masks. Couldn't see hair. But yeah. Big guy. Bouncer type. Hada ring. Felt it when he hit me." Ken winced as he raised his hand and touched his cheek.

I remembered the ring. It had to be the guy Ida had called Dr. Morgan.

"Other guy held a gun on us and watched."

"Other guy?" I said. "How many were there?"

Ken raised two fingers, grimacing with the motion.

"What did he look like?"

" 'Bout my 'ite," Ken said between the wires holding his jaw together. "White. Bowf white. Dressed nice."

"Did they talk to each other? Give names?"

"Little guy called the big one Morgan. I remember him telling the guy not to kill us. I passed out after that. Dey gone when I came to."

Morgan. So Ida was right about the name after all. Except maybe Morgan was the man's first name, not last. And maybe he wasn't a doctor after all.

I stared down at the battered body on the hospital bed. "Oh, Ken, what can I say? If I'd known this was going to happen, I never would have given you that phone. Now we'll never know what was on that phone."

"Didn't you get da pictures?"

His question took me aback. "What pictures?"

"The ones I sent." Ken made what I decided was a grimace. "Der awful dark. Must've been taken at night. Jer didn't want me sending 'em. Not without brightening 'em up some. But once I figgered out what dey showed, I was 'fraid we might lose 'em, so I emailed 'em to you."

"I haven't checked my email," I said. "Not for days."

"Sent dem udder night, from da cell phone. Look at 'em.

Police need to see 'em."

"Why, what do they show?"

He didn't have a chance to answer before three doctors—at least I assumed they were all doctors from the stethoscopes around their necks—and a nurse came into the room. "If you don't mind stepping out for a few minutes," the nurse said to me. "The doctor wants to show these interns what he did to rebuild Mr. Paget's jaw."

"She's leavin'," Ken said, motioning with his good arm for me to go. "Look at da pictures, P.J.," he insisted. "See if you tink der what I tink dey are."

Thirty-Six

I wanted to know what the pictures Ken had emailed me showed, if they would explain why people were being killed and attacked. My grandmother's house wasn't far from the hospital, and I headed that direction. I'd given her my old computer the year before. I'd even given her a printer. All I needed to do was go online and download the pictures. If they showed something the police should see, I could forward them on to Detective Ferrell or Daley and make some prints.

To my surprise, no one answered the doorbell at Grandma's house. Or my knock. And the doors—both front and back—were locked.

And then I remembered.

My mother was working, and Grandma had said she was thinking of driving Ida out to my place. I'd assumed she would call before she came. Evidently I'd been wrong.

I was walking back to my car when my cell phone rang. The phone number shown was mine.

"Grandma?" I answered, a bit surprised since I'd locked my doors before leaving.

"Where are you?" she responded.

"At your place."

"Well, I'm at yours." She sounded exasperated. "I told you we were coming out to visit with you."

She'd told me she was "thinking" about coming out, but I

wasn't going to nit-pick. I was curious. "How did you get inside?"

"You think a piece of plastic is going to stop a woman when she needs to use the bathroom?"

Her *hrumph* said it didn't. "Your dog acts like he needs to go out," she said. "We were wondering if we could take him for a walk in the woods. I want to show Ida what a mess that pack rat of an in-law of mine made of the property."

I didn't answer right away. Not because I didn't want Ida in my woods. That was no problem. My reluctance was due to my dog. A walk would be good for him, but ridgebacks need to be handled with firm control. Although I knew my grandmother never allowed me to get away with any misbehavior, whenever I took Baraka over to her house, she spoiled him terribly. Being a puppy, he would test her.

"I can handle him," Grandma said, a hint of pleading in her voice. "I won't let him run off or get hurt."

I couldn't say no. "Don't let him near the road," I ordered. "Meanwhile, I'll head back. I should be there in a half hour."

"We'll be waiting for you." She laughed. "That is, if we don't get lost."

"It's only ten acres, Grandma. I don't think you'll get lost. See you in a bit."

My car needed gas, so it took me a bit longer than a half hour to make the drive. Grandma's fifteen-year-old Buick sat in my driveway, a series of bumper stickers covering dented and rusted areas. My favorite is—*I believe in life before death.*

A breeze ruffled my hair the moment I stepped out of my car and flapped a corner of the plastic that was no longer securely taped over my broken window. I did need to get that fixed. Back in the woods, crows were squawking, their caws bringing back bad memories.

I hurried inside, hoping my grandmother and Ida would

forgive me for rudely ignoring them until I had a chance to turn on my computer and download the pictures Ken had sent. "Grandma," I called out the moment I stepped through the doorway.

Silence.

The old house felt cold and empty. No one responded to my greeting. No dog came dashing up to sniff my legs, and the door to Baraka's crate hung open.

"Grandma?" I called again, just in case she'd taken Ida Delaney upstairs or down to the cellar.

Again, no response.

I headed for the window that looked out the back and saw the gate that opened to the path through the woods was unlatched and ajar. For a moment, I was glad. With them still out on their walk, I could download the pictures without having to explain what I was doing or feeling rude. I turned on my computer, but as I waited for it to load, an uneasy sensation forced me back to the window. I opened it and listened.

The crows were still cawing.

I recognized the short, sharp bursts of sound as alarm caws, the warnings crows give in the presence of a soaring bird of prey or unwelcome humans. I assumed the humans were my grandmother and Ida. What bothered me was the cawing seemed stationary. Two older women might walk slowly, but that slow?

Had one of them fallen?

Icons dotted my screensaver, but I didn't click on any. The pictures would have to wait until I knew my grandmother was okay.

I half-ran along the path that took me past oaks and pines, sumac and wild cherry. The crows continued cawing, their harsh cries mingling with my frantic shouts for my grandmother and Ida. I thought I heard someone answer, but I wasn't sure. And then I saw my dog, racing toward me. "Baraka," I shouted, and stopped so he wouldn't knock me over.

He hopped around me, tail wagging and tongue lolling out the side of his mouth. I patted his head and sides, happy to see him. "Where are they," I asked. "Where's my grandma? Where's Ida?"

He headed back the way he'd come, stopping a few yards ahead and looking at me as if to say, "Aren't you coming?"

I followed him.

Most dogs don't respond like they show in movies. Unless they've been trained for search and rescue work, you can't simply ask a dog where someone is and expect him to take you to that person. It does happen on occasion, but Baraka was still a puppy, and I didn't really think he would lead me to my grandmother. Therefore, I didn't get upset when he journeyed off the path to cock his leg at a tree, stopped to sniff a log, and then went dashing after a butterfly.

As I'd told my grandmother, the woods behind my house weren't that large. Even without Baraka's help, I was sure I'd find Grandma and Ida somewhere ahead of me. My biggest problem was navigating several decades of junk and seeing through the overgrown underbrush.

I hoped one or both of them hadn't gone off the path, tripped and fallen, and broken a bone. Getting an injured, older person back to the house wouldn't be easy.

Because I had made the assumption they were alone, I wasn't prepared when I did find the two of them. They were sitting on a log, looking my way when I came into view. Standing a few feet in front of them was Nora Wright, a shovel in her hands. She swung it at Baraka when he came bounding at her, tail wagging. The flat side of the shovel hit his side.

He yelped in pain and slunk back toward me.

"What do you think you're doing?" I yelled and ran toward

her, ready to grab the shovel from her hand and maybe use it on her.

If I'd been looking down and not at Nora, I would have noticed the box she'd been digging around. As it was, the toe of my right shoe hit the metal edge, and I went careening forward. I instinctively put out my hands to break my fall, but the moment my palms touched the ground, I knew that was a mistake. Pain radiated up my arms and twisted through my shoulders. My chest hit something hard, knocking the breath out of me, and my shin ached from where my leg had come in contact with the box.

"Damn you!" Nora screamed above me, waving the shovel in the air. "Damn all of you."

I covered my head, afraid she was going to hit me with the shovel, and heard my grandmother cry out, "P.J." From the edge of my vision I saw her rise from the log she'd been sitting on.

"You. Sit down," Nora ordered above me, pointing the shovel at my grandmother. "Both of you. I've had enough meddling from you Bensons."

"My grandmother's not a Benson," I mumbled from my prone position.

"I don't care who she is," Nora spat back. "I don't care who any of you are. This should be my land. Paul promised me. He said this would be a good place for our son, that he'd watch over him, and if anything happened to him, the woods would be mine."

I rolled to my side so I could look up at Nora. She held her shovel like a baseball bat, her expression and stance aggressive. What she'd said didn't make any sense. "What are you talking about?"

She glared down at me. "I'm talking about that double-crossing, two-timing father of yours. That's what I'm talking about. And his father. I told that old man why the woods should be mine. Told him everything. And he promised me they would be."

I heard the emotional stress in her voice and noticed a slight trembling near her mouth. She kept looking directly at me as she continued. "These woods would have been mine, you know," she said, "if your father had married me, like he should have. As his wife, I would have inherited these woods. And if our baby had lived, he would have inherited this farm, not you."

"Baby?" I knew the fall had jarred my brain, but I'd never heard any of this. "What baby?"

"Your brother," Nora said. "Actually, he would have been your half brother."

"Oh, shit," I heard Grandma Carter say. "It was you?"

Nora looked at her, a sneer twisting her mouth. "Yes me. All the girls in school thought he was so great, so perfect. No one thought I could seduce him, but I did. And if I hadn't lost that baby, he would have married me instead of your psycho daughter."

"But you're a—" I stopped before I said lesbian, but Nora understood.

She snorted. "I was young back then. Confused. It wasn't until after I lost the baby, after I joined the army that I realized why being with a man didn't turn me on. That 'Don't ask, don't tell' bit might work for the brass, but we can tell. I wasn't through boot camp before I was approached. No more confusion." She laughed, then turned serious. "Your father was a prick."

Once I would have argued with her, but not anymore. "So I've learned."

"He probably didn't even bury him here. He probably just threw him away."

Nora's eyes glistened with unshed tears, and for the first time since I'd met her, I felt sorry for her. "You didn't have a funeral for him or anything?"

She shook her head. "We didn't dare. If my parents had known I was pregnant . . ."

Nora didn't finish, and I wondered how she explained an enlarged belly. "How far along were you when you lost the baby."

"Five months." She sighed. "I'd just begun to show."

"Did you give him a name?"

Nora nodded. "Timothy. Timothy Archer Benson. He would be thirty now."

"I never had any children," Ida said, speaking up for the first time. "But my nephew, Donald, is like a son to me. He worries about me, thinks I need someone to watch over me. He's probably worried now." She started to push herself up from the log. "I need to get back."

"Sit down," Nora demanded and thumped the end of her shovel against a broken metal bed post, making a loud clanking sound.

Wide-eyed, Ida sat down.

"What are you going to do, keep us here until you figure out where my father buried that baby?" I asked, pushing myself up to a seated position.

Nora looked at me, then at my grandmother and Ida. "I don't know. I don't know what to do," she said in a voice strangely pensive. Her gaze turned to the box I'd tripped over, then to the area surrounding us. "He said he was going to put him in a container that animals couldn't get to, that it would be like a real coffin. Something water and bugs wouldn't get into. He said he'd put a marker on the spot where he buried him, but I've looked and looked, and I can't find anything to indicate a burial site."

"I've never seen anything that looked like a grave," I said.

"If there is one, it's probably buried under a pile of junk."
She kicked at a nearby pair of bald tires. "Damn your grand-
father. The lazy bastard should of taken all of this to the dump.
But no, not him. He had to go and drag everything back here.
Thirty years of junk. How am I ever going to find my baby?"

"So you don't find him," Grandma said. "Just tell yourself
he's here."

"Oh, yeah, fine. And what do I tell myself after your granddaughter throws my son in a Dumpster and has him hauled
away? No." She took a step closer and pointed at me. "Either
you give me these woods or . . ."

I don't know what the "or" would have been because at that
moment, something about the way Nora was standing and
pointing at me must have triggered Baraka's protective instincts.
Up until then, my dog had been cowering back by my feet, but
suddenly he was seventy-five pounds of pent-up energy. Hair
standing on end, a deep-throated growl erupted from his throat,
and he plowed into Nora.

She yelled and stumbled to the side. Raising her hands in
defense, she dropped the shovel. I scooted forward and grabbed
its handle, pulling it away from Nora's reach. While she was in a
tangle with Baraka, I brought my knees under me and scrambled
to my feet. Grandma also sprung into action, grabbing a pipe
that had been lying on the ground near the log and stepping
toward Nora.

Baraka was off Nora by the time I was standing, but both
Grandma and I were ready, me with the shovel and Grandma
with the pipe. "Stay right where you are," Grandma ordered,
reminding me of times when I lived with her. When Grandma
gave an order, you obeyed.

Nora did. With a sigh of defeat, she sank onto the ground
and looked up at us. "What are you going to do with me?" she
whimpered.

I didn't know what to do with her, and I looked at my grandmother. "Did she hurt you? You or Ida?"

"No." Grandma shook her head. "She did a lot of threatening, but that was all."

I looked back at Nora. "You hit my dog."

"Evidently not hard enough."

Baraka had come over to my side, but I could see the tension in his body, his gaze focused on Nora. As far as I could tell, hitting him with the shovel hadn't done any serious damage, other than spurring him into aggressive action, which wasn't so bad in this case.

"Did you give my grandfather an overdose of sleeping pills?" I asked.

Nora snorted. "You think that old codger would take anything from me?"

Not exactly an answer, but I had a feeling she was right. Not that I knew Grandpa Benson that well, but I couldn't imagine him accepting any food from Nora.

"More than once, you've tried to kill me," I said.

"Tried to scare you, that's all. If I'd wanted to kill you, you'd be dead."

I remembered bullets whizzing over my head and a visit to the emergency room, but decided Nora might be telling the truth. From what I'd heard, she was an expert marksman—markswoman. If she'd wanted to kill me, would those shots have missed?

"Get out of here," I said, and nodded the direction of her house. "Maybe I'll help you look for that baby, but not today."

Nora frowned and slowly pushed herself up to her knees. Grandma stood ready with the pipe, and Baraka growled a low, throaty growl. I brushed my fingertips over his head and murmured, "It's okay, boy. It's okay. We're going to let her go."

"I think I'm ready to go home," Ida said and stood and

looked around. "Did Donald bring me out here?"

"No, I did, Ida," Grandma said, keeping her gaze on Nora. "We'll go home soon."

"Did I miss my shows?"

"No, it's Saturday. No soaps on Saturday."

"Oh, that's right."

I watched Nora walk away as Grandma talked to Ida. Twice, Nora looked back. She wasn't smiling.

I'd let her go mainly because I didn't know what else to do. I ached in enough places to know if Nora decided to attack, I might not be able to subdue her. And even though Baraka had knocked her down, he hadn't tried biting her, and I wasn't sure I wanted him learning to bite people. Grandma Carter could inflict some serious damage with the pipe she held, but she was seventy-some years old. If anything happened to her, I'd never forgive myself.

My promise that I would help Nora look for her son didn't mean I wasn't going to report what she'd done. As Wade kept telling me, I needed to leave the law enforcement to the people trained to do that. The sheriff's department would be getting a call from me.

I used Nora's shovel as a cane on the way back to my house. The palms of my hands burned from scraping them on the ground, a bruise was forming on my shin, and a puffiness around my right ankle indicated I'd pulled or twisted it.

Stay out of trouble, Wade had ordered. Good thing he couldn't see me now.

Back at my house, the three of us washed up, and I wrapped my ankle with an elastic bandage to give it support and stem the swelling. The more I'd walked on it, the better it had felt. Grandma stepped out on the porch for a cigarette, taking Ida with her, while I called the sheriff's office and reported what had happened. They promised they'd send someone out for a full report. I hoped it wouldn't be Chambers.

Next I clicked on the icon for my Internet server, and while I waited for it to load, I checked the two new messages on my answering machine. The first was from a client, who once again, it seemed, had forgotten to make his quarterly estimated payments to the IRS and the state. What bothered me was I couldn't remember if I'd sent him his usual quarterly reminder. With all that had been going on, my work was suffering. Not that those reminders always resulted in him mailing his checks on time, but he would blame me if I forgot.

The second message was from my vet. "P.J.," he said, sounding excited, "I think I know what the problem is. Give me a call."

So I did.

THIRTY-SEVEN

"It's the water," Rick said, as soon as we'd exchanged hellos. "We tested the sample you brought twice. Unless the jar you used was contaminated, that water has levels of benzene and carbon tetrachloride that are way too high. The benzene alone would cause low levels of red and white blood cells. Nausea. All of the symptoms this dog is exhibiting."

"Would it cause headaches?" I asked, remembering how Abby kept complaining about a headache.

"Definitely."

"Except," I said, remembering what Abby had told me. "She didn't drink the water. She said it tasted funny and sometimes smelled like gasoline. She bought bottled water and tea."

"If benzene is in her water supply, she probably would smell it. And it's a good thing she didn't drink the water, but that chemical can be absorbed through the skin."

I understood. "So every time she washed her hands . . ."

"Or took a shower or bath," Rick continued for me, "she'd be absorbing a little."

"If I have either a Detective Gespardo or Detective Kingsley call you, could you give him that information?" I didn't like being considered a suspect, and I wanted both of them to understand I'd had a good reason for taking Abby's dog. Dexter might be the key to finding why her house exploded.

"Before you call anyone, P.J., I need another sample. You need to make sure it's a clean sample, that the jar or whatever

259

you use is sterile. And, if possible, get it from a different location. You said what you brought me came from the holding tank of a toilet. There is the possibility she used a toilet boil cleaner in the tank that would give us these readings. If that's true, then what I've found would have nothing to do with what the dog drank."

Oh great. I'd had trouble getting the one sample. Finding another source wasn't going to be easy. "How soon do you need this?" I asked, wandering back to my office.

"Yesterday," Rick said and then chuckled. "Actually, the sooner the better. That transfusion I gave the dog helped, but I need to know exactly what we're dealing with if we're going to save him."

"Okay, I'll get a sample as soon as I can."

I sat down at my computer. It had gone into sleep mode, but a click of the mouse brought the screen back to life. I hoped I could download the pictures Ken sent before the sheriff's deputy arrived. In addition to reporting Nora's attack, I might have a reason for Donald Crane's death.

My computer—or more specifically—my Internet provider changed my plans. Instead of loading my log-on page, it delivered a message: *Due to technical difficulties, service has been temporarily interrupted.*

This wasn't the first time "technical difficulties" had interrupted service. Changing servers seemed my best option, but today wasn't the time to make that move. As long as I couldn't download the pictures Ken had sent—at least not for a while—I decided not to wait for the deputy, but to return to Abby's place.

I stepped outside and asked Grandma if she would mind hanging around until a sheriff's deputy arrived. She could report what had transpired in the woods as well as I could. Probably better since she and Ida had made the initial contact with Nora, and I'd come in later.

Grandma glanced through a window at Ida, who had gone into my living room and turned on the television. "She's looking for her soaps," Grandma said, watching Ida flip from channel to channel. "In a minute she'll start complaining."

Sure enough, a minute later Ida came to the door, "I can't find my shows."

"It's Saturday," Grandma said, winking at me before she stepped back in the house. "But there should be a baseball game on soon."

"I like baseball." Ida grinned and returned to the TV.

We watched until she found a game. For a second she stared at the television screen, then she waddled over and sank onto my old sofa, sitting in Baraka's favorite spot. Grandma touched my arm and in a low voice said, "Five minutes and she'll be asleep, so go do whatever you have to do."

"I won't be too long," I promised. "If you're hungry, there's lunch meat in the refrigerator. You can make a sandwich. Or there's canned soup."

"A sandwich," Ida said from the sofa.

I grinned. Obviously there was nothing wrong with Ida's hearing.

"What about your dog?" Grandma pointed at Baraka who had gone to his crate and was lying with his head on his paws, a worried look on his face. "Do you feed him anything at this time of the day?"

"No." Baraka's behavior worried me. Normally after a walk I gave him a treat, and he'd bug me until I did so. The crate was his safety area, the place he went when he was tired or naughty . . . or not feeling well. Even coming back from the woods, he'd been subdued, had walked behind us instead of bounding in front or to the side.

Nora had given him a solid whack with her shovel, and even

though I couldn't see any external signs of injury, she might have injured Baraka internally. "I'm going to take him with me," I told Grandma. "I want my vet to look him over."

"Okay." Grandma followed me into the kitchen as I started looking for a container for a water sample. "By the way," she said when we were sure we were out of earshot of Ida, "I heard from that lawyer who brought her to the house, the one you hired."

I started going through my cupboards. "And . . . ?"

"He said the nephew had a will and a life insurance policy. A bank is named as executor of Crane's estate and a person—a woman—as Ida's guardian. Hicks is contacting the woman. Evidently she moved a few months ago, so she may not want that responsibility."

Grandma grinned. "Hicks also said I'll be compensated for the days she stayed with me. I'm getting to like that man."

"That's great." I'd figured on giving my grandmother some money for the time and energy she'd spent caring for Ida. She deserved it. Having someone else pay was all the better.

Grandma solved my search for a jar when she asked if it would be all right if they finished up the applesauce I had in the refrigerator. As soon as she dished out what remained in the jar, I washed it, then gave it and its lid a quick bath in a pan of boiling water. I dried both with paper towels, and hoped my efforts proved satisfactory to Rick.

By the time I was ready to leave, Grandma and Ida were sitting down to turkey sandwiches, applesauce, and iced tea.

On my way to Abby's, I saw Leon Lersten. He'd parked his tan car at the end of his drive, near his mailbox. As I passed, I tried to decide if his was the same car I'd watched drive away from my house just the week before . . . or the same one that had followed me from Ken's shop the day I gave Ken the cell phone.

The license plate was still impossible to read, and too many cars looked the same, I decided.

I left Baraka in the car when I parked in front of the yellow police tape that still surrounded the burned-out shell of Abby's home, but I rolled down all of the car's windows. Although it wasn't as steamy hot as it had been earlier in the week, I knew how quickly the interior of a car could heat up. Every year there were stories of dogs and young children dying after being left in cars by forgetful or ignorant people. Some think cracking the windows will be sufficient, but even with the windows rolled down a ways, the interior temperature can rise to over a hundred degrees within minutes. I hoped having all four down all the way would counter that.

"Stay," I ordered, and held my hand in front of Baraka's face.

I hoped he would. During our daily lessons, he'd been getting better about staying in place when commanded, but I'd never asked him to do so for an extended period of time. I didn't want him jumping out and cutting a pad on a shard of broken glass. The fact that he made no effort to escape the car, even when I stepped over the sagging police tape, bothered me. I needed to find a water source and get it and my dog to Rick as soon as possible.

Wade had accompanied me on my last investigation of the site, distracting and worrying me with his presence. I'd checked the water faucets outside of the house before he pointed out the toilet inside. I never did check for a water bowl inside of a dog house.

One by one, I went along the backs of the kennel's dog houses, unlatching each, lifting the hinged roof, and looking in. I found cedar-chip bedding and cedar-filled dog pillows, but no water bowls. No water.

There was a pail of water in the kennel run nearest the lean-to, but the water in it could have come from the firemen's hoses or rain and wouldn't prove a thing about the water Dexter normally drank.

Discouraged, I limped back to the house. No miracle had suddenly fixed the inside or outside faucets. Only the toilet remained standing and undamaged. I was feeling totally discouraged when I heard a quavering voice behind me. "My my, what are you looking for?"

"Water," I said and turned to face Olivia Halsted. "Water that Abby's dog might have drunk."

"You don't have any water at your house?" She frowned.

"I don't have the dog. My vet does. He's trying to figure out what has made Dexter so sickly. He thinks it might be the water. The water he was drinking here."

"Oh." Olivia Halsted looked concerned. "That wouldn't be good. Not good at all."

"I did get some water out of that." I pointed at the toilet that could barely be seen from where we stood. "But my vet wants me to find another source."

"Ah." She nodded. "I see." For a moment she paused, fingering the cell phone she held in her hand. "I saw you pull into the yard. I wondered what had brought you back."

So she'd come over to find out. I smiled. *How typical.*

"What about her hot water heater," Olivia asked. "If it wasn't destroyed in the explosion, it would have water in it."

Of course. Why didn't I think of that? I looked inside the shell of the house, trying to locate a hot water heater.

"Probably in the basement," Olivia said, edging toward a part of the house that I hadn't explored. "I think it's over here."

A charred portion of wall and an opening in the floor indicated the way to the basement. The door itself lay on the floor, chopped to pieces by the firemen's axes. I took my time walking over to the area, testing the flooring with each step. I wasn't sure how much damage the explosion and fire had caused to the stairway or any structures below. In my house, I'd thought my grandparents only had a Michigan basement—a small, dirt-floored area that housed their water heater, furnace, and some storage shelves—but I'd discovered there was more to that old house than I'd ever imagined.

At the doorway, I paused and looked down. The stairs were still there, along with a cement-block support wall and hand railing. Everything looked intact. I turned back to Olivia Halsted. "I'm going to go down. If you hear a crash or me scream, call nine-one-one, okay?"

"Okay," Olivia said, standing by the edge of the house, her cell phone already up to her ear.

I took my time going down the stairs. Every board that creaked made my heart jump. A slight vibration and I clung to the hand railing, as if it could help if the entire stairway collapsed. The farther down I went, the more I wished I'd brought a flashlight. Although most of the structure above the cellar had been burned or blown away, and there were holes in the flooring, the amount of light that filtered down below was limited.

I could see that Abby's basement was larger than the main part of mine, the walls poured cement, as well as the floor. Cardboard boxes were stacked on the far end, a good fifteen feet away from the furnace and water heater. But distance hadn't protected them from the water that had poured down the steps and through the holes in the floor above. The bottom boxes had water stains up the sides, and I was sure they would fall apart if lifted. No windows provided any additional light, and I doubted the single bulb in the center of the area would work. Nevertheless, I gave the string hanging from it a tug.

Nothing.

The water heater stood near the wall facing me. I made my way over and gave it a tap, then another. As far as I could tell, it still held water.

It took me a minute to find the drain tap. Applesauce jar ready, I gave the handle a twist and let a little water escape before I captured a sample for Rick. As soon as I felt I had enough, I closed the tap and sealed the jar. Now all I had to do was get it to Rick.

To my surprise, Olivia now stood at the top of the stairs. "Stay down there," she said, a strength to her voice that I hadn't heard before.

It looked like she was pointing her cell phone at me, which didn't make any sense. "Why?" I asked and started up the stairs.

"No. I said stay down there."

She moved her arm, giving me a better look at the object in her hand. Darn if it didn't look like a gun. I stopped midstep. "Olivia, what is going on?"

"I want you to stay down there." She moved her hand, and I could clearly see it was a gun she held. "My grandson is on his way. I called him when I first saw you. He'll know what to do with you."

I didn't take a step back, but I didn't move forward, either. "I don't get it, Olivia. What's wrong? What do you mean your grandson's on his way?"

"You're what's wrong," she said. "Nosing around. Taking things you shouldn't."

"You mean this water?" I held up the applesauce jar.

"Not that. The briefcase. The cell phone."

A cold chill ran through me as I began to understand. "Are you talking about Donald Crane's briefcase? His cell phone?"

"Exactly."

"What do you have to do with those things?"

"So you never did see the pictures?"

I thought of my computer. If my Internet server had worked, what would those pictures have shown? "What about the pictures?"

Olivia half-laughed. "Oh, if you'd seen them, you wouldn't have to ask. Not that it really matters. Not now."

"What would I have seen?" I slowly placed my right foot on the next step and eased myself up. I hoped, if I kept her talking, she wouldn't notice I was closer.

I saw the flash from the muzzle before I heard the gun's explosive crack. Almost immediately something went ping behind me. I didn't feel any pain; nevertheless, I stepped back, losing my balance and stumbling down the steps. I dropped the jar of water as I did, the glass shattering the moment it hit the cement. I glanced down at the floor. The water I'd collected was rapidly spreading away from the broken container.

Even worse, water now sprayed out of a hole near the bottom of the water heater. Soon it would be empty.

"I told you to get back down there," Olivia said from the top of the stairs. "I will shoot you if I have to."

Gone was the helpless, frail little old lady I'd met at the township hall. Ma Barker now held me in her sights, and I didn't doubt for a minute she would shoot me. I just wanted to know why. "What's in those pictures that's worth killing me for?"

She snorted. "Answers."

"Answers to what?"

"To what happened to a nosy drain commissioner, and who buried him along with ten barrels of chemicals."

"You're saying the drain commissioner is dead?" So far the media had simply reported the man as missing. "That you killed him?"

"Me? No. My grandson did."

"I called my grandson," she'd said. *"He's on his way."* I did not like what I was hearing.

"He has a temper," Olivia added, as if that explained everything.

I looked around, hoping I'd missed a way to escape, but four very solid walls of concrete surrounded me. This cellar had no hidden doors. No secret room and passageway. I was in a hole with only one way out, and Olivia Halsted wasn't about to let me by.

I needed to find something I could use in my defense.

"None of this would have happened if Miss Busybody over here hadn't started complaining. Evidently she not only called the county, she told Crane, and he snuck over and took soil samples. I think he was the one who got the drain commissioner to come out." Olivia chuckled. "Guy came to my door. Said he had a sample of her water. Wanted one of mine. Then he started asking questions: What did I know about the company that owned the land next to me? Did I think someone might be dumping chemicals over there?"

She sighed. "When he said he was going to check into it, Morgan really didn't have a choice."

"Morgan is your grandson?"

"My daughter's boy," Olivia said, her pride evident. "Margo moved to Arizona, but Morgan stayed here in Michigan. He watches over me."

"And kills people."

I didn't realize I'd said it aloud until Olivia spoke. "Only if they get him upset."

"And Donald Crane upset him?"

"Crane upset everyone." From the top of the stairway, she waved her gun at me. "I couldn't believe it when I opened the letter and saw those pictures. If we'd known Crane was sneaking around when we buried that county guy, Morgan would have eliminated him then."

She snorted. "Idiot said he wanted a half million dollars, or he'd show the pictures to the police. Did he really think we'd pay, that we'd let him hold something like that over us?"

Ida Delaney had been right. Her nephew did try to blackmail

someone, that someone being Olivia Halsted and her grandson. "So Morgan went to Donald Crane's house and killed him."

"We couldn't let him send those pictures to the police, could we?" she said, as if killing Crane was the only alternative. "Morgan thought he could convince Crane to forget what he'd seen, could scare him into keeping quiet, but Crane wasn't buying."

I remembered Ida had said two men came to see her nephew. Two men had also beaten up Ken and his friend, and Ken had described the other man as white, about his height, and a nice dresser. That description fit one person to a T. "Was the other person Neal?"

"My lawyer?" Olivia made a face and shook her head. "That wuss might bore someone to death with words, but there's no way Morgan would take him anywhere." She gave a small chuckle. "Neal did help us. Not that he knew he was. We weren't sure Crane's cell phone was actually in his briefcase until I talked to Neal Tuesday morning, and he said you'd mentioned finding one."

I squeezed my eyes closed. Me and my big mouth. If I hadn't told Neal about the cell phone, Olivia and her grandson would never have been sure where it was . . . or had been.

"How did you know about Ken?" I asked, once again looking up at her. "That I'd taken the phone to him?"

"You mean that computer guy?" She gave a slight smile. "You led us to him. Morgan saw you buying some beer in Kalamazoo and followed you after you left the gas station. He saw you hand the phone to Paget. He called me when you left the shop, said he was going to follow you, but I told him to forget it. I figured if you knew what was on the phone, you'd have taken it to the police."

"I'm surprised your grandson didn't go back and just take the phone from Ken."

"He did go back," she said. "But there was someone else with the guy, and right after that, Paget closed up and took off."

Forcing her grandson to hire some kids to do his dirty work, I guessed. "What about the other guy?" I asked, remembering both Ida and Ken had said Morgan had another man with him.

"You mean Paget's pothead buddy?"

"No, the other one with your grandson when he killed Crane and when he beat Ken and his friend to a pulp."

"Oh yes, Walter." She smiled. "He and Morgan have been friends since high school. Nice kid, but not too bright, if you know what I mean."

I was beginning to think that description fit me. I still had questions. "Did one of them cause Abby's death?"

"Oh no." Olivia lifted her chin with pride. "I did that. I didn't really want to kill her, but if she wasn't going to sell to Leon, that meant she was going to keep on pushing for them to straighten the road. And that meant they'd be digging up those barrels we buried years ago, back when my husband was still alive."

Knowing Olivia Halsted had killed Abby sent a shiver down my spine. My chances of escaping alive were slim, which was probably why she was telling me so much. She wasn't worried that any of this would reach the ears of the police. My coming back to the scene of the crime had sealed my fate, so I guess it was morbid curiosity that made me ask the next question. "How did you cause the explosion and fire?"

"Put out the pilot lights and turned on the stove," she said, giving a chuckle. "She said she had a headache. I used her fry pan and gave her a bigger one. After that, I closed all the windows and poured some gasoline I found in her garage on anything that would burn. Getting out of this house and back to mine before it exploded was the hardest part. I wasn't sure if the timer on her stove would work . . . but it did."

She glanced around. "Didn't think there'd be this much damage. Guess that's the problem with old houses. They burn like paper."

The woman was sick. Deranged. And I was her prisoner.

Wade, where are you when I need you? I almost laughed. He'd told me to stay out of trouble. I wasn't doing a very good job of that.

THIRTY-EIGHT

In the distance, I heard the crunch of tires on gravel. Olivia looked over one shoulder and smiled. With her attention distracted, I pushed myself to my feet and started up the steps. Doing so brought her attention back to me. "Just stay where you are, Missy."

"I was getting wet," I complained, gesturing toward the floor where the hot water heater had emptied enough water to cover the cement.

"Tough." Her gaze wandered back to whatever she'd heard or seen out in the yard.

I considered making a dash up the stairs while her attention was elsewhere, but my body ached from my earlier fall in the woods and from tumbling down Abby's stairs. I wasn't sure I could make it to the top steps before Olivia had a chance to take aim and shoot. The alternative, however, was to do nothing and wait for her grandson to finish me off.

Not a good alternative.

My chance came when the tension in her body relaxed, and she lowered the gun. "He's here," she said with a sigh of relief.

Ignoring my protesting joints and painful ankle, I took the stairs two at a time. Olivia heard me and turned back. I saw her raise the gun and point it toward me. I didn't pause. Didn't breathe.

But I did duck.

The bullet whooshed over my head, the sound of the shot

immediately following. I kept going, arms extended, hitting her in the stomach with the palms of my hands and driving her off balance. She screamed and fell, the gun flying out of her hand.

I lunged for it, saw it bounce against a charred stud and plummet downward and out of sight. A clunk and small splash identified where the gun had landed, but I wasn't going to go back down to retrieve it. My luck, either the fall or water would have damaged the gun, and there I would be, once again trapped in the basement.

"Hey!" I heard a man yell.

I scrambled to my feet. A tan sedan sat parked next to mine, the bruiser who had come to my house just last week running toward me. Knowing what I did, he seemed bigger—scarier—than I remembered.

"Morgan! Help!" Olivia shouted and grabbed for my legs.

I jerked free, did a quick scan of my position, and started running, heading off at an angle toward the road. Adrenalin must have kicked in because I didn't feel any pain in my ankle or joints, and I'd cleared the house and made it past the kennel before Morgan caught me. He grabbed my right arm and flung me to the ground, knocking the breath out of my lungs and smashing my face into the dirt.

Now I felt pain . . . and terror. My heart was beating so hard and fast, I could barely hear Baraka barking. "Bitch," Morgan said above me and kicked me in the stomach.

The taste of bile filled my mouth. I gagged and curled into a fetal position as tears slipped down my cheeks. At the edge of my vision, I saw a blur of red.

Baraka hit my assailant at a dead run, the full force of my dog's seventy-five pounds knocking Morgan-the-bruiser off balance. The man stumbled, tripping over my legs, and fell, landing on his side. He swore and grabbed for my dog's neck before Baraka had a chance to jump away.

Baraka's gurgled yelp of pain spurred me into action. I rolled to my side and kicked at Morgan's crotch, the toe of my sneaker extracting a higher-pitched yelp from him.

My sense of satisfaction was short lived. Morgan released Baraka, but then immediately arched forward and grabbed me, his fingers encircling my neck and squeezing. I barely heard Olivia screaming or saw Baraka go for my captor's face. I was fighting for consciousness when the grip on my throat loosened.

A ringing in my ears sounded like sirens; a loud, explosive bang vibrated through the air. Baraka yelped, and I helplessly reached out, unable to help him.

In the span of an instant, memories flashed through my mind. Baraka as a puppy, all wrinkles and energy. Baraka playing growly, racing by and bumping my side with his body. My dog playing tug-of-war with the old socks I'd knotted together. Licking my face.

Licking my face.

My mind cleared, and I realized my dog *was* licking my face. And people were talking. Shouting.

I opened my eyes and ran a hand over Baraka's head, his silky ears, solid neck and shoulders. Slowly I rose to a seated position, still touching my dog, looking for blood or a gaping wound where a bullet would have entered his body. Around me people moved, a uniformed deputy jerking Morgan to his feet while another stood back, his gun drawn and pointed toward Leon Lersten.

Assured that Baraka hadn't been shot, I noticed the shotgun lying on the ground by Leon's feet. When my gaze met his, he mouthed, "Are you all right?"

I wasn't sure how to answer. My head still felt funny, my throat ached, and the parts of my body that weren't numb throbbed. But I was alive.

I nodded yes.

"What the hell is going on?" I heard off to my side, the familiar voice causing the usual flutter of my heart.

Baraka left me and, tail wagging, trotted over to greet Wade. I simply stared at him. He was supposed to be at a baseball game with his son. Nevertheless, I was glad to see him.

Wade flashed his badge, and Leon Lersten and one of the uniformed deputies started talking in unison. "He grabbed her, and the dog attacked him," Leon said.

"We received a call of someone trespassing," the deputy stated. "Heard the shotgun blast as we were coming around the curve."

"I shot over their heads," Leon said. "As a warning."

"Saw him holding the shotgun," the officer continued, "this man—" He nodded toward Morgan. "—on the ground, the woman and dog beside him."

"He killed Crane," I said, my voice hoarse and the words barely audible as I pointed at Morgan. "She. . . ."

I looked for Olivia Halsted and saw her slyly working her way toward her house. "Stop her," I croaked. "She killed Abby."

Morgan made his move then, snaking an arm around the nearby deputy's neck and jerking him back and off balance. I saw him grab for the deputy's gun, and I reacted without thinking. Still seated, I threw myself forward, hitting Morgan's legs with my shoulder and wrapping my arms around his ankles. He kicked one leg loose, flinging me to the side like a flea, but I'd given the deputies enough time to act.

The one in Morgan's grasp twisted to the side, moving his weapon out of Morgan's reach and hitting him at the same time. Within a second, Wade was there, standing beside me, his weapon drawn. "Hands above your head," he ordered. "Make one move, and I'll shoot."

Morgan glared at Wade, then down at me. Slowly he lifted his arms and the deputy stepped behind him, taking one arm then the other and securing Morgan's wrists in handcuffs.

"Olivia," I said, looking toward her house for her.

She had been walking at a fast clip toward her house, but the moment I said her name, she started running. Which was a mistake on her part.

For Baraka, this was all a game. Our game of tag. She ran, and he took off, dashing after her. Because I expect it, I know when to step or angle my hips aside. If he touches me at all, it's merely a brush of his shoulder. The moment Baraka reached Olivia, she turned toward him.

He ran right into her, and she went down.

Baraka stopped a few feet in front of her supine body and trotted back. He started licking her face, and for a moment I was worried that he might have knocked her out or truly injured her. But then she started moving . . . and yelling.

She hit at his head and slapped at his sides. She called him every swear word I knew and a few I'd never heard. My poor dog stepped back, out of striking distance, and stared at her, head cocked. I could just imagine his puppy brain going, "That's not how you play the game."

Wade told the other deputy to get Olivia and bring her back. Then he looked at me. "Okay, who are the good guys, who are the bad?"

"I think he's a good guy," I said, pointing at Leon. "They're the bad ones."

Wade nodded at Leon. "Leave the shotgun where it is for now. Tell me what's going on."

Leon came closer, his gaze on Olivia. He shook his head. "I really don't know what's going on. I saw her." He pointed down at me. "Park there." He pointed at my car. "And cross the police line. So I called nine-one-one and reported it. I mean, that yellow tape means no one's supposed to be over here, doesn't it?"

At Wade's nod, Leon went on. "Anyway, I figured I'd leave it up to you guys to take care of her, but then, a little later, as I was on my way out to the barn, I heard a shot and soon after that, a dog barking. So I grabbed my shotgun and came over here. Saw him—" Leon pointed at Morgan. "kick her. Then her dog went after him. When I saw the guy grab her neck, I fired my shotgun—over their heads—and right after that, the deputies arrived."

Wade looked down at me and shook his head. "How do you get yourself into these messes?"

I shrugged. What could I say? I never meant to get involved in this. A talk on how to protect yourself against scams shouldn't have ended in a gunfight.

"You say he killed Donald Crane?" Wade said, nodding toward Morgan.

"That's what his grandmother told me." I slowly rose to my feet, brushing the dirt off my clothes and body. "And according to her, the county drain commissioner is buried somewhere over there."

I pointed at the property across from Abby's.

THIRTY-NINE

I repeated what Olivia Halsted had told me, and both Morgan and his grandmother were taken away in handcuffs. Leon confirmed that he'd been curious about the property next to his and on occasion had heard trucks or heavy equipment working over there. The one time he'd tried to investigate, he said, he'd been stopped by a couple of burly guys who reminded him, in no uncertain terms, that the *No Trespassing* signs posted around the property included him.

Wade followed me back to my house, where we found Deputy Chambers talking to Grandma Carter and Ida Delaney. Wade kept shaking his head as I explained what had happened with Nora, and that I thought there might be the body of a baby buried somewhere in my woods.

Grandma and Ida left after giving their statements, and so did Deputy Chambers. Wade stayed. "I'm almost afraid to leave you," he said, and headed for my refrigerator.

I watched him grab a beer, but shook my head when he offered me one. I was glad for his presence, but also confused. "I thought you were taking Jason to a baseball game this afternoon."

Wade grimaced. "So did I. Linda, however, decided it was more important for him to visit her parents this weekend. She took him up north last night."

"Without telling you?"

He nodded. "I was on my way out here, to cry on your

shoulder, when I heard the call for backup at the site of the explosion. Somehow I knew you'd be involved in whatever was going on there."

I remembered wondering where he was when I needed him. I guess he was on his way.

"Rick wanted another sample of the water," I said. "When Mrs. Halsted came over, I never suspected she was involved in any of this."

"What exactly did she say to you?" he said, settling in one of my dining room chairs and motioning toward the one next to him.

"She said . . ." I paused, remembering exactly what Olivia Halsted had said. "She said I would have known if I'd seen the pictures."

"What pictures?" Wade asked as I headed for my office and computer, not the chair.

"The pictures on Donald Crane's cell phone." I clicked on the icon for my server, praying whatever problems they'd been having had been resolved. "Ken emailed them to me before he was attacked." I looked at Wade while the program loaded. "It was Morgan and a guy named Walter who attacked Ken and his friend. They were after the cell phone, not drugs."

I logged in and crossed my fingers.

"And what are these pictures supposed to show?" Wade asked, coming over to stand beside me as I waited for something to happen.

"I'm not exactly sure," I admitted, "but Olivia said the drain commissioner is dead, buried somewhere on that property next to hers along with barrels of chemicals."

To my relief, a list of my current emails appeared. I was on-line, and there was a message from ComputerMan. Several messages to be exact.

Maris Soule

"Did she say how he died?" Wade asked, watching my every move.

"I guess Morgan killed him." I clicked on the first email, and watched as a picture slowly appeared on my screen. Dark and grainy, it showed three people standing by a mound of dirt. No—four. I'd missed the body lying on the ground.

"Can you make it any lighter?" Wade asked, leaning closer.

"I'm not sure." I right-clicked my mouse and selected the option to edit the picture.

As I brightened the picture, the four figures became more distinguishable. Although their features weren't clear, I could identify two of the silhouettes—Morgan's and Olivia's. The third man standing by the mound physically fit the description both Ida and Ken had given of Morgan's accomplice. I'd never met the drain commissioner, so I had no idea if that was his body on the ground or not.

"Can you print that?" Wade asked. "Send a copy to me?"

I could do both and did. The sequence of emails that followed showed the body being dumped in a pit. With each I made a print and then forwarded the original to both Wade's email address and Detective Daley's.

"I'm not sure how those pictures will stand up in court," Wade said, "but if we can find the body, I think they, along with your testimony and your computer friend's, will put three people in jail for a long time. Will you be all right for a while?" He set his unfinished can of beer on the table. "I want to get these prints to the station."

"I'll be fine," I said, suddenly very tired and sore. "I think I'll take a hot bath, then just chill out for a while."

"You're sure?"

"Positive."

I walked with him to his Jeep. Although he had the pictures I'd printed in one hand, he gave me a one-armed hug that took my breath away. "I'll be back," he said close to my ear, imitating Arnold Schwarzenegger in *The Terminator.*

I limped back to my house, smiling. All was well in my world. The bad guys—and gals—had been caught—or soon would be—Ida's needs would be taken care of, and my lover still loved me. Even Baraka seemed happy, his tail wagging when I opened the screen door. Being hit with a shovel and nearly choked didn't seem to have caused any lasting damage.

I left the front door open to air out the lingering smell of cigarette smoke. Although Grandma steps outside to smoke, I swear the odor follows her inside. Everywhere she sits and whatever she touches seems to hold the smell.

A beer hadn't sounded good when Wade offered, but a glass of iced tea did. As I poured some from a pitcher, I remembered my promise to bring Rick a sample of water from Abby's place. I left my glass of tea sitting on the dining room table and dialed Rick's home number.

Several hours passed before Wade returned. "You," he said, tapping my chest with his index finger, "are giving me gray hairs. You need a bodyguard."

"I have one," I replied and rose on my toes to kiss him. "You."

It didn't take long before the T-shirt and shorts I'd put on after my bath, along with Wade's shirt and khaki pants, were lying on the floor by my bed. Baraka whined outside the closed bedroom door, and my box spring creaked as Wade levered his body over mine. I hadn't put on a bra, and for a short time Wade was content to kiss my breasts as I rubbed my palms over the muscles of his back and luxuriated in the knowledge that he did want to be with me, that maybe he even loved me.

I don't know exactly when touching and kissing no longer satisfied the throbbing of our bodies, or how my underpants ended up on the floor. I know I was ready when Wade entered me. Each thrust of his hips took me to a new level of pleasure, a new sense of passion. We were one, united in body and spirit.

FORTY

Wade was softly snoring, one bare leg draped across mine, when Baraka barked. The sound was different from his usual "I want to be with you" bark, and I eased my legs out from under Wade's. I heard the click of my dogs toenails on linoleum and knew he'd left his post at the bedroom door. Quickly I slipped on my shorts and T-shirt, not bothering with underwear.

The moment I stepped out of the bedroom, I heard the rap of knuckles on my screen door. Considering everything that had happened the last few days, I cautiously peeked around the bathroom door toward my front porch.

I'd left the door open, to allow the evening air to help cool the house, and hadn't bothered to lock the screen door. Not that locking it would have stopped anyone who seriously wanted to enter my house. For that matter, all anyone would have to do was remove the plastic from the window next to the door, as my grandmother had when she wanted inside.

My tension eased when I saw Baraka wagging his tail. Neal stood on the other side of the door, his face pressed against the screen in an attempt to see inside. I could tell the moment he noticed me. He stepped back and straightened to his full height.

"Hey," he said. "You okay? I just heard what happened today."

"I'm fine," I said and stepped into my dining room. Slowly I walked toward the door. I knew how I must look, my hair all mussed and my cheeks red with whisker burn. If Neal couldn't figure out what I'd been doing before he arrived, he wasn't as smart as I thought he was.

"Good. I . . . ah . . ."

I smiled. He'd figured it out.

"I was just over . . ." He pointed behind him, toward Abby's, Olivia's, and Leon's places. "That is, I had some papers for Mrs. Halsted to sign." He paused and shook his head. "The farmer told me what happened, what she'd done. I just can't believe it."

"Believe it," I said. "She was ready to kill me."

"That's what he said." He looked me up and down. "And you're all right?"

"She's fine," Wade said from behind me.

I glanced back as he came up beside me and slipped an arm around my shoulders. He'd put on his trousers, but not his shirt or shoes, and his hair was as mussed as mine. The way Wade eased me even closer to his body, I knew he was sending a message. And Neal obviously understood.

"I, ah . . . I didn't mean to interrupt you two," he said. "I just stopped by to make sure she was all right."

"As I said, she's fine."

I glanced between the two men and grinned. Wade was rigid in his posture, his nostrils slightly flared, his gaze steady. An alpha male ready to fight for his woman. I liked that.

Neal took another step back from the screen door and looked down at the porch. An obvious sign of submission. If I'd had deep feelings for Neal, I would have been disappointed. As it was, I was glad he wasn't about to challenge Wade. I also knew I wouldn't be getting any more calls from Neal, at least none that involved a date. "Thanks for asking," I said.

A week later, a crew of ditch diggers and law enforcement officers—court order in hand—discovered not one but several locations on Land Right Properties where barrels of chemicals had been buried. They also found a body, later identified as that of the missing county drain commissioner. After the sheriff's department released the crime scene, the EPA and DEQ took over. Preliminary soil and water tests showed toxic levels of benzene, picric acid, and tetrachloride, along with several barrels testing positive for radioactive materials. I had a feeling those wine-stained pages I turned over to the police would show the same results, that those boxes of dirt I found in Donald Crane's briefcase were from the property owned by LRP Incorporated, and the map with the Xs indicated sites where barrels of chemicals were buried.

A search for the owners of LRP Incorporated resulted in new revelations. Olivia Halsted had retained ownership of the land under the guise of the shell corporation, and had a storage arrangement with a chemical plant in the Detroit area that provided the capital she'd needed to resolve her late-husband's gambling debts. The chemical company swore they had no idea the barrels had simply been buried and were now contaminating the soil. I wasn't sure I believed that, but I doubted the public would ever know the full story.

With additional blood transfusions, Dexter improved. Rick wasn't sure how much internal damage had been caused by the chemical and decided to keep the dog for himself. And since he was doing that, he said he'd cover the expense of the transfusions. My bank account blessed him.

I felt I owed Leon Lersten my life, so one day after I finally caught up on my work, I stopped by his farm and offered my services as a CPA. He said he might just take me up on my offer. Seemed he'd been doing his own tax preparation, and the year before had made a major miscalculation. "Totally forgot to include a big check I got," he said. "Thought we'd had a windfall that year. Spent it taking my wife and sister abroad. Not sure now how I'm going to pay this." He showed me a recent notice he'd received from the IRS. "Much less the interest they want."

I promised I'd help him, and he gave me a tour of his place. As Wade had said, the odors coming from Leon's barn were the basic smells associated with farm animals. I also knew the sheriff's department had checked out the locked smaller building just off to the side of Leon's barn. The "meth" Wade had smelled had turned out to be a sewage problem, now corrected. "Sewer trap kept drying out," Leon said. "Allowed the gases from the septic tank to come up in here. I was lucky the place didn't blow up."

Over the next few weeks, Ken was released from the hospital—he'd lost several teeth, but said that was okay, they'd been giving him trouble anyway. Once his jaw healed, he'd be fitted for dentures. He also bid on and won the contract for the job with Zenith Township, and opened his shop again. His friend came out of his coma, but was facing drug charges. Ken said not to worry. His friend had a good lawyer who would get both of them off.

In addition to catching up on my own work, I'd continued cleaning the chicken coop. I'd also been taking daily walks in the woods behind my place, choosing a different route each time, looking for anything that might indicate where my father might have buried Nora's baby—my half-brother. So far I hadn't found anything, but when I visited Nora in jail—because she'd violated the previous conditions of her release, the judge wouldn't grant bond—I assured her I wouldn't throw anything away until I knew for sure it wasn't her son. I'm no longer afraid of her—a little understanding can go a long way.

The trials for Olivia Halsted and Morgan Anderson are scheduled for this fall. Walter Barker, Morgan's high school buddy, hasn't been found, but there's a warrant out for his arrest. Wade said I'll be called as a witness during the trials, which means I'm still being involved. I've made notes so I remember what happened and what Olivia told me while she had me at gun point in Abby's cellar.

Meanwhile, as I expected, Neal hasn't called or stopped by again, and Wade and I have been getting along quite well. However, as the day his ex moves to California and takes Jason with her draws closer, Wade has become moodier. That's probably why, when he asked if I wanted to go out on the boat today, I declined. His other passengers will be Linda, her new husband, and Jason, and I don't want to be stuck out on Lake Michigan if tempers flare. I also wasn't sure how my stomach would handle the waves. Lately I've been waking up sick to my stomach . . . and I've missed my period.

ABOUT THE AUTHOR

Maris Soule graduated from U.C. Davis and U.C. Berkeley and taught art and math for four years in California. She was attending U.C. Santa Barbara when she met the blue-eyed redhead who became her husband and talked her into moving to the small town of Climax, Michigan. There they raised a son and a daughter, several Rhodesian Ridgebacks, and a slew of farm animals. Although she taught art for four more years, a love of reading led Soule to writing. She started with romances (twenty-five published, several winning awards) but over time found murder and suspense equally intriguing. Melding the two genres, she's now writing mystery/suspense with a touch of romance. In addition to novels, she's had several short stories published.

Learn more about Maris Soule at her web site: www.Maris Soule.com